THE
BILLIONAIRE
AND HIS
NANNY

THE
BILLIONAIRE
AND HIS
NANNY

SADIE BLACK

Copyright © 2022 by Sadie Black

All rights reserved.

No part of this book may be reproduced in any form or by any electronic or mechanical means, including information storage and retrieval systems, without written permission from the author, except for the use of brief quotations in a book review.

Paige Press
Leander, TX 78641

Ebook:
ISBN: 978-1-953520-93-7

Print:
ISBN: 978-1-953520-94-4

Also by Sadie Black

HIS NANNY TRILOGY

The Billionaire and His Nanny

The Billionaire and His Scandal

The Billionaire and His Forever

About This Book

The first time I saw Graham Ratliff, I swear the earth shook.
But I was just a teenager with a crush on my father's best friend.

Now he's divorced, a single dad with an adorable daughter. I'm nineteen, ready to leave home, and desperate to see if Mr. Ratliff is as hot as I remember. Becoming his nanny is the answer to all my problems. I didn't expect him to treat me so coldly... or to see such heat in his eyes when I tan by his pool. Bet he didn't expect me, either...

Prologue

Abbie

The first time I saw him was the first time I experienced an earthquake.

Not the kind where the ground rips apart and buildings collapse. Not the kind that destroys cities and knocks out electrical grids. It was a sexual awakening. One unlike anything I'd ever known, or even heard about, before.

It was like I was asleep, and then suddenly my eyes were wide open. One minute I was naïve and innocent, and the next, everything I knew got turned on its head.

Graham Ratliff. Dark, sophisticated, world-stoppingly handsome, with an upper-class British accent that could melt an iceberg. The second he took my hand in his and smiled at me, he changed my life.

The only problem? He was my dad's best friend from college.

The summer I turned sixteen, Graham had just moved his main offices from London to the States, so he could spend more time with his glamorous American actress wife, Natasha. The Ratliffs invited my father, my mother, and me to spend a month at their new sprawling summer estate in the Hudson Valley to welcome them, help them settle in before they went back to city life in NYC.

I had fully expected other kids my age to be there. In fact, I had imagined a fantasy vacation full of horseback riding, late-night swims in the lake, sneaking sips of vodka (and secret kisses) beneath the full moon. But it turned out that other wealthy families sent their sons and daughters *away* for their summer breaks, to exclusive horse camps and on chaperoned trips abroad, or to complete prestigious internships for senators. The only other kid around was the Ratliffs' little girl, Jude. Who was all of five years old.

Still, I didn't mind being her unpaid babysitter. Not when it gave me an excuse to watch her father from a somewhat safe distance. In a way, it was like having Graham to myself the entire month. No boys to distract me, no girls to gossip with, certainly no kisses beneath a waning moon—just a lot of face time with the man who rocked my entire core.

What I did mind was when Jude would want to play near Natasha, who either ignored me completely or spoke to me as if I was merely the help. Which I guess, in a way, I was. I don't think Natasha liked the fact that I hadn't been shipped off to camp, even if I provided the childcare that she herself was reluctant to give. I had to pay more attention to Jude when Natasha was around, had less time to daydream about what it would be like to play family with the handsome man strutting around the house.

But those times when she wasn't around? They made all my efforts worth it.

As I fell in lust with Graham, I realized he had a wicked sense of humor buried under the stoic Britishism. My banter with him, innocent though it was, made me feel like I was older, more mature. He was stern and firm for the most part, but often I'd catch a glint in his eye or a twitch at the corner of his mouth that said he was kidding. He made me feel like I was included, like I belonged there with him in the Ratliffs' lavish estate, surrounded by perfectly manicured trees and lush gardens.

And then came the moment—the car ride—that's been seared in my brain ever since.

My mother had talked Natasha into joining her and my dad on some fancy all-day winery tour upstate, and Jude was down in Manhattan with Natasha's parents for the weekend. Graham, of course, was in his home office hard at work. I'd been engrossed in whatever was on CNN when I got up to make myself a snack in the kitchen. It was while I was slicing up vegetables at the counter, trying to keep one eye on Ana Cabrera's news story, when footsteps suddenly came up behind me. Startled, I whipped around.

"Sorry, hadn't meant to frighten you," Graham said, gesturing to the empty coffee cup he'd brought to refill with a fresh brew. "Though I suppose this face would scare anyone."

His teasing grin fell away as his eyes dropped to my hand.

"You're bleeding," he said, moving closer.

I looked down and realized I'd accidentally sliced my finger with the knife. The blade was so sharp that I hadn't felt a thing, but the cut was bad enough that it was leaking little drops of blood on the floor.

Truthfully, I've never been a baby about blood. But for some reason, maybe a combination of Graham's proximity and the shock of seeing what I'd done to myself without even feeling it, I instantly got light-headed, and my legs went out from under me.

You can probably guess the rest. Graham scooped me up in his arms, drove me to the hospital, and stayed by my side for hours while I got four stitches in the ER. The staff must have assumed he was my dad, because he was allowed in the exam room with me and held my hand while my wound was cleaned, while I got shots of anesthetic in my finger—which hurt so bad, I actually cried out in pain—and then during the stitching and the bandaging and the dispensing of ibuprofen afterward. Graham was perfectly calm, cool, and collected the whole time.

On the drive home, I held my breath, reached over, and took his hand again. That warm, strong, reassuring hand. I knew I was crossing a line, but he let me do it. Every so often he'd give a little squeeze, or brush his thumb over my skin. It was all I could do to stare out the window and pretend I wasn't turned on, that he wasn't giving me goosebumps from head to toe. Pretend I wouldn't be masturbating to the memory of him touching me like that—and imagining him pulling over on the side of the road to touch me everywhere else—all night long.

Despite the stress of the ordeal (and how embarrassed I was to have ended up in the ER to begin with), my biggest takeaway was how utterly soothed and safe I felt in his presence. He made me feel like the incident was no big deal, like he wasn't inconvenienced at all by having to rescue me, like I wasn't just some silly teenager who'd practically chopped my finger off out of sheer clumsiness.

By the time we got back to the estate, my parents and Natasha had returned from their trip and were getting ready for dinner. Beyond a few comments from my parents, nobody seemed all that concerned about my little adventure with Graham that afternoon. But it has stayed with me ever since.

That drive back home, just the two of us holding hands, and the way I wished it would never, ever be over. I might even think I'd dreamed the whole thing up if I didn't still have the scar on my finger to prove it.

So in the end, I didn't mind not getting my first kiss that summer. Instead, I discovered all kinds of new things about myself: I'm good with kids, pistachio ice cream is actually my favorite, blue is definitely my color, and I like touching myself in the privacy of my own room while dreaming of older, mysterious men.

It was a perfect summer with a perfect summer crush. Full of ice cream and beach days with their cool ocean breezes and hot sun. Full of laughs and late-night dinners and running my fingers across the spines of old books in the library. Hearing stories about British nightlife and wild Hollywood parties and Broadway drama. Private nights where I let my dirtiest fantasies play out in my head, gasping softly as I came so hard it felt like flashes of lightning striking my body, my pussy clenching tight and fast around my fingers.

Jude loved to swim in the pool in the afternoons when the heat was at its peak, so I'd make sure to join her and wear my skimpier bikinis on days when Graham was around, opting for a basic black one-piece when Natasha was there. I tried new makeup styles, fussed with my hair. Even borrowed clothes from my mom. Graham must have noticed the effort I was putting into my appearance, because one day he told my father, "I think your daughter has a little crush." They both laughed.

I was completely humiliated.

And yet.

Graham had *noticed* me. Really noticed. He'd picked up on the tiny details, had paid attention to what I wore, how I looked at him, how I presented myself. He knew I was attracted to him. Acknowledging that, even in jest, was an incredible turn-on. He *saw me*.

And even though Graham and I never touched again, there were times the back of my neck would tingle, and I could swear I felt his eyes on me across the room. I'd whip around, only to find him looking somewhere else entirely, his neck muscles taut, his interest in me almost glaringly obvious simply based on how hard he was trying to seem nonchalant. I wasn't imagining things—something was pulled taut between us. Like a rubber band waiting to snap.

Sometimes he'd brush past me casually, yet unnecessarily, and just the feel of his finely textured linen shirt against my bare skin would send a shockwave straight through me, making me instantly wet. It didn't matter that he acted neutral toward me after the hospital incident—some part of me was convinced he was forcing himself to act indifferent because he knew something had passed between us. Something dangerous.

But maybe it was wishful thinking.

Regardless of what was really going on in the impenetrable mind of Graham Ratliff, those four weeks changed me in ways I'd never even imagined were possible.

And then we all went back to the real world.

Chapter One

Abbie

Three Years Later

Memories are funny things, pulling out the best or worst moments of your life and magnifying them through self-reflection.

Most of the time, things from your past seem bigger than they actually are. Fights are more vicious and cinematic than they really played out. Monuments grow by miles. Scenery is more vivid, more picture-postcard perfect. The impact of people is greater by how you've built them up in your mind over the years.

But this house, the Ratliff summer house? It's actually maybe bigger than my memories.

As the private car I'm sitting in glides up the gravel driveway, the imposing outline of the expansive Tudor swells up out of the ground before me like a great, toothy beast. There's the ivy-covered brick exterior, the countless arched windows with their diamond-shaped panes, the dark wood double doors on the front porch flung open like a gaping wound. Even the gardens around the property feel a little dangerous, with their tall topiaries and walls of sculpted boxwoods. When I was last here, Jude and I played in them like it was a maze, even though we knew the property so well that we rarely got turned around much. On the drive up, though, the place feels foreign and new, even a bit intimidating.

I can't believe this is going to be my actual residence for the next three months. Thank God for the friend-of-a-friend of my dad, who had thrown a ritzy fundraiser in TriBeCa where an acquaintance of the Ratliffs had casually gossiped to Dad about Graham's difficulty finding an "appropriate" summer nanny for Jude. When Dad got home from his New York trip and told me about it, I instantly felt like fate was smiling on me.

"Thank you so much," I tell the driver, Ronaldo, as he unloads my suitcases from the trunk of the car. I try to dig a tip out of my wallet, but he waves me away.

"That won't be necessary. Mr. Ratliff is a quite generous employer," he says.

Immediately, I feel my face go hot. Of course Graham pays his private driver well. I guess rich people don't tip their household staff, do they? I feel like an idiot.

Not that I'd know how this all works...my family has money, but not the kind that affords full-time, live-in help. For my dad, it's always been more about presenting an outward picture of wealth, and keeping up with his cronies—driving the latest brand-new luxury cars, living in the ritziest neighborhoods, wearing expensive designer

Chapter 1

clothes, going on exotic vacations—than actually being able to maintain the kind of lifestyle that people like Graham Ratliff don't even give a second thought. The man has so much money he probably doesn't even know what to do with it all. Must be tough.

Standing before the mansion's massive front doors now, my bags at my feet, the memories come toppling like Jenga blocks. The corners where I'd tuck myself away to spy on Graham while the adults were sharing cigars on the balcony. The rose garden where Jude and I picked the most fragrant blooms for our bedrooms. The long-winding paths we led horses down in the blazing summer sun...

"Hello?" I call into the house, my voice echoing in the foyer. "Mr. Ratliff? Jude?"

I feel awkward crossing the threshold without being properly invited inside, but as I take one small tentative step onto the polished marble tile of the grand front hall, familiarity zings through my veins. A double staircase sweeps up before me, christened by a two-story chandelier with a thousand dazzling pieces of cut crystal. I remember asking once how they dusted it, and one of the housekeepers told me it was a full day's job.

Even the scent of the fresh-cut flowers in tall vases—hydrangeas and stargazer lilies, with their heavy perfume—evokes a sense of nostalgia. It's all here, almost exactly as I left it. And yet somehow still...*more*.

Maybe I just spent more time committing Graham's face to memory than his home. But his face isn't the one that greets me—it's the housekeeper. Which is for the best, probably, because I'm supposed to be an adult now, and I can't be acting like a teenager with a schoolgirl crush over my new boss.

"Welcome, welcome! You must be Abbie." An older woman with a thick gray bun and warm eyes with deep-etched laugh lines bustles into the foyer with a smile. "I'm Esmeralda, the head housekeeper. Do you need help with your luggage? I can have it brought up to your room."

She looks past me, out the front door, examining the pile of bags waiting.

"Um, yeah, that'd be nice," I say. "I brought a lot of clothes."

Nodding, she calls to someone and then goes on, "How was the drive? We've been so eager for your arrival. Especially Jude! I know you haven't seen her in ages, but she seems to remember a great deal. You really left an impression on her."

As her brisk chatter echoes off the empty vault of a house, I try to keep up with smiles and appropriate responses. Despite her age, Esmeralda is a whirlwind. No wonder she's in charge. Meanwhile, I'm already feeling completely overwhelmed. To say my home is nothing like this is an understatement.

Esmeralda offers a curious look, and I realize I've spaced out. "Sorry, what?"

"Shall we go up to your room now?" she repeats. "Your things should be there, and you can freshen up."

"Oh, yes. That's perfect. Thank you."

"Excellent. And then I'll give you a tour. It's been several years since you were last here, and as I'm sure you know, the estate is quite large. Ronaldo joked about

Chapter 1

making you a map." She stops abruptly on the lavish stairs and turns back to look at me. "We can do that if you like."

"I should be fine after the tour," I reassure her, soaking in the exquisite decorations and the stunning view from the bank of windows framing the front door. "My memories are coming back already. Isn't there a library down the hall, next to the dining room?"

"Very good!" She grins approvingly at me and continues up the lengthy, curving staircase. "I knew you'd be the perfect fit."

"Thank you," I say, because I don't know what else to say.

"Things are a little different from the last time you were here," Esmeralda says as she leads me down a bright hallway loaded with closed doors, framed art, and pedestals with sculptures. How does a little girl play in a house like this? I can't remember. Her voice lowers as she adds, "Mr. and Mrs. Ratliff divorced a year ago, very messy, I'm sure you read about it. Honestly, the staff was a bit relieved. I don't know how much you recall about Mrs. Ratliff, but she could be quite...severe. Not that I'm one to gossip, of course."

Which means she is, naturally. I *knew* I liked her. As the older woman goes on, I keep quiet, eagerly soaking up all the dirt. Esmeralda clearly sees me as an ally, which is to my benefit.

Of course I knew about the divorce. Not only did it make the rounds of my parents' social circles less than a year ago, but it was front page and center in the entertainment magazines and tabloids, not to mention the social media storm. Celebrity actress Natasha Ratliff and one of her directors, both caught cheating on their longtime partners. Page after page of glossy photos detailing scandalous trysts by the Aussie seaside and at luxury hotels in Italy were plastered all over. The news was almost unavoidable. Natasha was a stunning woman, tall and model gorgeous, with a full set of pouty lips and a glorious mane of hair that most people would kill for. It wasn't the first time rumors had swirled of her infidelity, but it was the first time there was irrefutable photographic evidence.

And the first time Natasha walked out on her family.

Her former husband, my new boss, was portrayed as the grieving betrayed, with photos of him protectively escorting their daughter away from the paparazzi while they harassed him for comments. Which he, of course, refused to give.

My heart broke for him, just a little, when I saw the stoicism etched in his dark, brooding face. The rest of me was overjoyed that he was suddenly free from that horrible woman. It's easier to fantasize about a man when he's single, I learned.

"This is you!" Esmeralda pushes open a pearly white door near the brightest end of the hall and gestures for me to enter. "I hope you find it to your liking."

"It's beautiful." I spin in a slow circle, already picturing my new life here.

There's a large bed with a canopy against the far wall, the expanse of windows next to it overlooking the gardens. To my left is a large wardrobe that will no doubt dwarf my belongings, and an oversized desk for

Chapter 1

my laptop. Everything is plush and cozy, with large pillows and throw blankets adorning every surface. I inhale the scent of freshly cut roses in a vase on the desk.

"Really lovely, Esmeralda, thank you."

She beams. "We're very excited to have you here, Abbie. If you need anything, please don't hesitate to ask. We're all here for you. Shall I give you a few minutes?"

"Actually." I take a deep breath before turning back around to face her. "Is Mr. Ratliff here? I'd like to reintroduce myself. It's been so long."

"Of course, of course. He'll be expecting you in his office after the tour."

Esmeralda leads me back down the hall and through the rest of the house. It's full of more chandeliers, more art, with plenty of gorgeous antique rugs to cushion my feet. And it's all gleaming and spotless, not one speck of dust to be found. The staff is obviously very attentive. We pass a few of them, dressed in black and white, fluffing pillows in the formal sitting room.

A sharp twinge hits me in the gut, but I ignore it to refocus my attention on Esmeralda. She's been very forthcoming in all her responses to my less-than-professional questions.

"So...it seems no one was particularly fond of Mrs. Ratliff?" I hazard as I drink in the ornate library. There's a bar cart in the corner and ladders to access high shelves. It looks like something Belle would have if she lived in a slightly smaller castle.

"Oh. What gave you that impression? I must have misspoken." Esmeralda offers a tight-lipped smile, but her eyes betray her. "The former mistress was...a very nice woman."

"It's okay." I lean forward conspiratorially. "I don't have many fond memories of her myself. I don't think she liked me very much."

Esmeralda relaxes. "Well. The former Mrs. Ratliff didn't like *anyone* very much, except Mr. Ratliff. And even then..." She lets her voice trail off as she leaves, and I reluctantly follow.

Admittedly, I don't read much for pleasure these days—too busy cramming and cursing my textbooks—but I don't know how anyone couldn't be shocked into reverent silence by the sight of such a gorgeous library. I plan on sneaking in here as often as I can, nicking booze from the cart and poring over Jane Austen's finest or my trashy magazines (with their many quizzes and articles on the best sex positions), depending on my mood.

"This is Mr. Ratliff's office." Esmeralda pauses in front of another impeccably white door, framed by celadon Chinese vases and more works of art that have no choice but to be original. The Ratliffs never owned anything mass produced. "It's best to not interrupt him, even when the door is open. Though it's usually closed. He's a very busy man, and been all the busier since Mrs. Ratliff took her leave."

Esmeralda knocks on the door in a pattern and waits patiently until a deep voice, one with a sultry British accent, calls out, "You may enter."

Esmeralda opens the door with a cheery smile. "Mr. Ratliff, good morning."

Chapter 1

"Good morning, Esmeralda." He doesn't look up, but in that moment, my heart stops.

His crisp white sleeves are buttoned at his wrists, and he's bent over a laptop, frowning slightly so a crease appears between his dark brows. His full lips are pursed as though he's deep in thought, a lock of hair falling over his forehead. My God, the man is somehow impossibly more gorgeous than I remembered or saw in every last one of those paparazzi photos. Thank God Esmeralda isn't paying attention to me, because for just a moment, my knees buckle.

"Abbie Montgomery has arrived," Esmeralda tells him from the doorway.

"Send her in, then." He still doesn't look up from his work.

My heart careens against my chest. *Look at me. Please, look at me.*

I take one shaky step into the office. "Hello, Mr. Ratliff. Good to see you again."

I use my most professional voice and clasp my hands in front of my designer sundress, borrowed from my best friend Amanda. It's pale yellow with dainty flowers across it, one I thought I looked pretty damn good in until I was faced with his overwhelming presence.

That feeling of not belonging here creeps over me again. I square my shoulders and lift my chin, silently telling myself that I do belong here. I belong here and I have a job to do.

"Miss Montgomery. Welcome back." He glances up at me without a smile, but the brief moment of eye contact gives me a thrill. His crisp accent is better than

Abbie

any music. Everything about him makes me want to fall at his feet. "Jude has been eager to see you."

"So I've heard. I'm excited to see her again as well," I somehow answer without moaning.

"I trust Esmeralda has shown you your quarters?"

"She's given me a wonderful tour. Most everything matches my memories."

"I trust you won't have any problem finding Jude?"

There's a slight edge to his voice I can't decipher. "No, sir."

"Very well. I'll see you at dinner, then. Consider tomorrow your first official day."

Graham goes silent and begins typing away on his laptop again, his long fingers flying across the keyboard like he's playing piano.

"Thank you, Mr. Ratliff." I hesitate, but Esmeralda motions for me to follow her. It takes an extra second for my legs to work again.

Once I'm back out in the hallway and the office door is closed, she turns to me with an apologetic smile. "He's very busy."

"I understand."

"Shall we go find Jude?"

I look back at the closed door and try to steady my heart. "Absolutely."

Chapter Two

Abbie

It's my first dinner with my new boss and I don't know what to wear. Everything I brought looks shabby now that I've been back in the presence of Graham Ratliff.

Exasperated, I take pictures of myself in a number of different outfits and send them all to Amanda for help. She's been my personal wardrobe guru ever since we met on our first day of ninth grade at Suffield Academy. The private school's dress code was somewhat strict, but it was still the first time since I was five that I hadn't been required to wear a school uniform. During our lunch period, Amanda bluntly pointed out that I'd obviously never learned how to dress myself outside of plaid skirts and cardigans. She's always had a flair for patterns and accessories.

While she muses over my options, I loosely curl my hair and swipe on some blush and a quick coat of lip gloss.

That red number is HOT!!! Amanda texts back. *I'm*

not sure it screams "I'm here to take care of your daughter" though.

She has a point. I put it back in the wardrobe just as my phone chimes again.

Go blue! And pull your hair back. It'll make your eyes POP.

I pick up the blue summer dress. It has cap sleeves and a modest hemline, just above the knee. It's more conservative than what I'd normally wear, but she has a point about how I'm supposed to look. I slip it on and do a quick spin in the mirror. I only have a few more minutes before I'm supposed to be downstairs, so it's going to have to work.

You're a lifesaver <3, I text back, and then slip my phone into one of the desk drawers.

When I open the door, I nearly run headlong into Esmeralda.

"Don't you look lovely!" She beams cheerily. "I just came to see if you were ready."

"Thanks. I was a little nervous about what to wear."

"Don't be. You did well." She steps back to allow me into the hallway. "Mr. Ratliff and Jude are in the dining room."

Shit. "Are they waiting on me?"

"You're not late, dear," she says gently, but firmly, in a way that basically means yes.

We head down the hall in silence. No more gossip from Esmeralda, which is disappointing. I want to know if Graham said anything about me after I left his office today.

As for Jude, she was overjoyed to see me, and

Chapter 2

wrapped herself around me like a sloth on a branch as soon as I entered her room. A far cry from how her father regarded me.

Downstairs, I catch the scent of something delicious. "Oh, wow. That smells amazing."

"Crab cakes, chilled asparagus bisque, and a citrus summer salad. Mary wanted to make sure you felt welcome on your first night, so she called your parents to ask about your favorite foods." Esmeralda smiles. "Don't want you to be too homesick on your first night."

"That was so kind," I hear my voice go soft with emotion, which is embarrassing. But she's right—having some comfort food tonight just might help the ache in my gut. I can't tell if it's nerves or homesickness or both. "I can't thank you all enough."

Esmeralda pats my arm and gestures toward the dining room. "Off you go."

She doesn't follow me in, and for a second, I wish she would. But it's time to pull myself together and start acting the part. I'm here to do a job, after all.

"Good evening." I offer my brightest smile as I make my way across the room, relieved to find it absent of any firing squads. Not that I expected one. Mostly.

Graham sits at the head of the long table in the same sexy getup as earlier: crisp white shirt with the top two buttons undone, dark slacks, gold watch. Jude, her brown hair in stubby little braids, sits next to him in her cute daisy-print Stella McCartney overalls. Her face lights up when she sees me.

"Abbie!" she gushes and starts to get up.

"Jude," Graham warns. "Manners. We're at the dinner table."

"Sorry, Daddy." She settles back into her seat. "Sit by me, Abbie."

"Of course." I want to sit by Graham, but I take a seat next to the girl I'm going to spend all summer with and give her a quick side hug. "Thank you for the welcome."

"I trust the staff has attended to all your needs?" Graham looks at me with an expression I can't read. "You've found everything?"

"Your staff has been wonderful." I carefully lay the cloth napkin in my lap and offer another smile. "And yes, I'm settling in well."

"Good." He gestures with two fingers to a corner of the room. A few of the house staff bustle in a moment later to lay out bowls of soup, a steaming basket of bread, and a bottle of wine. Is one of them Mary, perhaps? "I'm glad to hear it."

He doesn't sound glad, but the words are close enough.

I glance down at the soup, which has a dash of cream and fresh herbs on top, with two grilled asparagus spears for garnish. "This looks incredible," I can't help saying out loud.

"I hope you enjoy." The staff member smiles back and takes her leave as Graham raises two more fingers dismissively.

"*Green* soup?" Jude asks tentatively, her brows knitting.

"Just eat it," Graham tells her, voice dropping an octave into something deep and rumbling that instantly

Chapter 2

intimidates me, even though he's speaking to his daughter. Turning to me, he adds, "I hope you find the meal acceptable, Abbie."

The way he says my name sends a fresh wave of tremors down my spine and I have to take a deep breath to keep myself together. Suddenly, my job feels bigger than ever. Graham is like an iron strongbox, impossible to get through. Everything about him is stern, impenetrable.

"It's perfect," I assure him. Jude dives into the bread and butter and barely touches her soup. "I can help you with yours, if you want," I whisper to her with a wink.

Jude's face perks up, but then Graham clears his throat and she slumps back in her seat. She dutifully spoons up a bite of soup, places it against her lips, and sips it down before shivering and setting the spoon back in the bowl. Graham clears his throat once more, and she shoves another bite into her mouth, looking utterly miserable.

I feel terrible, but I didn't actually ask for this dinner...right? I'm about to ask Jude what her favorite foods are when Graham clears his throat and pulls a slip of paper out of seemingly thin air, sliding it over to me.

"This is Jude's schedule," he says.

At first glance, I try to keep my eyes from bugging out of my head. It's a high-gloss calendar packed full of activities from morning till night. I have a sudden memory of my own summers when I was her age, being shuttled off to a million different lessons and tutoring sessions and mandatory social gatherings. Some things never change, I guess.

"Goodness," I say, picking it up and carefully following the lines. Even her bath time is scheduled. "This is a lot."

"The house rules are quite simple," Graham says, ignoring my comment. "I expect the schedule to be adhered to by the letter. Jude is a very busy child, and the only way we get things done is by the calendar. Is that understood?"

"Yes, of course." I take another look at the color-coded chart before me and feel my stomach drop. There isn't much free time built in at all. Tutors, tennis, piano lessons, horseback-riding lessons, swimming lessons, more tutors. When is she supposed to actually just...play?

I remember so looking forward to summers as a kid: swimming, running around in the sunshine, playing with friends. Sure, I did a lot of what Jude is doing, but I don't remember it being quite so oppressively scheduled. Graham continues listing out her activities, gesturing to the calendar as he talks. I'm getting dizzy just thinking about everything we have to do.

"Your days off are Saturday and Tuesday. Esmeralda will attend to Jude on those days. You are free to leave the grounds or stay here, but either way Jude is not to bother you." Graham dabs the corners of his mouth with his napkin. It feels so...British. "You're expected at breakfast each morning at seven sharp to begin the day. Your work ends when Jude goes to bed, but you are not to leave the house without my express permission unless it is your day off. Understood?"

"Understood." I smile and try to swallow down a

Chapter 2

mouthful of bread, but I don't feel so hungry anymore. My entire summer is now locked down to the exact minute. So much for lounging in the library or laying out by the pool in the afternoons.

Graham's expectations are sky high and unrealistic. This is a summer house, during summer vacation, and he's acting like I should be running a military school. What kind of fun is that for Jude—for either of us? This poor kid is overscheduled to the max, and now so am I.

The next course of crab cakes, potatoes, and salad are brought in, and Jude chats about her day as she dives into the food. She's a sweet kid, though maybe not as energetic as I remember. I guess losing your mom will do that. Poor thing.

"Is Jude allowed to have playdates this summer?" I ask during a break in one of her stories about her favorite horse. "In the event a parent should ask, at one of her lessons?"

"All of her lessons are private, and unfortunately Jude's friends are down in Manhattan." Graham looks at me like I have eight heads. Of course they are. Can't have his baby girl slumming it with the local children, I guess. "Did you see a playdate on the calendar?"

This feels like a trick, so I take another glance at the calendar and shake my head. "No."

"Then it won't be a concern, Abbie."

God, if he could say my name forever. Forever. I'd die happy. Even if he acts like a military sergeant.

Still, no playdates for his daughter? What kind of lonely summer is this? Thinking back, though, I don't remember any other kids around the first summer I met

Abbie

the Ratliffs. It was just us then, and it's just us now. Maybe this area is populated solely with wealthy adults. Poor Jude.

We keep mostly silent after that, with Jude taking extra care to eat as if she's at an etiquette lesson. Once her plate is clean, fork and knife placed on top side by side to signal that she's finished, Graham excuses her. Esmeralda waits outside the dining room to take Jude to her bath and put her to bed, leaving me one final evening free before I dive into the chaos that is the littlest Ratliff's life.

Following Jude's lead, I place my utensils over my plate and gently push my chair back.

"Before you go, do you have any questions about my expectations?" Graham asks.

"No, sir." I shake my head. "You've made everything very clear."

"Excellent. I'll see you in the morning, then." With that, he stands up and glides out of the room. He doesn't even say goodbye.

Asshole doesn't begin to describe this man. I don't remember him being so cold and impersonal. My stomach feels heavy, and it's not because of the meal.

Upstairs, I change into a comfortable set of pajamas and curl up in my bed with my phone, wondering if I made a terrible mistake. I should be spending my summer with my friends, chasing cute boys and lounging by the pool. This feels like I've marched into a hell house.

My phone chirps, a text from my dad. *Settling in?*

I roll my eyes and sit up. *STOP. At least let me unpack before you start hounding me.*

Chapter 2

I've barely been here five hours and he's already up my ass. This is going to be a painfully long summer if he keeps going like this. All I want is a pair of headphones, some loud music, and social media to take my mind off of everything that happened today.

Can't a dad just check on his baby girl?

We both know that's not what you're doing. I sigh heavily. *He's not like I remember.*

It doesn't take a minute for my dad to answer back. *Divorce changes people.*

Are you sure he wasn't always an asshole?

Dad sends several laughing emojis. *You know what you have to do.*

"Thanks, Dad," I mutter under my breath.

He's the one who got me into this mess, and now there's no way out of it. I recline against the pile of cushy down pillows and try to envision the perfect summer—hot, wet, and full of attractive boys. Every one of them wears Graham's face, except this time they smile.

Familiar urges swell through me, so I settle under the covers, turn off the light, and slip a hand down the front of my silk shorts. Then I let my imagination take me away.

Chapter Three

Abbie

My alarm blares at six a.m. and I hate everything. I haven't had to get up this early since I was living in the dorms at Suffield and there was never enough hot water to go around for morning showers.

Isn't this summertime? After busting my butt to make straight A's every semester of my freshman year at freaking Cornell University, aren't I supposed to be sleeping in for the next few months and being generally useless? I slap a pillow over my face and groan loudly. I want to hit the snooze button six or seven more times, but the reality of my new job quickly slams over me.

I have to be up, dressed, and ready to impress in an hour. I have priorities, and unfortunately, sleeping in is no longer one of them.

After a quick shower and change, I head downstairs with ten minutes to spare. Not bad for my first official day! I breeze into the dining room, happy to be early, and find Graham already drinking his coffee. He doesn't notice me at first, so I take the time to soak him in. He's in

Chapter 3

another crisp button-down with the sleeves neatly pinned at his wrists with gold cufflinks, and this time he's wearing a pair of dark-rimmed glasses as he pores over a newspaper. Delicious.

And a hard-ass.

"Early is on time," Graham finally says by way of acknowledgement, barely looking up over his paper. "I like to see it."

Was that a compliment? For once I'm glad he's basically ignoring me, because my cheeks are on fire. I hate how he does this to me, even after all this time. I should be over it by now, but my crush appears to have only multiplied over the years.

"My father always impressed upon me the importance of being punctual," I explain, grasping for something to say to Graham and sounding like a Stepford Wife for all my trouble.

"Your father is a smart man," he says.

"Morning, Abbie," Jude croaks from behind me, stifling a yawn as she walks into the room to join us, effectively putting an end to my ogling.

"Good morning, Jude." I smile at her. She does her best to muster up a smile in return. "How did you sleep?"

"Okay." She takes her seat next to Graham. "Morning, Daddy."

He finally sets his paper down and gestures at the seat across from Jude, flashing those dark eyes at me just long enough to make my stomach tighten into a knot. "Sit," he commands.

I do.

We're served by one of the same women from dinner

Abbie

last night, who Jude addresses as Mary, and then we quietly dig into breakfast. A scone and coffee for Graham, multigrain pancakes with sliced banana for me and Jude. Jude doesn't have much to say, I've noticed. She plays with the syrup on her plate and takes dainty bites of pancake while Graham intones her schedule for the day, but not much else.

After he's done, I ask Jude, "Are you looking forward to your day?"

She has a tutor, she has tennis, she has piano lessons—and judging by her scowl, she hates it all.

"Of course she is," Graham answers for her. "I wouldn't be paying for all of this if she didn't like it."

Right. I recognize the lifestyle, but I can see that it isn't working for Jude. She silently drags another piece of pancake through syrup and doesn't look at either of us.

I don't know what else to say, because it seems like almost everything that comes out of my mouth is wrong when I'm around Graham. I honestly don't remember him being this terse when I last saw him. Maybe my dad is right. Maybe divorce changes people.

What would make him softer, more tender?

"I have several meetings today and won't be back until dinner." Graham, finished with his breakfast, wipes his mouth tidily and straightens his newspaper, his tablet, his cell phone. Everything in its place. Another routine. "I trust you will be able to provide Jude everything she needs today without issue?"

"Of course." I nod a little too eagerly. "If I have any questions, I'll ask Esmeralda."

"The calendar should be quite plain." Graham looks

Chapter 3

pointedly at me. "But yes, ask Esmeralda for assistance if needed."

He gets up from the table and kisses the top of Jude's head on his way out. She smiles up at him but continues her silence. Yet again, he didn't say goodbye to me, which burns a little. I don't want him to view me as invisible, just another member of the help he commands.

I want him to think I'm smart and capable. I want him to acknowledge me. I guess I'll just have to work harder, find the right things to say. Mom always said I had a good read of people, but Graham is all but a brick wall.

It'll just take time, I tell myself. *This is all new. You'll figure him out soon.*

"How was your breakfast?" I ask Jude, once she's finished. "I love pancakes."

"It was okay."

"Just okay? What's your dream breakfast?" I ask, trying to coax some personality out of her. In my head she's still five years old, but it's obvious that she's grown up a lot over the last three years. Maybe too much.

"I like eggs best," she answers with a slight head tilt. "Mary makes these baked eggs with cheese mixed in, and toasted Italian bread to dip in it."

"Sounds like something I need to try," I tell her. "Mary seems really nice."

Jude nods. "She is. You're nice, too. I'm glad you're going to be my summer nanny. Are you a grown-up now, or do you still go to school?"

"Well, I'm nineteen, so I guess I'm technically an adult. But I am still in school—I go to college now, at

Cornell, but I'm on summer break just like you until the fall."

"Cornell...that's an Ivy League school, isn't it?" Off my surprised nod, she goes on, "Daddy's always saying I have to go to an Ivy League or else Oxford. I don't care where I go, as long as they can teach me how to be an animal doctor."

"I'm sure wherever you end up, you'll do great. But it might be a little early to be worrying about college, no?" I smile at her, and she manages a small one back. "I still can't believe how much you've grown since the last time I saw you."

"I'm three inches taller than last summer! Mary measured me in the kitchen doorway. Daddy says I need to stop growing." She twirls a lock of fine hair around her fingers. "But I just want to be grown up already."

"Why's that?"

Jude turns to look out the windows and sighs. "Just because."

The poor kid looks depressed. I start to gather up our dishes, but Jude stops me.

"Mary does that. Don't you have someone at your house to do that?" She looks back at me. "My dad said you come from a big house, too. In Connecticut."

"We do," I say smoothly. "But sometimes I like to help."

"Oh," Jude says, as though it's a revelation. "I like to help, too."

"I bet you do. You look very helpful."

Jude slumps in her chair. "You don't have to talk to me like I'm little."

Chapter 3

Well, hello, mini Graham. "Sorry, Jude. I forget sometimes that you aren't so little anymore."

"It's okay." She shrugs easily. "Anyway, we should go. It's time for Spanish now."

I pull out her calendar. "You are correct. It's like you don't even need me."

"I'm still only eight." Jude looks blankly at me for a moment.

What is going on in this house? "Right, right. Off we go."

The Spanish tutor meets us in the library, arms loaded with books. Last time I saw Jude, the girl could barely read, and now she's conjugating better than most of the kids in my own high school Spanish classes ever did. She politely answers all the questions, repeating the phrases over and over as the tutor corrects her accent, and dutifully works until the hour is up.

Then we shuttle off to tennis lessons on the Ratliffs' private court. There's a covered area with comfortable lounge chairs next to the court for viewing, so I kick my feet up and watch Jude's sweaty little pigtails bounce. Same as before, she dutifully performs all her tasks and runs around the court as needed. Yet never once do I see her smile.

Esmeralda brings us lunch by the tennis court while Jude cools down, so she has time to eat before piano lessons. Jude plays with her food while I try, again, to make conversation.

"You're really good!" I say, picking at sliced veggies and hummus. "Have you been playing long?"

"For like my whole life." Jude takes a thoughtful bite

of her pita sandwich and chews slowly. I swear she counts bites.

"I started playing when I was eight," I tell her. "You're much better than I was at eight."

"It's just because I've been playing for such a long time."

"Right. Makes sense." I nod. What happened to this poor kid? Yesterday she was excited to see me, but today she's locked down tighter than my dad's office portfolio. "Do you play tennis with your friends when you're in NYC?"

Jude only shrugs, and it makes me wonder just how many "friends" she really has. And then it's off to piano lessons. Piano is exactly like every other lesson today: she performs whatever task is requested of her without much effort, but she never looks like she's enjoying herself. Probably because she should be playing a massive game of hide-and-seek instead of studying all summer, but what do I know?

Except I *do* know. I grew up just like her, shuffling between private schools, with a million different activities scheduled and private tutors coming out of my nose, but the thing is, I have fond memories—because I at least got to choose my lessons, and there were plenty of other kids around. On top of that, my parents never made me do schoolwork over the summer like this. Jude clearly isn't happy. She looks like she's just going through the motions. At eight years old. It isn't until three in the afternoon that she finally perks up, a little bit.

I'm waiting at the bottom of the stairs when she appears in full riding gear. "I'm ready."

Chapter 3

"Is that a smile I see?" I ask.

Jude frowns. Okay, not the way to go with her. Got it.

"Which horse is your favorite?" I ask as we make our way to the stables.

She shrugs.

"Come on, everyone has a favorite!"

This time, Jude looks like she's mulling it over. "Probably Desi. She's a British Vanner. My dad bought her for me the last time we were in the UK."

"Wow." Vanner Horses are both very rare here and very expensive. "I've never seen a Vanner in person. I can't wait to meet her."

"She's good with people." Jude looks at me side-eyed. "Like you are."

The compliment stops me in my tracks. I've been convinced all day that I've been doing nothing but annoying her. I try to find something nice to say, but we've entered the stables and Jude takes off down the row of stalls. It's the most energy I've seen her have all day, too. Tennis lessons excluded, where she was expected to run around.

"Hey, Jude!" a friendly female voice sings. "Don't make it bad."

"Take a sad song and make it better!" Jude sings back.

"You're Abbie, right?" A short, athletic brunette walks around the corner and I nod. She doesn't look much older than me. "I'm Cassie Conner, Jude's equestrian coach."

"Nice to meet you." I shake her hand with a smile.

"You can head out to the corral. There's a seating area there." Cassie nods toward an open door at the back of the stables. "We'll be just a minute getting the horses ready."

"Perfect, thanks. See you out there, Jude!" I call out.

"Okay!" comes her little voice from the depths of the stables.

I turn around to walk out and promptly collide into something massive and solid. We both share an, "Oh!"

"Sorry!" I feel my cheeks heating with embarrassment. "I didn't see you."

"That's okay." The owner of the body I just rammed into grins a pearly white smile. He's got deep blue eyes, a full head of blond hair, and is built like a truck. A sexy truck. "I was hoping a pretty girl would run into me today."

Don't get me wrong, the guy is beautiful—but he clearly knows it, which kind of ruins the appeal. Still, having him smile so intently at me makes my stomach feel a little funny.

"You must be here with Jude."

"I am. I'm Abbie, by the way." I try to restrain the smile on my face, but he's so damn cheery and it's been a while since someone looked this excited to see me. "Jude's a sweet kid."

"She's really good with the horses. Quiet. They like that."

"That must explain why my parents' horses all hate me," I joke.

His eyes practically sparkle with amusement. "I find that hard to believe."

"Oh, I'm very unlikeable." Why am I flirting with this

Chapter 3

guy? I don't know, but I can't seem to stop it, either. "It's a gift."

"Quinn!" another deep voice hollers from the stalls.

"I better get back to work. Nice meeting you, Abbie," he says, sauntering away.

I shake out my limbs for just a moment to re-center myself. I'm not here to flirt. I have a job to do.

"So you met Quinn?" Cassie says with a smirk when I join them at the corral. Jude is working on dressage today. "He's got a knack for running into all the nannies."

"Jude's had other nannies?"

"Every summer. None of them stuck around long because of the former Mrs. Ratliff, but that didn't stop Quinn from trying to leave his mark." Cassie gives me a knowing look.

I laugh. "Noted. Thanks for the warning."

Jude performs a series of walks with Desi, and Cassie directs her for the next set. Jude does an excellent job and actually has a smile, a real smile, on her face. Her horse is a beautiful piebald beauty with an excellent mane. The pair move together seamlessly. Quinn was telling the truth—Jude is great with the horse.

"She seems to really love this," I tell Cassie.

"She does. It's probably the only time I see her happy around here," Cassie says, and then immediately looks like she regrets it. "That came out wrong. What I meant was—"

"It's okay," I assure her. "I spent the summer here when Jude was five, and it seems she's changed a lot over the past few years. Or maybe just since the divorce...?"

Abbie

Cassie shrugs. "She's been like this for a while. It wasn't just Mrs. Ratliff leaving."

"Poor thing." Jude used to be so loud and...sparkly... but now she's reluctant and shy.

"She's a good kid. Just really quiet," Cassie explains. "But if you ask me, what she really needs is more fun in her life."

"Perfect. Because that's exactly what I'm here for," I lie.

Chapter Four

Abbie

I stand in front of my wardrobe again, video chatting with Amanda, on a mission.

"Okay, I have to make a better impression at dinner tonight," I say, shoving clothes around unhappily. "It's like he doesn't even see me. I don't want him treating me like the rest of the staff, you know? He needs to view me as an adult and a professional. Not just the girl babysitting his daughter."

"What about the black one?" Amanda offers. "You look hot in that."

"Real professional, Amanda!" I roll my eyes with a laugh. "I mean, yes, I also want to look hot. But he needs to respect me first and foremost. A man like that won't give anyone the time of day unless he respects them."

"God, I want to be as good at reading people as you are one day. How do you do it?"

"I've spent a lifetime around my parents," I say bitterly. "But I don't know that I'm all that good, anyway. Getting through to him is going to be rough. Jude barely talked to me all day, too. She's like his depressed little mini me."

"Wow, that's sad."

"It is." And I mean it. I may be paid to look after her, but that doesn't mean I'm heartless. She seems miserable, and I want to help change that. "Okay, what about this one?" I pull out a turtleneck sleeveless number in stretchy red knit. "With my Nana's pearls?"

"Ooh!" Amanda squeals. "Perfect! If you curl your hair and pin it up, you'll look like Sharon Stone!"

"Who?"

"This old actress from the 90s. My parents love her. She was totally hot back in the day. My dad says she still is."

"If she's hot, I'm in. I gotta go get ready. Call you later?"

"I want all the details!!" Amanda squeals again.

I take a quick shower to wash off the stink of horse and style my hair up in a way that I imagine Amanda meant. Whoever Sharon Stone is. Maybe Graham knows who she is and will make the connection? I apply a little more makeup this time, and a little darker, to age myself up. My favorite lipstick goes on last. It took me forever to find exactly the right red for me, but this one's a knockout —it's semi-sheer and the color of fruit punch, with a hint of blue undertone.

In the mirror, I look confident and professional. Let's hope Graham thinks so, too.

Jude waits in her room, freshly changed, flipping through her tablet. Massive stuffed animals, as tall as I am, sit in a corner, and even her bed is huge and

Chapter 4

vaulted. Sitting there, she looks much smaller than eight.

"Want to walk down to dinner together?" I ask brightly.

Jude carefully lays down the tablet and obediently walks down the hall without waiting for me. Guess I still have a long way to go with this one.

It's only the first week, I tell myself. *There's plenty of time.*

An empty table awaits us in the dining room, though three place settings are laid out.

"Where's my dad?" Jude asks with a frown. "Is he missing dinner tonight?"

My heart sinks. "Um—I'm not sure." Does Graham miss dinner often?

"He'll be down in just a few minutes," Esmeralda says, popping her head in. "Mr. Ratliff just arrived home."

"Thank you, Esmeralda," Jude says, sounding older than she should.

"You're very welcome." Esmeralda winks at me before disappearing back into the hall.

"You really kicked butt out there on that horse today," I tell Jude, trying to cheer her up.

Her face goes a little pink, and pieces of my heart anchor onto her tiny cheeks. "Cassie is a really good coach."

"I'll bet, but I saw how hard you worked." I point playfully at her. "Dressage isn't easy. You have to really connect with your horse to do it properly. Desi seems to trust you a lot."

Abbie

"I've been working on our bond," she says sagely. "Cassie says that's the most important part of our training. We have to connect. It's harder during the school year, since I only get to ride on the weekends. But when we're here for the summer, I can see Desi every day."

Well. That's at least one plus for her being stuck here, I suppose.

"Keep doing what you're doing, Jude. You looked absolutely awesome out there."

"Sorry I'm late," Graham announces in a booming voice. He kisses Jude's head on his way to his chair. "My meeting ran long."

"That's okay. We were just talking about Jude's riding lessons today." I give him a bright smile and channel my most professional look. "She has such an amazing bond with her horse. She really knows what she's doing."

Graham says nothing. Mary comes in with our dinner, salmon and wild rice with a rainbow of summer vegetables, and serves us in a pleasant silence. When she leaves, I continue with my rundown of Jude's day, determined to impress him with my level of attentiveness.

"In Spanish, she worked on conjugating *dar*. I remember having trouble with that one myself back in high school, so I was very impressed with how well she did."

I pause and take a few bites, waiting for Graham to engage. When he doesn't, I try again.

"Jude was all over the court during tennis, too. She's got a wicked backhand, which I'm sure you already know."

Chapter 4

Still nothing.

"And in piano—"

"I receive detailed reports from all her tutors, Abbie," he interrupts. My *God*, the way he says my name. Will it never not be my undoing? "As such, I am not interested in a rehash of my daughter's day."

I blink back the shock and try to keep it clear from my face. Unsuccessfully. "You don't...want to hear about Jude's day?"

"If Jude wants to tell me, Jude will tell me." Graham looks pointedly at me, and then turns his attention to his daughter, who looks like she wants nothing more than to be buried under her rice. "Do you, Jude?"

Jude stares at her plate with large, unblinking eyes, and shakes her head. Her fork gently shifts her rice around the plate.

"Don't play with your food," he says, a little on the stern side for something so benign.

"Sorry," Jude says softly and puts her fork down.

Anger starts creeping up my chest. Doesn't he see how miserable his child is? I would hardly call that playing with her food, and he had to get on her because I asked him a question?

No wonder his wife left. He's a dick.

You just got here, I remind myself. *Do not blow this.*

I have to get my anger in check. My dad warned me Graham was "particular," though I had no idea what that meant at the time.

Understatement of the year.

"You're going to have to grin and bear it, baby girl,"

my dad had told me. "Working for a man like Graham isn't for the faint of heart."

"But he's your best friend." I frowned at him. "Shouldn't you be able to just...give me all the secrets to making him happy?"

"*Was* my best friend," he corrected. "Still a friend, but life and time has a way of pushing people apart. You're a quick study, Abbie. You'll learn him. But there will be times you'll just need to bite your tongue."

Bite your tongue, Abbie.

I send a mental apology to Jude and take another bite of my salmon. He doesn't want to know about his daughter's day? Okay, fine. I can find other ways to talk to him and show him just how grown I am. I've sat through enough of my parents' horribly boring dinner parties to know what "adults" like to talk about. Safe topics, like the goddamn weather.

"The weather was just about perfect today," I offer in a cheery voice. "It made for a pleasant afternoon. Were you able to enjoy it?"

"I was in meetings," Graham answers in a kinder voice. He still doesn't exactly sound like he's in the mood to converse, but at least his harshness is gone.

"Maybe you should host the next one outside, before it gets too hot." I force a smile. Being an adult is so damn boring. "It probably won't be this nice for much longer."

We fall back into silence. Damn. Okay, fine. I know what will get him talking.

"What is it that you do, again?" I ask, all but batting my eyelashes. "It's been so long since I was last here, I don't remember."

Chapter 4

"I own banks both here and in the U.K. The family business, which I expanded to the States." I must be on the right track. He looks a little livelier. Jude, however, looks more bored than ever.

"Wow. That's impressive," I say honestly. "Managing all that must be a lot of work."

"It is." He takes a drink of water and the way his Adam's apple bobs does things to me. Everything he does causes a reaction somewhere in my body. Too bad he's a massive assbag. "But it affords the lifestyle we have. I am able to give Jude the best of everything."

"I can see that. You must be very busy."

Silence again. This pie is going to take longer to crack, to borrow a phrase from my Nana. I remember Graham being so much more lively three years ago. He's always been stern, of course, but he was also generally enjoyable to be around. My dad used to laugh, actually laugh, around him. My dad hasn't really laughed in the years since.

Graham was supposed to be so different. So was Jude. Natasha leaving must have completely destroyed them. How terrible. I can't even imagine. If my mom left, I'd be heartbroken. We may not always get along, but she's *my mom*. She's a part of me. And Jude is so, so young to have lost that. I spend the rest of the meal brooding along with them.

"It's bath time, Jude," Graham says, interrupting my thoughts.

"Okay." Just like all day, the girl gets up obediently and walks out of the room.

She works so hard to be good, and I suddenly realize

Abbie

what's been right in front of my face since I got here: Jude doesn't want to give anyone (else) a reason to abandon her.

My heart breaks for this girl. She deserves a happy life, one where she can be carefree and loved without reservation. Then again, maybe I'm assuming too much. Maybe this isn't about Natasha at all. Maybe Jude's just grown into a shy kid. Maybe.

Then I realize I'm all alone with Graham. Butterflies flood my veins and fill my stomach. His shitty demeanor frustratingly adds to his allure. Between that and the accent, my fantasies barely have a chance to feature anyone else. How can he be so attractive, yet so freaking awful?

Men. Men are the worst.

I try to think of another topic to discuss, but he busies himself with his phone. Unsure what else to do, I linger over my meal in silence. Why did he send Jude away before she was done eating? Last night, we all finished dinner together.

My stomach flips again at the reasons he might have wanted the two of us to be alone.

So he can privately tell me how great a job I'm doing, since he's a man of little fanfare.

So he can compliment my outfit, and tell me how much I look like Sharon Stone.

So he can tear me a new one about my attentiveness to Jude's schedule.

The last one makes my stomach turn from butterflies to a sour pit. I hope it's not that.

"I wanted to thank you for your kindness, Mr.

Chapter 4

Ratliff," I say. "You and your staff have been so wonderful since I got here yesterday. I think I'm really going to enjoy my time here."

He nods thoughtfully and then gives me a slow, searing once-over, from my head to my feet and back up again, that makes everything inside me run hot and still.

"I need a word after you put her to bed," he says.

The very air I breathe stops in my throat. And then, like last time, he gets up and leaves.

As soon as he's gone, I let out a quiet little squeal of a giggle. He wants to see me privately. After *clearly* checking me out. Oh my God.

I did it. I really did it.

It worked.

Chapter Five

Abbie

JUDE GOES DOWN without much of a fight. I read her a book I remember from my childhood, *Pinkalicious,* and she drops off by the time the imaginary golden unicorn shows up. Poor kid is so busy during the day, she doesn't need much help going to sleep. As she lays there curled around a horse stuffed animal, breathing softly, she reminds me of a tiny angel.

I'm going to get through to her, one way or another. She needs a friend. *I* need a friend. Sure, it's not ideal to have an eight-year-old be your bestie, but at least she's a sweetheart.

I take a few minutes to clean up her bedroom, shelving wayward books and heaping the stuffed animals back in their piles, but there isn't much to do. She's a pretty tidy child. Before I leave, I sneak one last glance at her. Jude snores, just a little, and it's sweet.

The urge to hug her swells through my veins. I don't, because it's weird to hug someone when they are uncon-

Chapter 5

scious, but it doesn't stop the want. I just want her to know someone cares.

I pause, hand on the doorknob. Why do I care so much about this girl? I'm here to do a job, not get connected to anything. I shake my head a little, trying to knock loose the gum that's sticking Jude to my brain.

"Abbie?" Esmeralda says, coming up behind me. "Is she asleep?"

"Out cold." I shut the door silently and turn around. Esmeralda looks tired, but she keeps a smile anchored to her face. I really do like her. "It didn't take long."

"Jude doesn't take much work." Her voice sounds a little wistful, but she keeps up the smile. "Mr. Ratliff is waiting for you in his study. Do you need help finding it?"

"I think I can manage. Thank you, Esmeralda."

"Of course."

Before going into the lion's den, I stop by my room to refresh my makeup. New coat of lipstick, new layer of blush, quick re-curl of the hair. I want him to take one look at me and know I mean business. I want him to take one look at me and want me like I want him.

The thought sends chills down my spine and I nearly burn myself with the curling iron as I shiver.

What would I do if a man like that actually wanted me? So many things. So. Many. Things. I hike my dress up a little and change into a strappy pair of heels instead of my flats.

"You have a job to do," I tell myself in the mirror and do a quick spin. I look professional. I look mature. I look hot as hell. "Just let him try to tell you no, looking like this."

But I have to take a deep breath to steady myself before I leave my room. I grasp the doorjamb and inhale deep, trying to still the nerves coursing through me. Graham is as delicious as ever, but he's so much older. So mysterious, and almost...dangerous. He was married to a famous actress, for heaven's sake. His tastes are exquisite.

And I'm—what? A nineteen-year-old still hoping "second puberty" is a thing? With tits too small and an ass too flat and that beautiful optimism that seems to evaporate after youth.

I steady myself and square my shoulders. I'm beautiful. I'm smart. I'm determined. I'm young, yes, but there is power in youth. I just have to find it. Tonight is my first test.

Done with my mini pep talk, I walk to the study, head held high and my shoulders back. I walk with purpose. With poise. Looking like a sexy badass. To, you know, meet with my boss.

The door is shut, even though he was expecting me. I roll my eyes. Doubtless it's some power move. They must teach this garbage in the rich-boy fraternities, because my dad does the same thing. I knock clearly and loudly, and take another deep breath to keep my nerves at bay.

"Enter," he calls through the door.

God, he can't even say "come in" like a normal person. Why is that so attractive? Why is it so hot when he asserts himself? I have to steady myself to keep from tripping over the entry.

"You wanted to see me." I manage to keep my voice

Chapter 5

level as I open the door, and pop a hip out, just a little. Just a touch of assertiveness.

"Please, come in." He gestures without looking up from his laptop. Something about him looks different, but I can't quite put my finger on it.

The study is as lavish as the rest of the house, but with a more masculine style. There aren't bookshelves in here, but there are plenty of books sprawled across an antique table, a few leather chairs, a sofa, and a fireplace. I see some framed certificates and diplomas on the wall, along with photos of Graham with Jude.

And...Jude on a horse. Toddler Jude dressed for some kind of dance recital. Slightly younger Jude posing with Princess Tiana at Disney. Actually, most of these are Jude. It makes me feel all warm and fuzzy to see all these photos of her, which speaks volumes about how much Graham adores his daughter, despite the fact that he seems so stern with her. I also notice that there's not a single picture of Natasha anywhere.

And in the middle of all this, sitting there like a god, is Graham Ratliff himself, behind an equally imposing and behemoth desk that gleams in the warm light spilling from the brass floor lamps in the corners. My God, the man is stunning. He's literally glowing right now.

I take a seat in a straight-backed chair in front of his desk and cross my legs slowly. I want him to look at me without knowing I want him to. It has to be a suggestion, slow, coy.

His sleeves are rolled up—that's what's different. His exposed forearms are toned and luscious, the muscle definition making my mouth water. This is like Graham

Abbie

Relaxed, or Graham 2.0, and it is sexy. Really sexy. He's got his glasses on again too, which I absolutely love. Dark rimmed and thick, framing his penetratingly blue eyes. His hair is slightly tousled, like he may have been tugging on it a little.

I cannot overstate how turned on I am at this exact moment.

And he wanted to talk to me. Privately. Like this. There's already a scotch on his desk. Graham has wound down for the evening and invited me into his private quarters. There can be literally nothing bad about this tonight.

Butterflies hit my stomach again, hard and heavy.

"And...done." Graham closes the lid to his laptop and finally looks at me. Nothing on his face betrays what he's thinking. No poker tells about my dress or my leg draped across my lap. Nothing.

He stands and makes his way to a fancy liquor cabinet on the other side of the room, drink in hand, for a refill. He still hasn't properly acknowledged me yet and my skin is crawling in frustration. How hard is it to say hello? He pours another finger of scotch and then sits on the couch. Taking his lead, I get up and cross the room to sit next to him.

This is the closest we've ever been, since the summer I was sixteen. He smells musky and woodsy and clean, everything I expected him to smell like, and I immediately plan to steal a bottle of his cologne and spritz my pillows with it.

"Old enough to drink yet?" Graham asks, finally looking at me. "Or does it matter?"

Chapter 5

He turns his body to face me.

I can barely breathe.

"Doesn't matter," I say, proud of how put together I sound.

"That means no." His lips quirk upward, just slightly, into something that might maybe one day be considered a smile. Well, well, well. I cracked the giant. I feel ten feet tall myself.

"I didn't think men like you obeyed the rules." I gesture to the numerous frames on the walls amplifying his achievements.

"There are always rules to follow." He takes a slow sip of his scotch and pleasure washes across his features. It's intoxicating to watch. The bob of his Adam's apple, the purse of his lips, the way his forearm flexes, God, it's like he's doing it all on purpose.

Graham Ratliff is definitely sexier than he was three years ago.

Faced with him like this, I'm suddenly feeling very unprepared. He's so much older and more experienced. All my shortcomings come crashing around me once more and I'm not sure how to swim out from under them. Everyone on the debate team says I'm great at reading people, at thinking two steps ahead of my opponents and at presenting myself confidently even when I'm actually not feeling confident at all. My father said no one else had the ability to do this job. But here I am, and I don't know if he's right.

Everything feels so wrong.

"That shade of lipstick?" Graham says, his voice almost a growl.

Abbie

His question eviscerates my thoughts and brings me back to the present. The way he's looking at me, studying my face, the hunger in his eyes—he wants to kiss me. There aren't butterflies anymore, this is a full force cyclone erupting in my veins.

"Yes?" I lean in, like a magnet drawn to his impenetrable metal.

"Is it called whore's red?"

I blink, letting his words wash over me. The sultriness in me is gone, shock in its wake. This definitely isn't what I thought it was.

"Excuse me?" I choke out.

He takes another sip of his scotch, but this time the sex appeal is gone. "The people I hire to work with my child are expected to be appropriate role models."

I clear my throat. "Mr. Ratliff, I'm not sure what you are insinuating, but—"

"I'm not insinuating anything, Miss Montgomery," he says coldly. "I assumed the child of one of my oldest friends would have the presence of self to maintain her respectability." Graham stands and walks back to his desk, drink in hand. "Am I incorrect?"

"No. Absolutely not," I manage.

I feel hit by a truck. *Whore's red*? Who even says that? Who acts this way? Natasha Ratliff may not have won any friends here in the house, but how did *he*? I guess loyalty is easy enough to buy when you have more money than God.

"To be absolutely clear, you are expected to adhere to a certain level of decorum. Understood?" He cuts a rough look at me.

Chapter 5

"Yes, sir," I say miserably.

"Does Ford know you walk around painted up like that?"

"My father has seen me in makeup, yes," I say, my teeth on edge. This is not how this was supposed to go, and I'm quickly being sent downstream. I need to rectify this, but I have no idea how. "I'm sorry if it offended you, Mr. Ratliff. I had no intention of being disrespectful."

I measure out my words carefully, but inside? I'm livid. How dare he talk to me this way.

He gives me a hard look, his eyes raking over my body, and I'm suddenly very self-conscious. I want to take off this dress and hide in a hoodie. I want to hide from his cruel, judgmental gaze. A smaller part of me wants to strip naked, right here in his "respectable" office, and sully his space. I want him to fuck me on the desk, lose every ounce of this bullshit decorum.

"And that dress." He gestures with his glass. "It's entirely too short. I expect you have other clothing you've brought with you?"

"I—"

"Do I need to get you a uniform, or can you assure me that I don't need to worry about how you'll dress?"

I'm straight up insulted now. Fuck this guy. Fuck him and his big house and his big money and his big fucking attitude. I take a deep breath and stand up, drawing myself up taller.

"I can dress myself just fine, Mr. Ratliff. Thank you very much."

Turning my back on him, I storm out of the room

indignantly, but I stop just at the threshold of the doorway. I can't help it.

"Teenage Fantasy," I say over my shoulder.

"What?" he asks, almost bored.

I lock eyes with him. Very carefully, enunciating each word, I say, "That's the name of my lipstick. Teenage Fantasy."

I don't look back again as I stalk away. I know I've fucked this up, but I couldn't help myself. What a condescending ass. Still, I've basically burned the bridge I was building, and I have no idea how I'm going to get on his good side now.

I'll have to try other methods.

Chapter Six

Abbie

As much as I want to show Graham Ratliff exactly what a whore looks like, I dress like a freaking nun for the rest of the week. Polos buttoned up to my chin, hemlines halfway down my calf, cropped jeans instead of my trusty daisy dukes and light cardigans over my sleeveless tops. I look longingly at the short, cute summer dresses I'd hung up in the wardrobe, wishing for relief from the heat and the excessive amount of clothing.

"Soon, my babies," I promise them.

Graham, however, doesn't seem to give me even a passing glance. In fact, he has very little to say to me during the week, despite being a total asshole in his study. I can't figure out what to talk to him about. He doesn't want to know about Jude's lessons, he doesn't want to make small talk, and he has zero interest in tooting his own horn about his business prowess.

I'm getting absolutely nowhere and it's frustrating. How can I move forward when he won't even talk to me? The worst part is, the crueler he is, the more I want him.

Abbie

The more I want him to be interested in me. The more I want him to bend me over and punish me for being a wanton little hussy.

I think about strutting around the house in one of my string bikinis and heels just to get his attention. Wearing my shortest dresses and accidentally dropping things in front of his office door. At this point, anything is better than nothing. But nothing is exactly what's happening.

Jude, on the other hand, has been clinging to me like a koala. Not that I mind. We've spent a lot of time together this week, and I've done everything I can to get her to come out of her shell. Slowly but surely, she's starting to crack. Between her litany of lessons and myriad of practices, we've formed a little bond.

It's sweet. She needs some joy in her life and I've tried to give it to her, although having a child all but cling to your leg can be a bit much sometimes. I have to learn how to balance.

"Hi, Abbie!" Jude beams at me at breakfast on Thursday.

Graham's at an early meeting and doesn't show up at all. Disappointing, but also a relief.

"Morning, Jude. Ready for Spanish? You have a quiz today, right?" I ask her, digging into my eggs benedict.

Mary is an excellent chef and having exquisite food every day has started to spoil me. It makes me long for the old days at my house.

"*Si*," she says with a nod. "Can you speak Spanish?"

"*Un poquito.*" I smile at her. "I took four years of it in high school. But I stopped practicing about a year ago and it's a little rough now."

Chapter 6

"You can practice with me." She smiles a little, and then looks timid. "I mean, if you want to."

I give her a happy grin. "I would love that. I mean, *me encantaria*."

This time a real smile, small but present, blooms across her face and she buries herself in her food. This girl just wants some damn attention. How hard is it to give it to her? For all Graham's posturing about the quality of people he allows into his daughter's life, he doesn't seem to care very much about being involved himself.

When I was growing up, my dad worked all the time, too. I felt like I was nothing but an inconvenience to him—he barely paid attention to me, and when he did it was usually to scold me—and that I wasn't worthy to spend time with him. Needless to say, it took a long time for us to form any sort of connection.

The first time he seemed to take an actual interest in me was when I was in sixth grade, doing a project on Alexander Hamilton's contributions to the Federalist Papers. It led to us having a lot of complex discussions about law and government, which impressed him enough that he started sharing his morning newspaper with me and asking me what I thought about the articles. It's no surprise that I'm now an American Studies major at Cornell; my area of concentration is legal and constitutional studies. Still trying to impress Daddy, I guess.

Maybe that's why I care so much about Jude. I see a lot of myself in her.

Spanish lessons go well, and Jude aces her quiz. I pay more attention than usual so I can refresh my knowledge.

Abbie

My mom desperately wanted me to be multilingual, hoping I could live out her dream of traveling the world and becoming an interpreter for the UN. Sadly for her, I was too busy flirting with Aidan McAdams to really care much about my foreign language courses. But now? I'll remember how to conjugate some verbs.

Maybe Jude and I can speak Spanish at the dinner table and impress Graham. He can see my dedication, see how serious I am about this whole thing. Maybe a girl who can speak multiple languages is a turn-on for him, too. It's worth a shot, at least.

I sling my arm around Jude's shoulders on the way to tennis and she doesn't flinch once. Instead, she leans into it with that same crooked smile from breakfast. I wonder whose smile she has: Natasha's or Graham's? It's hard to tell after only seeing Graham's frown for a week.

While Jude is bopping around the court, I take advantage of my break to text Amanda.

Tell me something fun. I need something fun.

Aidan McAdams is back in town ;)

I pause, waiting for the familiar McAdams butterflies to come flooding through me, but they don't. I guess since I've set my tastes on higher things, he doesn't feel as delicious anymore.

Are you going to ask him out?? I text her back.

It takes her a minute to respond. *Girl code, bitch. Plus, he's too clean-cut for me. I like it when they're a little dirtbaggy.*

This makes me laugh. Amanda did always go for guys who were a little rougher around the edges. Our differences are part of what makes us such good friends;

Chapter 6

there's never any overlap in wants. We just support each other on our own paths. Amanda has been my best friend for five years, and I can't imagine my life without her.

After a lunch of probably the best lobster roll I've ever had in my life, and Jude's piano lesson, Jude takes my hand on the way to the stables. She's working on jumps today, on a muscled Irish Sport Horse, a gorgeous imported thing. I'm astounded by the horses here.

"Welcome back," a smooth voice calls after Jude walks her horse out to the corral.

"Hi, Quinn." I give him a friendly grin. He used to be my type, before permeating thoughts of Graham hijacked my brain. "How are you today?"

"Better now that you're here," he says. Was that a wink? "Having fun?"

"All day, every day."

"Do you ride?" He's polishing a saddle, making it gleam in the afternoon sun. "You look like you ride."

"I do. We didn't have quite the assortment of horses as you do here, but I grew up riding."

"Riding is great exercise."

"Uh, sure." I laugh.

"You look like you're in great shape already, though."

My cheeks flush a little. It's been a while since someone was so direct with me, and I'm especially susceptible to the flirting after spending the week on lockdown in a house with a man who apparently hates everything I am. So yeah, the attention is nice. Especially when I know I'm dressed like an old lady in a pair of mom jeans and a long-sleeve polo.

Abbie

"Well, I should get out there to watch." I lean over and whisper, "I think you missed a spot."

His laugh follows me out of the stables.

Jude struggles a little with the jumps, but still does an exceptional job for someone her age on such a big horse. Cassie leads her around, firm and encouraging in her instruction.

"Abbie! Watch me!" Jude calls out, just before she takes another jump.

I shield my eyes from the sun and watch her soar over the beam, easily maneuvering the horse through the difficult stunt. I clap and cheer for her, and she grins easily from atop the monster horse. She seems to be happiest when she's on a horse. This, I can definitely understand.

That's how the rest of the lesson goes—"Watch me! Watch me!" as she performs jump after jump. It makes my heart feel warm and fuzzy, even if it does get a bit repetitive.

After, we walk her horse back to the stable where Jude removes the tack, brushes her horse down, and gives her water, chatting to her all the while like she's a friend.

"What's her name?" I ask.

"Lucy," Jude says fondly, scratching the horse's nose and feeding her an oatmeal treat. "My mom really loved Lucille Ball."

"Desi and Lucy." I nod. "I get it. That's really cute. My mom loved that show, too."

"Have you watched it?"

"Some of them. I really liked her neighbor, Ethel. She was funny."

"Lucy is the best." Jude looks up at me with big,

Chapter 6

sweet eyes. "We should go for a ride tomorrow! You can ride, right?"

"Of course I can." I give her a high five. Sure I can help her have a little bit of fun for once in her life. "Let's do it. Where do you want to go? I'll bet there are some really nice trails around here."

Just then, Cassie joins us. "I can set up a trail ride for tomorrow if you'd like, Jude."

"Yay!" Jude claps her hands and gives me a hug.

After dinner, another meal that's mysteriously absent of one Graham Ratliff, I get Jude bathed and read-to and put to bed and then call my dad.

"Any progress?" he asks, instead of saying hello.

"Jude is really warming up to me." I recline on my bed and close my eyes, tired from the full day of activities. "She's a very busy little girl."

"That's not what I'm asking."

"Just ship me my riding clothes, will you?" I don't want to talk about this right now. "Overnight, please. It's important."

"I expect to hear more next time."

"Thanks, Dad." I hang up without saying goodbye. If he can answer without saying hello, I can hang up without the same formalities.

Esmeralda brings me my package the next morning, bright and early. "This just arrived for you, Miss Montgomery!" she chirps.

"Please, call me Abbie." I take the package gratefully. At least he sent it. "Miss Montgomery makes me feel like an old spinster."

"Ah, youth," is all she says. "Enjoy your ride."

Abbie

Mary meets us downstairs with two picnic backpacks that are full of delicious food, I'm sure. Cassie waits in the stables with a pair of gorgeous horses that I haven't seen Jude ride yet. The Ratliffs must have at least ten horses here. Jude chats nonstop the whole time, clearly on cloud nine to be taking a ride out and skipping her lessons for the day.

"This is Daisy." Jude pats the nose of a gorgeous dapple grey. "I got to name her when I was little."

"She's beautiful." I let her smell me before petting her massive, velvety nose. "What a perfect name."

"And this is Donald, but we call him Donnie." She points to the matching dapple grey next to Daisy. "I got to name him, too."

"Donald and Daisy?" I grin at her and give her a little head rub. "I like it."

"They really like classic pairs in this house," Cassie says with a wink. "Are you ladies ready?"

"Yes!" Jude squeals.

She climbs up on Donnie. I take Daisy. Cassie takes another deep brown thoroughbred and leads us through the grounds to the trails. Jude, who was so forlorn and quiet when I first got here, talks a million miles a minute as we maneuver over the estate grounds.

Cassie turns back to look at me, grins, and dips her head in Jude's direction, mouthing, *Love it*. Apparently I'm not the only one who's noticed the change in Jude.

The path takes us past the house, which somehow looks impossibly bigger from the back of a horse, and something twitches between my shoulder blades, that feeling when you're being watched. I look up toward the

Chapter 6

bank of library windows and catch a figure standing there.

Graham Ratliff. He's home, which is surprising, given his absence from our meals lately. And he's staring right at us.

The pinch between my shoulders intensifies.

He's not just watching us. He's watching *me*.

The cruelty is absent from his face, as though he likes what he sees.

Interesting.

I look down at my very modest riding gear, and the wheels start turning in my head.

Chapter Seven

Abbie

Sunday morning breakfast is a small feast of eggs, sausage and bacon, fruit, and fresh baked croissants. I'm getting spoiled more and more by the minute.

Graham graces us with his presence today, dressed in a pair of slacks and a dark blue button-down. The man must never relax. He's always buttoned up tight, like an oyster that doesn't want to crack.

"You should come horseback riding with us sometime, Daddy." Jude chews thoughtfully on a strawberry. "It was really fun with Abbie."

"It looked fun." He glances at me, for just a moment, before returning to his tablet.

"Can we go today?" she asks.

"Not today. Soon." Graham's right thumb flies across his screen while he drinks coffee with his other hand. He never stops working, it seems. Always tied up in phones or laptops or newspapers, making notes and looking grim. Owning a multibillion-dollar banking empire clearly comes with a lot of high stress.

Chapter 7

Stress that keeps him from his daughter. I frown into my own cup of coffee with cream. Jude's face wilts a little, and she crams another strawberry in her mouth.

"I could take her." I say the words before the thought finishes in my head.

"Cassie is off today." Graham still doesn't look up from his screen.

"That's okay. I remember where the trails are," I counter. I don't like how quickly he dismissed me. "I may not be a riding instructor, but I've taken riding lessons my whole life. I can handle her just fine out there."

"Ooh! Say yes, Daddy!" Jude perks right up. "Please!"

He looks up, finally, at me. His mouth is tight. "My answer is no. Cassie is a trained professional familiar with both the property and the livestock, and as such she's the only one qualified to supervise my daughter on the trails. That's final."

Wow. This man really doesn't want his child to have any fun. He loads her up with lessons and classes and tutors and schedules, but the moment she wants to do something for herself, he digs in his heels. What is his problem?

"Maybe we can watch *Spirit* today, instead," I offer, trying to erase the sadness from her face. "And we can plan another ride soon. Maybe Cassie can show us some new trails."

"Okay." But Jude doesn't look as enthused as she was a few minutes ago.

Esmeralda comes in just then and clears her throat, looking perplexed. "Mr. Ratliff? Sir?"

Abbie

"What is it?" He looks up to acknowledge her, I notice sourly.

"There's, um." She frowns and looks like she's unable to string together a series of words. "There's a situation in the foyer."

"A situation?" he repeats.

"Yes, sir."

Graham frowns. "So handle it."

"Unfortunately, sir, the situation is not listening to me."

"The situation is..." His frown deepens. "I'll be right there."

"Ohhh Judey!" A singsong voice calls out from somewhere within the depths of the house. It's followed by the steady click of heels on marble.

Graham's face does something I've never seen before. It transforms completely with rage, just for a split second, and then settles back into its usual state of blank impenetrableness. He immediately rises and makes for the door, Esmeralda looking utterly pale, but before he can reach the threshold, a tall woman appears in it.

"Mommy!" Jude squeals, tearing out of her chair to throw herself into the woman's arms.

"How's my little Judey girl?" Natasha Ratliff looks absolutely stunning in a herringbone suit jacket rolled up to her elbows, a pair of dark designer jeans, and a white silk blouse. Her fingers are loaded with rings and her neck is ensconced in half a dozen gold chains of varying sizes and shapes. She wears a pair of oversized cat eye sunglasses, even though she's inside, and her ruby red lip color looks vaguely familiar.

Chapter 7

"Teenage Fantasy," I whisper to myself. Or at least a close match.

"What are you doing here?" Graham asks her, his voice betraying nothing.

"I'm obviously here to see my child." Natasha's voice is harsh but the smile never leaves her face. "What kind of question is that, Graham?"

My eyes dart back and forth at their verbal volleying. It's like watching a championship tennis match. Neither of them pays me any mind all the while; I didn't realize I could get any more invisible, but apparently that moment has arrived.

"This was not discussed," Graham says.

"I didn't think there would be a need for a discussion to see my darling *daughter*."

"You know exactly what you've done here."

"You flatter me, Graham." Natasha wraps her arms around Jude, who clings around her middle like the koala she's been imitating with me all week. "How thoughtful."

"You did not inform me of your intended arrival." Graham remains anchored next to Jude's chair. "This is unacceptable."

Natasha's grin grows wider, showing off her gleaming white teeth. I start to sweat a little under my dress. This woman is the devil. "I wanted to surprise her. Surprise, Judey! I'm taking you out on a mommy-daughter date."

"This is the best surprise ever!" Jude exclaims. "Can I go, Daddy?"

"You can't just walk in here and take her whenever you deem convenient." He flashes a tight smile, likely for

Jude's sake, but it looks just as predatory as Natasha's. "Surprises are not part of the arrangement."

Natasha turns her sharp gaze to me, finally, and I feel six inches tall. "You've surprised me as well, Graham. I was unaware you were dating high schoolers."

I feel my face go hot. "I'm not—"

"Must have slipped your mind while you were dating your colleagues," Graham says.

"At least the colleagues had some class," she shoots back sweetly.

"That's an interesting way to explain infidelity."

"Is this all a big show for your new girlfriend? Think you can give Jude a younger mommy to help your aging bones?" Natasha's smile looks like it's about to split her face apart.

Shame licks at my face, mixed with angry indignation. First of all, I'm here as an employee. Secondly, I already graduated high school. Third, I have no part in this domestic dispute and I don't appreciate being dragged into the middle of it.

No wonder Jude was so miserable all the time. It's obvious she must have been relentlessly used as a pawn between these two childish adults.

Graham suddenly switches to neutral again. "Natasha, you remember Ford Montgomery's daughter, Abbie. She's Jude's nanny for the summer, as Jude's mother abandoned her."

Jude and I exchange glances. She looks absolutely terrified. Her hands start to droop around her mother, her chin starting to wobble, but Natasha grabs hold of her.

"Abandon is an interesting word choice for 'got ran

Chapter 7

out,' don't you think, Abbie?" She doesn't look at me, doesn't look at Jude, doesn't look anywhere but at her ex-husband. "Graham always was one for dramatics."

"And yet you're the drama queen."

"Stage actor is the appropriate term." It's almost like they live for this. Natasha is positively gloating. "But I know how hard it is to keep up with those pesky word differences from one country to the next."

"You are not welcome here," he enunciates slowly. "You are no longer welcome to invade my house on a whim."

"But darling, this is simply a visit. It's not invading." Natasha takes off her glasses with one hand and wears them like a crown atop her head. "I don't invade. Only the British do that."

"The Americans have always been quite good at being notorious copycats."

"Oh, that's cute," Natasha interrupts with a smirk. "Yes, the American colonies, with all that pesky open land and history of abuse. But we're not here to talk history, are we, Judey? We're here to get ready for a fun trip!"

"A trip?" Graham's voice slips, just a little. "You aren't taking her anywhere."

I glance over at Jude and we exchange a look of mutual panic. It's like neither of us is even in the room right now. I want nothing more than to scoop her up and protect her from the barbs being hurled, but that wouldn't look good with Natasha here, and she's still got an iron-talon grip on Jude.

"I'm not here to argue, Graham, dear."

Abbie

"Your entire presence contradicts that. And don't call me dear, Natasha." He stresses the syllables in her name with an agonizingly fierce look.

I can feel the heat from across the table, where I sit too terrified to move. I haven't taken my hands off my coffee mug since she came in, as if it's some kind of anchor. Beyond the awkwardness of bearing witness to this argument, I'm also having some flashbacks of my own.

There was a period of time where I was sure my own parents were going to get divorced. They would have loud arguments in the middle of dinner (one of the only times they were consistently in the same room together), Mom throwing picture frames or dishes across the room, both of them yelling obscenities. During one of these fights, I learned my mother was sexually frustrated, which was both disgusting and traumatic to hear, and that my father allegedly spent more nights passed out on the couch surrounded by work papers than in their bed. I honestly thought they hated each other—that they'd never be civil to each other again. They somehow got through the rough patch, but as much as I've tried over the years, I still can't forget those fights.

These are the days Jude is going to remember. When she looks back on her childhood, she's not going to remember the lessons and tutors and classes. She's going to remember this right here: her parents weaponizing her very existence to prove some sort of ridiculous point.

The difference is, my parents stayed together. They went to ample counseling sessions and on even more private vacations, leaving me with my grandparents in

Chapter 7

their comfortable Windsor home, watching *The Price Is Right* and desperately trying to pretend everything was normal.

Jude doesn't have that luxury. Her parents had a very public divorce and possibly even more public disdain for one another. Though Graham is the quiet one, his venom is on full display right now, all for Jude to see. And she looks miserable.

"I'm not getting into this right now." Graham interrupts my thoughts. "You aren't taking her on a trip."

"You do not have exclusive ownership of our daughter, Graham Ratliff. Might I remind you, you're legally obligated to share custody." Natasha's words are daggers, betraying her still-sunny disposition. "So. Jude and I are going to have a fun mother-daughter date tonight. Judey, love, go pack an overnight bag. We're going to have the best time. Your daddy loves you and wants you to have some fun with Mommy."

Jude's face lights up as she turns to look at her dad.

"Abbie," Graham says, his jaw tensing. "Please see to it that my daughter packs her toothbrush."

Jude squeals with delight and runs out of the room. I know I should follow her, but Natasha Ratliff terrifies me and I'm nervous to breathe, much less scoot past her. Also, if I'm being honest, I kind of want to sit here and continue watching Graham and Natasha's dynamic.

Which Ratliff is the alpha? I have no idea.

"Of course." The words unstick from my throat and I get up and edge my way around Natasha, who shoots me daggers with her beautiful, large green eyes, to follow the little girl skipping up the stairs.

Abbie

On the way, I pass Esmeralda, who seems to be spending a lot of time dusting a vase near the dining room.

"They are so terrible to that poor child," she mutters under her breath.

I don't know if she meant to talk to me, and I don't know if it's appropriate for me to say anything, but I'd love to play fly-on-the-wall with Esmeralda instead of packing up an eight-year-old girl. But I have a job to do, so I follow Jude to her room, watching her bounce the whole way, hoping this trip with Natasha is exactly what Jude needs to lift her spirits.

Chapter Eight

Abbie

Natasha Ratliff's presence in the house sent Graham into a deep, dark spiral—but on the plus side, it gives me extra time off this week. I lay in bed, letting the weighty list of possibilities cascade over me.

Will I try to snoop in Graham's bedroom to look for his delicious cologne? Will I tour the library? Will I venture out into the city? Should I call my dad?

No, I decide, all that is good enough for a different day. Today, I want to be lazy. Today, I want to lounge by the pool with my favorite trashy magazines and social media apps and pretend the rest of the world doesn't exist.

In protest of the nun-like clothing I've had to wear for a week so I wouldn't get fired, I wear my skimpiest swimsuit, a white string bikini. "Nipple covers" is what my mother called the top. She was sort of horrified when I bought it, and then I think her childhood memories returned and she stopped complaining. "Well. If you've

Abbie

got the body, might as well wear it," is all she'd say after that.

I miss my parents, just a little. It's been a while since I've been away from them this long—during the school year at Cornell, I'd make the four-hour drive to visit them at home almost every weekend—and the homesickness has started to settle in.

True, I do love Mary's exquisite food, but I miss my mom's fried chicken and dumplings, her shrimp and grits, her crispy Sunday morning waffles with peach preserves. You can take the woman out of Georgia, but not the other way around. Even during my family's best financial years, we never had a cook because my mother was, and still is, "a strong Southern woman who knows where her roots are." Part of her roots involves feeding her family like she's feeding a small infantry. But I miss picking at the food and having her fuss over me. I miss watching baseball with my dad and cheering for opposing teams, having our weekly political discussions over weekend brunches.

Here, there's no family unity to be seen, and I think that's what I ultimately miss the most. Graham says he cares for his daughter, and I believe him—but it also seems like he'd rather dump Jude on a nanny and a bunch of expensive tutors than be truly involved. His job is too demanding, his life is too busy, his hair needs to be washed, whatever his excuses are for being so absent, it all puts a sour taste in my mouth.

But the sour taste doesn't last long, of course, because he's ridiculously beautiful and ridiculously assholish and ridiculously tantalizing in all the worst possible ways.

Chapter 8

Esmeralda helps me procure several magazines—the kind with articles on the best sex positions, the trendiest makeup, the most effortless summer styles—that I can gorge myself on by the pool, and Mary sends out a small charcuterie tray to snack on. I wonder if they wish they, too, could just relax by the pool and pretend their boss doesn't exist. Or maybe they, too, have a thing for him? How could they not? Have they *seen* him?

I settle into a chaise, dark sunglasses over my eyes and tanning oil at the ready, to spend some time pretending I'm back home and that none of this, not even the hot boss, exists. Where things are easier and I don't have to work twelve hours a day.

Even if that work involves a cute little kid, who can keep up with those hours? It's worse than school ever was. Truly, I'm exhausted after the week and want nothing more than several sun-baked naps. Sitting by yourself, though, no matter how lavish the scenery—and boy, is it lavish—gets very lonely after a while.

I wonder what Cassie does for fun around here? Or Quinn? The town seems so small.

Talk to me, I'm bored, I text Amanda after a measly thirty minutes alone poolside. My sparkling cucumber water is empty, my charcuterie tray is nothing but crumbs, and I've already run out of things to read. *It's my off day and there's nothing to do.*

Aren't you in a literal mansion with a literal snack? Stfu! she shoots back.

It makes me laugh. *Yeah, but I'm also going crazy all alone here. There's no one else our age to talk to at the*

Abbie

house and he barely speaks to me. I'm sitting by the biggest pool I've ever seen and I'm completely bored.

You embarrassment, she texts, adding four or five laughing emojis. *Send me a pic of the hot boss! I wanna get in on this snack. Ya girl is hungry, too.*

I haven't had time to take any pictures of Graham recently, because he's never around to spy on. And it's not like I can take a photo of him across the table at dinner. In some ways it makes my job easier, in others, exponentially more difficult. But it also means no photos to eat up during my, ah, private times in the evening. And in the afternoon. And any other time that I'm alone and he's asserted himself recently.

A familiar tingle runs through me and I have to push it away. Not here, not now.

Before I left home, I dug up a bunch of old photos from that summer I spent at the Ratliff estate and put them in my suitcase. I haven't looked at them recently, honestly, because having him in person is so much better than looking back on faded memories. Graham's got this very slight graying going around his sideburns now that absolutely destroys me. He didn't have that three years ago. Hell, he's more attractive in person than any photo of him. The pictures paparazzi have nabbed don't even do him justice.

I find one of him and me at the pool, a five-year-old Jude splashing nearby. You can see the hint of good humor he usually hides under his severely buttoned-up personality in the smile on his face, which is rare to see these days. He's shirtless and sculpted and tan, and I'm

Chapter 8

beaming next to him, shy and embarrassed but equally excited, in a modest swimsuit.

He's never around to get a recent picture, but here's one from like three years ago when I met him, I text her back.

I send the one of us in the pool, and a few others of him and my dad out on the balcony smoking cigars. In those, his sleeves are rolled up to his elbows and he looks relaxed. It's sort of foreign to think of him this way anymore because now he's the total opposite. The quality isn't great since I'm sending a cell phone picture of a glossy photo, but it's the best I can manage.

He's hotter in person, believe me, I add.

OMG!!!! Amanda has always been excitable—it's one of my favorite things about her. *He's TOTALLY checking you out in that pool picture. Are YOU still crushing???*

I frown at the question, because I don't know how to answer it. *I mean, he's only gotten hotter. Impossibly hotter. Ridiculously hotter. But turns out he's a complete asshole, so…*

Careful! She sends a wink. *Assholes are total kryptonite.*

Careful! Your women's studies professor might murder you for saying so. I pause, frowning a little. *Even though you're totally right. It's maddening.*

Gonna make everyone's dreams come true so I can live vicariously?

Idk. I'm sitting poolside in a hot bikini and he hasn't even noticed me. I'm probably just too young.

AND too hot. Maybe he's too shell-shocked by your own freaking beauty, MA'AM.

Abbie

This makes me laugh. She's always been a great cheerleader. *I wish. He treats me like furniture.*

Curse those hot assholes!

Exactly!

I hear the French doors open behind me, so I shove my phone away, embarrassed. It's not like anyone can read my text messages, but my face burns a little at the idea of Graham somehow knowing what I'm doing. Like he can see right through me, see how desperate I am for him. I don't want to be desperate; I want him to want me on his own.

Heavy footsteps come toward me and my heart immediately starts racing. I can smell his cologne before I can see him. Graham is here and I'm practically naked. How many fantasies have I had that started this way? Countless. Countless fantasies begin this way in my head.

He's wearing a pair of blue shorts and a polo that clings to his wide frame and promises more muscles beyond what I can see, and he's carrying something in his hand. He looks like he's about to go sail around on his yacht. I have never wanted to be on a boat more in my entire life.

Why is he coming out here, if not to see me? Every inch of my body is alive and very, very aware of his presence. Suddenly, an idea strikes. I've got him.

Sliding my sunglasses on top of my head and shading my eyes, I look up at him, arching my back a little. Hell yes, I'm going to be his teenage fantasy now.

"Can you oil my back? I'm a little...exposed," I say, batting my eyelashes. I tilt my head toward the bottle

Chapter 8

sitting on the side table, hoping he'll take the bait and every late-night movie I've ever watched about a teenage nanny comes true.

My adrenaline rushes as he heads purposefully toward me.

Come to me, Graham. Come—

"I'll put this on it instead." He drapes something heavy over me and then promptly walks away.

Shocked, I pick up the thing he all but threw at me. It's a robe. A big, heavy, white robe.

Okay. So on the one hand, the bikini didn't work. At all.

On the other hand, he sure must have been watching me after all. Otherwise, he wouldn't have brought the robe out here to cover me up.

Thrills explode through me. It's not what I wanted, but it's a start. A very nice start.

Later that evening, I look for him again, this time walking around in the robe—maybe this is a kink he likes—but I can't find him anywhere.

"Mr. Ratliff went out for dinner. He'll be back late, so he gave Mary the night off. You'll have to fix yourself something from the fridge," Esmeralda tells me, sounding slightly apologetic.

Without Mary, my own dinner is a sad affair, just me eating microwaved leftovers by myself in the kitchen as I brood. Not that the leftovers aren't great. But I miss the company.

Graham once knew I had a crush on him. Does he know it now? Does everyone? Do I look like one of those young girls who comes in, preying on the unsuspecting single father? Shit, shit, shit. That's not the vibe I want. I slink back up to my room, mulling over ways to get around this hurdle, but I'm coming up with nothing.

Everyone's always telling me how great I am with people, but now that I'm here? I feel like a child all over again. A child with a schoolgirl crush and nothing else to offer.

Depressed after hours of overthinking everything, I head back downstairs to the kitchen to look for some ice cream as a pick-me-up.

But a throaty laugh from the front room distracts me from my search. It's not a child's laugh. It's the flirty, breathless kind. What the hell.

Abandoning my search for a sugar high, I immediately tiptoe down the hall. Peering around the corner, I stop in my tracks.

It's Graham in there. With a woman. And they're all over each other.

Reality slams into me like a shock of cold water.

He went to dinner with a woman and brought her back here. The fragile little house of cards I'd built up internally comes crashing down with every second I stay frozen in the doorway, watching him and this woman paw at each other like horny teenagers without ever noticing me.

The man barely ever looks my way, but then he randomly goes out one night and brings home a lover? He doesn't look sixteen years older than me in the soft light, the way he kisses this woman. He looks much younger. My heart careens against my chest and my knees go weak.

Chapter 8

Overwhelmed with frustration and jealousy, I sneak back up to my room with a dark cloud hanging over my head. Then I pick up my phone and call Cassie.

"Hey, Abbie. What's up?"

"Hey...what are you doing tonight?"

Chapter Nine

Abbie

In situations like this, I'd usually video chat with my best friend and have her help me choose an outfit, talk about hair options, ponder over makeup. But I don't need Amanda tonight, because I'm officially now a woman on a mission.

I know exactly how to dress, what makeup to use, and what to do to my hair.

It's funny; I spent the week feeling completely lost and adrift, but all it took was thirty seconds of watching Graham make out with another woman like he was my age to get all the wheels in my head turning. Maybe I just needed a good reminder about what I'm here for and what all I have to lose.

Flinging open my wardrobe, I pick out the skimpiest dress I brought and my tallest pair of heels. Then I curl my hair and shake it out into loose waves. My fingers dance over the makeup lined up across the bathroom counter until my hands land on my favorite tube of

Chapter 9

lipstick. I'll take an extra coat of Teenage Fantasy tonight, thank you very much.

Cassie said she needed an hour, so I take my time getting ready. I've never worked so hard on a cat eye in my entire life, but after a few failed attempts, I'm finally satisfied that the wings look perfect. I take a second to size myself up in the mirror and get a little giddy. In this tight black dress with the obscene side cut-outs and skinny little spaghetti straps that cross over the chest, I look fucking hot. I look hotter than hot. I could put the sun to shame in this outfit.

Bless Amanda and her sketchy taste in clothes. This is absolutely perfect. Just let this man try to deny me dressed like this. Let any man try to deny me.

Something most people don't know, with the lone exception of my best friend who has been pinkie-sworn into secrecy for half a decade, is that I used to be a really awkward kid. I had long frizzy hair I brushed into a poof of a rat's nest every day and wore these gold-rimmed granny glasses that I thought were stylish, and I preferred the company of horses (and schoolbooks) to the company of people—at least until I met Amanda in ninth grade. In some ways, I relate to Jude so hard my heart hurts.

I never had many friends and my mom was constantly perplexed about what to do with her daughter, who would rather collect porcelain dolls and horse figurines and line them up on her bedroom shelves than go get her hair and nails done or swing by the mall for weekend clothes shopping. Even with Amanda's help, which I appreciated, I didn't really take a personal

Abbie

interest in my appearance—I was happy enough to just sit back and let her make me over.

Everything changed the summer I met Graham. Everything.

Something deep inside me woke up when I met him. Something raw and carnal, something that had been waiting in the dark for years, it seemed. I suddenly cared about my clothes, getting my hair to fall in soft, silky waves, and playing around with my mother's makeup. She was over the moon to have a girl to play dress up with, even if it was a bit late.

Since then, getting the attention of boys has never been much work. Turns out I just needed a little finishing, a little polishing, to turn into someone worthy of male interest. If I'm honest though, I never had the greatest self-esteem when it came to my appearance, so after my transformation I mostly ignored the catcalls and the flirting.

But now? Now I feel powerful.

Or I did, until Graham decided I was about as interesting as an ottoman. At least it seemed that way before he threw a robe at me this afternoon. And then brought home a throaty, moan-y woman who acts like she's half her age right along with him.

I think part of him wants me, and he's fighting it. I just need to figure out how to get to a man like Graham. He's not like the boys are at college, where it takes honestly so little to impress them. Have a pair of tits and a smile and half a brain and you can make these Ivy boys drool. Graham, however, has been exceptionally difficult to crack.

Chapter 9

Satisfied with how I look, I order an Uber and head downstairs. I can still hear Graham and his lady friend in the living room, her making that fake-ass orgasmic-sounding laugh and him talking. Graham sounds so sexy when he lets loose a little. He's not the authoritarian he usually is around Jude and me; he sounds like he's enjoying himself.

What do I have to do to get him to lower his walls like that? Walk around naked?

Then I remember the look on his face when I went riding with Jude a few days ago, the hunger in his eyes as I rode by his windows in full riding gear. Maybe his kink is fully dressed women? That can't be right either—he's all but ignored me in my nun garb this week.

Why are men so complicated?

"I'm going out," I announce to the living room as I pop my head in.

Graham's visitor is draped across his lap with one hand flat against his chest, cheeks flushed, her dress stretched so tight across her perfectly round ass that it's obvious she's not wearing underwear of any kind. Jealousy blooms in my chest, but I keep it tamped down. She can be pantyless all she likes. I still look drop dead amazing.

I catch Graham's eyes trailing down my body and back up, but he says nothing.

"Is this your daughter?" the woman asks. "You let her walk around dressed like that?"

I have to hold back an eye roll. Like she seriously has any room to talk.

"I'm not your father," Graham says, answering us

both. "You don't have to check in with me on your day off."

"Ooh, the nanny!" The woman's eyes go wide.

Before she can say anything else, I cut her a look and then coolly ask Graham, "Do I need a key?"

He clears his throat. He's definitely not looking at me like a father would look at his daughter, nor how a wealthy asshole would look at an ottoman. I pop my hip out a little farther but try to look bored.

"Someone will be here to let you in," Graham answers.

"Good." I turn on a heel and saunter out of the room.

"Well she certainly thinks she's cute, doesn't she?" I hear the woman say behind me.

I hold my breath, waiting for Graham's reply, but it doesn't come.

Jealousy continues to knot itself in my stomach. The Uber still isn't here yet, so I make a quick stop to the library bar cart. The decanted scotch smells delicious, so I pour myself a finger and shoot it all back at once. By the time my Uber arrives, my head feels better and the jealousy has subsided a little.

We pull up to a bar called The Flightless Pelican. The driver checks me out hard as I leave his car. I give him a friendly smile and toss my hair before walking into the bar.

See that, Graham Ratliff? I'm desirable, you asshole.

I hand the bouncer at the door my fake ID from college, but he barely looks at it before waving me in. The lighting inside is dim, and the music is distractingly loud, but I find Cassie pretty quickly. She's nursing a drink at

Chapter 9

the bar, in a much more subdued outfit than mine—a cream silk blouse and tight black pants—but she still looks fabulous.

For a moment, I feel a twinge of jealousy. I have to spend an hour in my room to get a rise out of the man I want, and she pulls off an amazing, effortless look without even flashing a hint of cleavage. But I doubt she cares about scoring the attention of her boss, or anyone else.

"Oh my gosh. I thought this was just girls' night. You look *hot!*" Cassie shouts over the music and hands me a martini that looks like the one she has. "Here. Figured I'd get you started."

"Thank you!" I give her a quick hug and take a deep drink. "It's been a very long day."

"I don't know how you do it. Jude is a great kid and all, but hanging out with a kid all day every day sounds exhausting." Cassie widens her eyes. "I'm surprised I don't see you here more often, honestly."

No way am I telling her I'm only nineteen. "Eh. My off days are weird." I shrug.

"So what's this favor you need?"

I take a deep breath. I really just needed Cassie as an excuse to get out of the house, but I managed to come up with a scenario to share with her on the drive over, between the Uber driver's lustful eyes and Graham's bobbing Adam's apple filling my brain.

"I feel so stupid." I take another sip of my drink. "I don't usually have trouble getting guys to notice me—"

"And you shouldn't!" Cassie cuts in, clinking my glass with hers.

Abbie

"Thanks. But this one..."

Cassie scrunches up her face, and then a realization hits. "Ooh. You mean Quinn?"

I freeze for a second, but then it hits me: Quinn is the *perfect cover*. I nod and bite my lip, hoping she interprets my startled reaction as pure bashfulness.

"God, he's adorable. And a total flirt. I've always just written him off as a player."

"That's exactly it," I lie, warming up to my cover story. "I can't tell if he's really interested, and I have no idea how to catch his attention. He seems like the type who makes passes at girls just for fun, and I'm not really into playing games. I need your help."

She laughs. "Yeah, your methods so far haven't really been...how should I put this? I mean, I couldn't tell you were after him, so I promise you there's no way he can tell. Men are a little dense most of the time, you know? What you need is some practice! Just look around."

Cassie orders us a pair of Lemon Drop shots from the cute blond bartender, who offers me a shy smile when he sets them down. Cassie nudges me with her shoulder.

"Did you see that? You could start real easy here with the bartender."

"I can't flirt with the bartender!" I squeal. "He's got like thirty people over here, all wanting his attention."

"Yeah, but he keeps looking over at you, so he's probably willing to give it."

Laughing, I shake my head. "He's not really my type."

Cassie cocks an eyebrow. "Seriously? He looks just like Quinn, woman."

Chapter 9

"That's probably why it's so hard." I laugh again.

We clink glasses and down the shots. As I suck on the sugared lemon, a guy at a table nearby catches my eye. He reminds me of Graham, but without the salt running through his hair. He's not a dead ringer, but he's close enough to make my heart race.

"What about that one?" I nod to him.

"Ahh." Cassie waggles her brows at me. "He's handsome. A little older than us, I think. And very different from Quinn, so he'll be good to get your feet wet. Here, get *him* a shot and ask him to dance. Guys like it when you chase them down a little. It removes the fear of rejection."

"I thought guys liked to do the chasing?" I flag down the cute bartender and ask for two more shots. "And direct women scare them?"

"Only little boys do that. You don't want them, anyway." Cassie shoots me a wink and swats at my ass. "Now go get you a man!"

I take a deep breath and approach the guy's table. He watches me the whole way, just waiting for me to get there, so it's not that hard to open my mouth and say, "Hey, I have an extra shot and I was looking for someone fun to take it with. Know anyone?"

Not the best line, but a co-ed at Cornell used it on me once and I'd found it pretty cute and low pressure, as opposed to an aggressive come on. Besides, this is just practice anyway.

The cutest dimpled grin spreads across the guy's face. "I might know someone. Who also happens to be looking

Abbie

for a beautiful girl to buy a drink for. Do *you* know anyone?"

"I might." It's so easy to picture him as a young Graham. I set down the shots and hold out my hand. "Abbie."

"Devin. I'm working on my MBA at NYU. Alpha Kappa Psi. You?" His hand dwarfs mine in exactly the way I like.

"American Studies at Cornell," I tell him. "Undergrad. No Greek affiliation, I'm afraid."

"Ah, but you're a smart girl. I love smart girls," he says.

We clink glasses and shoot the drink. Around sugared lemons, he asks, "Want to dance?"

"I thought you'd never ask," I lean in to say in his ear.

Devin leads me to the dance floor, his hand never leaving the small of my back. He's got pretty good moves for a frat boy, which is a nice change from literally every college party I've attended. The beat kicks up in the song, and soon we're pressed together, living out half my fantasies under a spinning disco ball. Even his cologne is similar to Graham's.

Between the heat of the bodies crushing in on all sides and the four drinks already under my belt, I'm soon leaning hard into Devin's chest, half dizzy and half floating. Letting the music carry me away, I quickly lose track of time. It's glorious—exactly what I've been needing.

When a popular hip-hop song comes on, the whole dance floor erupts in drunken cheers. Devin spins me around so my back is to him. As his hands rake up my

Chapter 9

sides, his fingers hot against my bare skin, I can feel the bulge in his pants pressing into my ass.

"I love this song!" a girl around my age says, grabbing my hands. She starts singing along to the Lizzo lyrics and I join in, both of us wasted and grinning.

The girl and I start dancing, Devin still grinding on me from behind. Finding myself turned into the middle layer of a sexy dance sandwich, I can't help laughing hysterically. I'm actually having more fun than I have in ages. I'm surrounded by colors and music and people and energy and everyone's having a good time—it's contagious. Cassie has found a hot guy to dance with too, though she's over at the edge of the crowd where it's less intense.

Another song comes on and then another. Suddenly, I notice the room starting to tilt.

"I think I need some water!" I tell Devin breathlessly, leaning back from him a little.

"What?" he shouts back.

I pantomime drinking something, then point to the bar.

But he just pulls me closer, hands firmly squeezing my ass now. Nuzzling my ear, he lowers his voice and says, "You need another drink?"

Shaking my head, still dizzy, I say, "No, I need—"

Just then, I feel Devin's body jerking away from me as a familiar voice cuts through the loud music, stern and British and angry as hell.

"Time for you to walk away," he tells Devin.

Chapter Ten

Abbie

I CAN FEEL Graham stewing in the driver's seat next to me as we head home. Anger permeates through the blasting air-conditioning, settling around the fringes of my vision like an aura.

Admittedly, I had more to drink tonight than I'd planned. I'm not totally drunk after sweating my ass off on the dance floor for the past few hours, but tipsy is probably an accurate assessment of my current state. Graham's voice rises and falls in wild crescendos, leaving me confused and frustrated and more than a little turned on.

His accent gets extra thick when he's angry, right on the verge of me barely being able to understand him. It makes him demonstrably sexier.

What's not sexy is the verbal lashing he's issuing, with its implication that he *is* my father, despite what he said quite clearly only a few hours ago. And, you know, the whole bit where he's my sexy boss instead of my angry father. I'm feeling like a chastised little girl and my

Chapter 10

frustration is slowly overtaking every other feeling I've got.

"Do you realize how stupidly you behaved? God only knows what could have happened to you."

"I was with Cassie! Having a good time on my night off!" I shoot back, though his concern warms me to my toes. "It's really not any of your business."

His jaw clenches. "You could have been hurt. You could have been taken advantage of. Or mugged."

"Oh yes, because Upstate Millionairesville, New York is soooo dangerous." I roll my eyes and let out a huff. "The horrors!"

I don't know what it is about this man that makes me act like a bratty thirteen-year-old. I just can't keep my emotions under control when it comes to Graham Ratliff.

He turns to glare at me, and I decide at that moment that I should try to get on his nerves every single day, on purpose, just so he'll be forced to actually look at me. Good, bad, whatever the reason, at least I'm more than a damn ottoman right now.

"You're wearing that lipstick again," he says. "You're asking for trouble."

"Are you saying this lipstick could get me into trouble?"

Graham shakes his head, frustration wrinkling his eyebrows. Then he falls silent. Shit, I'm losing him.

"Why'd you come looking for me?" I push. "You really think I can't handle myself?"

"You're underage, and there are only so many places in town you'd be going to dressed like that."

"Dressed like what?" I say, just to antagonize him,

even though my hem has ridden so far up my thighs that I'm practically flashing my underwear.

"That outfit is provocative and you know it." His frown deepens. "You're inviting prying eyes and roving hands."

"Maybe I *wanted* prying eyes and roving hands." I side-eye him, because two can play at the mean-face game. Even if all I really want to do is giggle at how he pronounced *provocative*. "In which case, I believe I succeeded. You know, you can get anything when you're pretty, Graham." I'm feeling just about bulletproof right now and I can't explain why, save for the vodka and sugared lemons still pumping through my bloodstream. "An. Y. Thing."

"That is utterly ridiculous."

"So is dropping in to crash my night off."

I kind of *did* get anything I wanted tonight. Except now my sexy boss has shifted from treating me as a footrest to treating me as a wayward daughter, and I'm really not feeling that right now. I already have a father, who is far superior to this piece of shit, regardless of his faults. At least he gave a damn and tried with me. At least he cares. At least he doesn't use me as a pawn against my mother the way Graham does with Jude.

"Are you crying?" Graham asks.

I wipe my eyes, suddenly furious. "What happened with your date? She walk out? Were you that boring?"

"I was that concerned about you running afoul with the law on my watch. Regardless of what you're 'pretty' enough to get, the police in this town are more than happy to arrest underage drinkers. You may recall that I

Chapter 10

am friends with your father, and I have no interest in calling him to come bail you out of a jail cell."

"How kind." I sneer.

"And in future, you'll respect the fact my dating life is private."

"So is my night off." I'm fuming now.

I should have told him to fuck off when he approached me on the dance floor. Devin should have punched him to defend my honor. Graham has no business tracking me down when I'm off his property and out on my own.

"I can easily rearrange your nights off if you're planning to be this irresponsible with your free time," he responds.

Irresponsible? I seethe. I want to storm off and get away from this absurd conversation, but I'm trapped in a car with nowhere to go.

So I try to swallow down the venom and manage, "Again, my free time is not yours to involve yourself with."

"Would you like me to discuss this with your father? Perhaps I'll call him tomorrow."

"Are you kidding me?" I have to pinch myself to stop from shouting. "I'm an adult and I'm handling myself as such, regardless of whether or not you approve."

I knew Graham probably didn't see me as anything more than a temporary employee, but somehow, having my suspicions confirmed just makes it feel worse. This is so demeaning. Disrespecting me is the least sexy thing he's ever done.

"Shouting is not necessary."

Abbie

"Neither is dressing me down like I'm your child." I cross my arms, feel like a child, and instead clasp my hands in my lap. "I am your employee, I get that, but what I do when I'm off the clock has nothing to do with your daughter and therefore doesn't concern you."

"Then why did you get in the car?"

Oh, he thinks he's fucking smart, huh? Well, I don't feel like playing his little games anymore. "Because I was worried you would fire me if I didn't. Don't pretend you're unaware of the power dynamic here."

That's enough to shut him up.

"You have overstepped, sir, not me," I conclude.

After a brief silence, he says, more quietly, "This may be hard to believe, but I do have your best interests in mind, Abbie."

"It's not your concern."

"So you've said."

"You don't get to control me. You don't get to tell me what to do, unless it involves Jude." I chew on my lip, tears forming in my eyes out of frustration. "Take me back to the bar, this is bullshit."

"I will regard these outbursts as a byproduct of your drinking." I can feel him looking over at me again and I don't turn to survey him back. "But this *is* the last time this will happen."

Fuck you, I think as loudly as I can. I'd love to say it. I'd love to just lose it on this man because holy hell, how *dare* he, but he's also my boss and I'm slowly becoming more and more sober the angrier I get. I say nothing for the rest of the car ride, busying myself with texts when Cassie messages me to ask if I'm okay.

Chapter 10

Graham doesn't say anything, either, which is for the best.

We get to the house, park near the front walkway, and continue our silence up to the door, though I purposely stalk ahead of him. I don't want to walk behind him, like a punished child, and I'm too pissed off to trail at his side. So I settle for sashaying my ass before him while gritting my teeth.

Esmeralda says nothing as she opens the door, but offers a kind smile.

"You may go, Esmeralda," he says behind me. She nods and scurries away.

I move to do the same, looking forward to calling Amanda and giving her the complete rundown of this nightmarish evening, when Graham suddenly grabs my shoulders and pushes me against a wall. I'm so shocked I can't say anything.

As I look up into his eyes, he takes his hands away, but he puts them on the wall on either side of me, caging me in. His dark expression is one I haven't seen before. It's...positively predatory.

Suddenly, my panties are very damp and I can't remember how to breathe. His brows knit together, his soft lips purse, and his eyes are on fire as they rake over me.

His head dips down toward me, and I go completely still. The space between is charged, electric, and my knees are so weak I have to lean into the wall to remain upright. I can feel the heat of his body, can hear my heart hammering in my ears. Every fiber of my being aches for Graham to put his hands on me. But he doesn't.

Abbie

Instead, he traces the tip of his nose softly along my neck.

"What exactly were you wanting to get tonight in this outfit?" he murmurs against my neck.

My skin instantly breaks out in goosebumps, a tiny intake of breath my only reaction. I'm too floored to say or do anything else. I can't breathe. I can't speak. I'm overwhelmed by the very nearness of him, static overtaking my brain and winning the fight.

Never in my life did I think today would end this way. With me deliciously trapped between his strong arms, him looking like the big bad wolf who wants very much to eat me, in more ways than one.

"You think you're a bad girl. Walking around my house half naked. Begging for someone to touch you," Graham whispers. His voice is hot, throaty. I'm melting against the wall. "Better be careful. You might get what you're asking for."

With that, he walks away.

Chapter Eleven

Graham

It's NOT good form to fuck your nanny.

Plenty of people do, but it's naff. Classless. The men who do it are fools, inviting trouble into their homes and lives. Not to mention that many of these women aren't chasing down love and affection—they're chasing money. They want tell-all interviews and TV specials, they want to spread their venom for the world to gobble up. They want to destroy things that are bigger than themselves. They want their fifteen minutes of fame, or else they want extra zeroes in their bank accounts in exchange for their silence.

Fucking your nanny is a terrible, terrible idea. Especially one that young. Especially *especially* one who is the daughter of a close friend.

Yet it's all I can think about.

As soon as Abbie left to go out earlier, it was impossible to concentrate on my date. So I'd sent Vivian home. She's a colleague who's been on my radar for some time, one who's made it abundantly clear that she is very interested in seeing what is beneath my suits and ties. Every time the company holds a meeting or a seminar or, God help me, a conference, Vivian is there at my elbow afterward with a drink and a smile. I like Vivian. She's attractive, successful, and witty. She keeps the work functions bearable and makes for a good drinking buddy. She's also the only way I've been able to keep my hands off Abbie. The whole reason I'd brought her home tonight was because I'd needed a distraction. Unfortunately, it had failed.

It's abundantly clear that Abbie wants me. Her schoolgirl crush has only grown stronger over the years, which was obvious from the first moment she stepped foot in my office. Sometimes I'm convinced she learned how to flirt by studying the kind of terrible romance movies Natasha used to force me to watch in the early days of our dating. The hair twirling, the ridiculous wardrobe choices, the incessant giggling. Abbie practically oozes desperation.

Her immaturity isn't the strength she thinks it is. I don't want a child and I don't want someone else to kiss my ass. I get enough of that, and I have enough staff, enough employees, enough ass-kissing. I like it when she's mouthy. I like it when she's frustrated. I like it when the anger eats at her cheeks and she flushes red. Those are the cheeks I want around my cock.

But I know better than to taste the forbidden fruit.

So I invited Vivian out for an overpriced dinner and drinks, and then brought her back to my estate for a relaxing evening of casual fucking to take my mind off of things. Between Abbie and my ex-wife, it had been a

Chapter 11

long, shit week. I wanted to have a good time, get my dick properly sucked, go to bed a happier man. Vivian promised to do all of that for very little in return. She's a smart, grown woman who is fully capable of handling her own life. She doesn't need me for anything. That's refreshing.

And then Abbie came downstairs in that shredded black frock, all her supple skin on display, those pouty red lips begging for attention. The way she held herself, the way jealousy ate at her as Vivian rolled around on my lap, it was clear what Abbie was looking for. It worked, too. Vivian no longer held the power to occupy my mind after seeing Abbie dressed like that.

Vivian was cross when I told her to go home, irritated that I'd "led her on," and she made a few pointed comments about Abbie's appearance as well.

"You men are all alike, you know that?" She smiled angrily, but didn't yell. Just slipped her heels back on and shook her head. "You can't think past your dick, no matter how old you are. Youth slips through your fingers and you're all so desperate to get it back. You think by fucking young beauties, you'll find the fountain."

"I don't need a fountain."

"We all want the fountain. It's absurd to pretend we don't." Vivian eyed me. "You're just terrified to age. Terrified to become something else."

"That's not what this is."

Vivian laughed. "That's absolutely what this is, Graham. Don't insult me. We've known each other a very long time, haven't we? You're afraid you're getting old. You're afraid your time is fleeting while your ex-wife is out there, fucking everything that moves. We aren't even old, Graham. We're adults. But we aren't old."

"Speak for yourself. I feel every one of my thirty-five years."

"Then take up jogging." Vivian rolled her eyes. "You're out of shape, not old."

I pulled up my shirt to showcase a row of abs I've spent entirely too much time working on between meetings and conference calls. "Yes, that seems to be exactly my problem."

Vivian ran her hand along my abs and then slapped them. "You drink too much."

"You drink too much."

"You get even more classless when you drink, you know that?" Vivian bared her teeth and grabbed her designer handbag from the chaise lounge in the corner. "You want to ride your nanny just as desperately as she wants to ride you. It's tacky. You can do better than that and you are better than that."

"Vivian. Enough. I've just developed a bit of a headache."

I could tell by her smile that she didn't believe me. Hell, I didn't believe me either. I took another swig of scotch and watched her smooth out her dress and hair. She really is an incredible woman. Poised. Intelligent. Aggressive and unafraid to go after whatever she wants, like a tiger. Unfortunately, we're too much alike. She knows me too well.

"We'll have to take a raincheck, as you Americans say," I told her after walking her to her car.

She grinned at me, a beautiful thing, and shook her

Chapter 11

head. "We've known each other too long, Graham. Please don't insult my intelligence. Fucking your nanny will land you in a world of trouble."

"I have no intention—"

"Right. And your divorce meant absolutely nothing to you, either."

"You saw the way she's dressed and how young she is, Vivian. Her father is a friend of mine. I'm responsible for her safety while she is under my roof. Someone is liable to take advantage of her."

She smirked. "And you're mad that someone isn't you."

"I'm offended by the entirety of this conversation."

Vivian cut me another look and ducked into her car, revving the engine and then lowering the window. "Well, whenever you purge her from your silly little head, I'll be here."

"You're too good for me, Vivian."

"I know."

She sped off without saying goodbye.

I didn't want to think about what she'd had to say. I didn't want to think about how obvious it was that I wanted Abbie. I am an adult and she's barely out of adolescence. She works for me. Her father is an old friend. She's too damn inexperienced. Everything about it is wrong.

The first time I met her, she was nothing but a gangly teenager with old-fashioned glasses and her nose constantly in a book. But she took a shine to me, and I didn't mind the ego boost. It had seemed harmless enough at the time. Three years has changed her quite a bit, though. Now, she's an adult woman who's blossomed into something undeniably fresh and stunning, and her desire for me has only grown ten-fold. My cock aches at the thought.

Abbie is better than Vivian. She's better than Natasha. She's better than the countless other women beating down the door to try to manipulate me. Because Abbie is too young to know how to use me.

I can use her.

How long did I wait to chase her down after she left? I practically caught up to Vivian's car as I raced down the driveway.

"She's too young for this," I told myself, pulling onto the highway at top speed.

"She could get hurt," I lied to myself, checking out the first bar in the city.

"Someone could take advantage of her," I said to myself, checking the bar across the street.

It was ridiculous. I was hunting for the proverbial needle in the proverbial haystack, yet deterrence was not an issue. I had to find her. No further arguments. She was in an unsafe situation, and it was my responsibility to look after her...as her employer and family friend.

I found her in the fourth bar I checked, visibly inebriated and being publicly molested on the dance floor. The hoodlum she was dancing with was pawing her everywhere, his clumsy hands in places they had no business being, and in her drunken state she was encouraging it.

The feelings it knotted in my gut.

I had to stop it.

Did I have to all but throw the pillock across the

Chapter 11

room? Likely not. That was a momentary lapse in judgment. But it was to protect the daughter of one of my oldest friends.

It didn't escape my notice that the kid she was dancing with bore more than a passing resemblance to me. She was fawning over a substitute of my likeness and it tore at me. As did her drunken smile, her easy laughter, the way her skirt was barely covering her ass.

No one should see her that way. No one but me. That boy wasn't fit to see her in that poor excuse for clothing, in that reckless state of intoxication, wasn't fit to grope her tight body the way he was. He was a boy, and I am a man. She deserves a man.

Her anger in the car was delicious. I like her mouthy. I like her feisty. I like the passion she shows for life and everything in it, because it means the world hasn't yet eaten her soul. She's still vibrant, with a zest for life most women my age no longer have. It's that passion I crave.

If she'd been sober, I would have had my way with her right there at the bottom of the stairs. I would have torn that dress off and savored everything bare and exposed to me, drunk in her sweet nectar.

I almost did. The alcohol on her breath saved her. Maybe it was a good thing she was drunk. I need control, and she's completely out of control.

Fuck. She's going to be the death of me.

After she stalked off to bed, good and angry, I returned to my quarters with a scotch and a raging hard-on. All I could think about was her in that riding outfit, wearing that bright red lipstick. I could imagine the way it would smear across my dick as she sucked me down. I could picture the way her pert tits would bounce as she rode me the way she rode her horse.

I tried a cold shower, but it only worsened my hunger. Imagining her body in that dress tonight, me ripping it off of her, finding her nipples perked and waiting for me. Her round ass bare and exposed, begging for a hit. Every time I closed my eyes, I saw her lying in my bed with her legs spread before me, desperate for me to break her in half.

Fucking the nanny is bad form, but doing so in my dreams was innocent enough.

In the end, I gave in to my desires. I jacked off in my room to thoughts of her with her face shoved into the mattress, her fingers in her pussy, and my cock in her ass.

Chapter Twelve

Abbie

ONCE, I drank an entire bottle of Malibu rum with Amanda and her cousin Emma in Amanda's parents' basement. The three of us spent the whole night giggling over trash television and stalking Amanda's celebrity crushes online, passing the bottle between us and chasing down every shot with orange juice. We gave each other makeovers, took tons of selfies, and passed out in a heap on the pullout couch. Rum! Greatest stuff on the planet!

The next morning, we took turns hugging the toilet and trying to keep down saltine crackers and ice chips in between bouts of vomiting. We all had horrible hangovers for the rest of the weekend, and I haven't been able to look at another bottle of rum since without feeling my stomach clench up a little.

This morning didn't go exactly the same way, but I still woke up with a sour stomach and a pounding headache. Which sucks, because Jude's still away on her mother-daughter trip, and I was looking forward to enjoying another day off. Instead, I feel like crap.

Abbie

I take a few ibuprofen with a full glass of water and then force myself into the shower to clear my head. Dad always says cold showers are nature's hangover cure. Last night's memories slowly unlock as I shiver under the arctic spray, hands wedged under my armpits for warmth. I didn't have that many drinks—four or five, max—but I also didn't eat much yesterday, and as much as I'd love to say I can hold my liquor, the truth is, I'm a cheap date.

Something about the citrus scent of my body wash brings back the memories of Graham, hard. The way he squared off against the poor guy I was dancing with. The way he demanded I go home with him. How he chastised me like an overbearing father for going out and having a good time.

How he cornered me by the stairs.

Better be careful. You might get what you're asking for.

I shiver again, but it has nothing to do with the cold. I can still feel the way his nose brushed my neck, something so intimate yet so dominating. Why didn't he do anything more? I've practically been throwing myself at him and he could have me eating out of his hand in point two seconds.

So why did he walk away?

I step out of the shower and stare at myself in the mirror. The circles under my eyes are a bit rough this morning, but nothing a little makeup can't fix.

Except I start to second-guess myself as I think back on the woman Graham brought home last night. She was stunning, self-assured, and an actual adult—clearly a good match for Graham despite the rude comments she

Chapter 12

made about me. Standing here in this towel, I feel every bit the nineteen-year-old. Immature and underdeveloped, still feeling like the secrets of adulthood continue to elude me. Maybe Graham really is just...out of my league.

I was so sure a man like him would prefer a younger woman. But between his reaction to my riding outfit and the age-appropriate company he had last night, maybe I pegged him all wrong. Maybe I need to channel Sharon Stone again. I should look her up.

Wrapping myself in a plush towel, I head back into my room to get dressed, but a package sitting on my bed stops me dead in my tracks. It's a medium rectangular box, wrapped in cream paper embossed with a floral pattern and tied with a blue ribbon. My pulse starts to race.

A gift. For me?

I gently touch the paper, excitement thrumming through me. No note, but it's exquisitely wrapped. Several thoughts hit me all at once.

1. Someone was in my room while I was in the shower.

2. Who in the house would leave me a gift so well-wrapped? It certainly wasn't Jude. And Esmeralda wouldn't have come in here on her own. It has to be from Graham. Which means—

3. Graham was in my room while I was showering. Only a wall away from my naked body standing under the water, ready for him, begging for him, if he would only say the word.

A chill trips down my spine. I almost don't want to open the gift, because I so enjoy this little Schrödinger's box scenario. I have no idea what's inside, but I can certainly dream. What would a powerful man like Graham buy the desirable woman he pinned down oh so intimately in the hallway?

Lingerie? A sexy designer dress for a date he's going to whisk me away on tonight?

Perfume?

Better be careful...

I run back to the bathroom to wrap my hair up in a towel so I don't drip on whatever luxurious magnificence awaits me in the box. Letting the anticipation be my guide, I climb onto the bed and give the gift a shake. It's not too heavy, but very slide-y. Definitely lingerie. I carefully untie the satin ribbon and take my time sliding my fingers under the pieces of tape so I can save the pretty cream paper.

This is my first ever gift from a man. A real one. I want the moment to last.

I carefully shake off the top of the box, peel back the layers of pale blue tissue paper...and stare down at the contents, confused.

Sitting there in the protective nest of tissue paper is one of the ugliest one-piece bathing suits I've ever seen. The fabric is printed with a hideous tropical flower design, bright magenta and teal and orange, with an unflattering square neckline and extra wide shoulder straps. It also has a freaking *skirt* on it. It's for grandmas. Grandmas with bad taste.

I search the rest of the box, hoping it's a joke, hoping there is something lacy and sexy buried underneath, but

Chapter 12

all that's in there is this hideous suit covered in neon flowers.

What the hell is this? His twisted sense of humor? Or does he actually expect me to wear this when I'm in the pool? Or maybe it's more of a statement, him telling me to cover myself up.

I don't understand this man one fucking bit. He chastises my wardrobe but then ignores me in my nun garb, only to come onto me last night when I was wearing that skimpy dress. He barely speaks to or even looks at me in the house but then chased me down on my night off.

And now he gives me a bathing suit meant for old ladies.

Amanda answers her phone drowsily after two rings. "This better be good. I was sleeping in."

"I need help figuring this shit out. I'm so confused."

"Ooh! Man drama!" I hear a muffled shifting sound, like she's getting more comfortable amid the pillows. "Worth my time, every time. Vent away, I want to hear everything."

I flop back on the bed, still in my robe. "So. I went out to the bar last night with Cassie. I was hoping she'd have some insight on how to get someone like Graham, you know?"

"Because why ask your best friend, right? Got it."

I laugh at the sarcasm and sass her back, "Does my best friend also work for my hot boss? No? Okay then."

"Fine. Fair point."

"Come on, Amanda. You know you're my number one, but this situation has required some…outside assistance."

Abbie

"I've gathered. So go on, you went to the bar, and then?"

"Okay, so there was this guy who was a dead ringer for Graham, if he were like ten or fifteen years younger and basically a frat boy."

"Please tell me you said hello."

"Obviously. We did shots and he asked me to dance. He was so hot. Not as hot as the real thing, but close. We were dancing for a while, and he was getting all frisky, although the place was so packed I couldn't even tell who was groping me half the time, and then just when I started to feel like I needed to sit down for a minute… you'll never guess who walks in."

"If you don't say hot boss, I'm going to die."

"Girl, he didn't just show up, he practically threw the guy I was dancing with across the room! I thought he was going to punch the poor kid. But he just dragged me home and yelled at me in the car like he was my dad. Then, he…" I pause, unsure how to explain what happened because I still can't explain it.

"He what? Stuck his hand up your dress? Made you give him road head? Come on, I'm dying over here. What happened?!"

"We got home and he…kind of pressed me against the wall and told me I needed to be careful, or I'd get what I was asking for."

"Oh my God," Amanda gasps, as breathy as I feel just talking about it again. "That is so hot, Abbie! Did you die? How are you alive to talk to me right now? Then what?"

Chapter 12

"He just kinda walked away after that," I say, my disappointment making me whine.

"Psh! He walked away because he totally wants you and he knew if he stayed, he'd have his way with you."

My insides do cartwheels and I have to steady myself against the bed. "*Stop*."

"I'm serious, Abbie, I can't believe you didn't get set on fire right then and there because that is some of the sexiest shit I've ever heard."

"You need to get out more." I try to act lighthearted, to distract myself from the intense pulses between my legs, begging for relief as the memories continue to flood me.

The way he smelled, the fire in his eyes when he warned me, what it was like to be so close to him in that moment. Amanda's right—how did I manage to not get set aflame?

"Anyway, like I was saying, I could have sworn there was a spark there last night. But then today I find this gift box on my bed and it turns out he bought me the ugliest bathing suit ever. Like straight up granny status."

"Wait, what? Why?"

"I don't know. That's why I'm calling you—" I move to sit up on the bed and freeze.

Graham is standing in my doorway, appearing so silently and suddenly that I have no idea how long he's been there. Listening to me. As I gossip to my best friend about him.

"Uh, I gotta go."

"What?" Amanda squeals. "Don't—"

I hang up and the phone drops to the bed as I do my

Abbie

best to look proper and respectable, sitting here in a robe with a towel wrapped around my head. Almost naked.

And meanwhile he's just *staring*.

I feel like a terrified gazelle cornered by a lion.

"Jude's home," he finally says, betraying nothing about what he may or may not have overheard. "She's upset, and I'm...frankly at a loss. I need you to deal with her. Please."

My stomach instantly knots. Jude wasn't supposed to be back until tomorrow. Now, I'm going to be fighting off my lingering hangover while trying to comfort an eight-year-old. And did Graham just say please? Is that a hint of fatherly vulnerability I detect?

Brushing away those thoughts, I try to focus on the job ahead of me. I need to prove to Graham that I can handle Jude right now, because I'm a mature and responsible adult. One who's unaffected by last night's drunken events.

"Of course. Let me just get dressed," I say. "By the way, thanks for the suit."

I'm expecting some kind of good-humored response, or at least a flash of that sexy smirk if nothing else. But instead he just turns on his heel and leaves without another word.

Once again, I'm left completely confused. What does this man want? And how long was he standing there, listening to my conversation?

I steady myself against the wardrobe, queasy again, and look at myself in the mirror. I need to find something to wear and put on a happy face for Jude. I can only imagine why her mother dropped her back here early.

Chapter 12

Important people to see? Fancy parties to attend? Did she even want to spend time with her daughter, or was it just a ploy to get under Graham's skin?

Either way, Jude's probably heartbroken.

And now it's my job to cheer her up the best I can.

Chapter Thirteen

Abbie

During the schedule block marked "loosely structured reading time," I decide to leave Jude to her stack of horse books and seek out Graham before the end of his workday. He wasn't exaggerating about being at a loss with Jude. She's been listless and despondent ever since Natasha dropped her off. I don't know what to do for the kid, but I have to do something.

Not that I blame her in the slightest. I'd be crushed, too, if my mom fobbed me off on a sitter the second a better offer came around.

I've suggested horseback riding, pool time, even offered to play dolls with her, but nothing seems to catch Jude's attention. She just shrugs or gives noncommittal answers. It breaks my heart. This girl deserves so much more than she's getting and I don't know how to fix it. I'm only the nanny, not a parent, and hardly viewed as a functioning adult around here, but I can't just let Jude's whole summer get ruined, much less her life.

A miserable Jude also means I'm not doing my job,

Chapter 13

which means I'm at risk of being sent home, which means I'll have failed. That's not an option. My father will be livid.

Also, if I'm being honest to myself, I just feel for the girl. It's one thing to grow up with gross amounts of money, all the privileges anyone could ever dream of, but it's another to be cast aside by your parents. All the horse toys in the world won't make up for the fact that Jude was abandoned by her mother and gets regularly ignored by her workaholic father.

"Enjoy your book. I'll be back!" I sing to her, slowly closing the door as I go. Jude doesn't move or acknowledge that I've talked to her, exactly as she's done the rest of the day.

The thought of talking to Graham after our altercation last night sends my stomach into knots. I stop by my room on the way down, to make sure I'm appropriately dressed for the part of Helpful and Concerned Nanny. I haven't seen Graham since he appeared in my doorway this morning, and I want to be sure I approach him in a strictly professional manner. My attraction to him can't play into this, or else he'll quickly dismiss me—and my worries about Jude.

I quickly touch up my makeup and pull my skirt down a little lower, so it's covering my knees. Then I fuss with my shirt, buttoning it all the way up to the neck. My hair goes into a neat bun at the back of my neck, and with one last mirror check, I finally feel ready to face the beast.

As for the butterflies gathering in my stomach as I head to Graham's office...they need to go. I should just forget about what happened last night. Regardless of

Abbie

what it may or may not have meant, I'm sure Graham won't mention it ever again. And neither should I.

Besides, this conversation is about Jude. The girl needs so much more from her father than he's giving. I'll be damned if that isn't something I also understand. I need to get him to listen to me.

I decide to treat this like I'm prepping for a big debate team competition. Cornell may not be the top-rated Ivy League college, but our Speech and Debate Society is ranked first *in the world*—which is a big reason I applied to the school. After reluctantly joining debate club with Amanda our sophomore year at Suffield Academy (so we'd look good on our college applications, she'd insisted), I realized how much I loved structured arguing. Not only that, but debate taught me how to listen better, be more persuasive, more self-assured, more assertive, more aggressive. It helped me blossom into the me I am now.

Taking deep, calming breaths, I run down the list of things I want to say to him on my walk from one end of the house to the other. How Jude gets lonely, how she deserves better, how she needs more one-on-one time with her dad. By the time I reach the closed door of his office, I feel confident and prepared and ready to rumble.

Taking a deep breath, I knock on his door, and his accented voice calls out, "Enter."

Keep your shit together, Abbie.

I open the door and take a step inside. Today, like every day, he's dressed in a crisp button-down and cufflinks. No glasses today, I'm disappointed to see, but the sight of him still takes my breath away. He's golden, liter-

Chapter 13

ally glowing, surrounded by windows and reflections from the numerous framed awards.

It's intimidating as fuck. Despite all my prep, my tongue sticks to the roof of my mouth as he drags his gaze from his laptop to me. Heat licks across every inch of skin his eyes graze past, and soon I'm sweating and can barely remember why I came here in the first place.

"Yes?" he prods, sounding impatient.

I close my eyes and take a deep breath. Jude needs me to not lose my shit right now.

"Do you have a minute?" I ask.

After a long, painful moment where I'm not sure if Graham wants to incinerate me or eat me, he gently closes his laptop and gestures to a chair in front of his desk. The same one I sat in so recently, before he all but called me a whore.

Today will be different. It has to be.

He watches me the entire time from underneath his dark brows, his expression betraying no hint of the thoughts running through his head. Is he thinking about me in last night's dress? Is he thinking about all the ways he can bend me over the furniture in his office?

Dammit, Abbie, focus.

"So. What brings you to my office this evening, Miss Montgomery?" He says my name and chills explode down my back. We're so close I can smell his cologne. My insides turn liquid and I have to take another deep breath just to focus.

"I wanted to talk to you about Jude."

He says nothing, only stares. This man really doesn't like to talk. Fine.

Abbie

"You were right," I go on. "She's been having a really hard time since Mrs. Ratliff brought her home. I could barely get her to eat today, she's been distracted in her lessons, she's not even enjoying her favorite books. I don't know how to pull her out of it. I'm trying, but—"

"Her mother's impromptu little outing has caused problems, yes, per usual," he interrupts. "Which is why, as her nanny, I expect you to be able to handle these things. That *is* what I am paying you for, is it not?"

I can feel my face go hot at the rebuke. Graham leans back in his chair, exuding a combination of intense power and disdain. How does anyone keep their shit together around him? Half of me wants to turn around and run for the door. More than half, if I'm honest.

"It is, sir." I nod, digging my nails into my palms so I don't get lost in the maelstrom that is Graham Ratliff. "But…this isn't just about me 'handling things.' Jude feels every bit the abandonment by her mom, which I get—but she can't feel abandoned by you, too. So I was—"

"I had *nothing* to do with her mother's tasteless display," he snaps. "I didn't want Jude going off with her to begin with, and I certainly did not encourage it in any way. The implication this issue is in *any* way my fault is asinine."

I wince.

"I'm not saying it's your fault. I know Mrs. Ratliff just…showed up out of the blue to whisk Jude away and then dumped her back here the second something else popped up. But as I was saying, I was thinking a little extra attention from you might help smooth things over. Maybe dinner tonight could be for two—just you and

Chapter 13

Jude. You could ask about her day, try to get her to open up. Maybe see if she wants to go to a movie this weekend, or—"

"It's really not in your job description to tell me how to parent my child," Graham says, inhaling sharply between his teeth.

My gut clenches. It's like everything I try to say is somehow offending him. "I'm not trying to do that. At all." I scramble for better words, but I can tell I'm already losing him. "I just thought Jude would benefit from some quality time with a parent who's willing to make an effort to show up for her. Instead of treating her like an afterthought."

Graham's gaze is deadly. "Are you insinuating that I don't show up for Jude?"

I was trying to be tactful, but yes. That's exactly what I was insinuating. And I'm not going to let him intimidate me out of speaking my mind. Because regardless of how he *thinks* he acts toward his kid, I know what I've seen with my own eyes.

"I don't know, do you? Because sometimes I'm not so sure," I continue, my voice getting louder as my temper rises. "Jude barely sees you apart from when you actually deign to make an appearance at the dinner table, which is hardly something she can count on. And even then, you can be pretty harsh with her. She's eight years old and she worships you. A little quality time would go a long way. In my opinion. *Sir*."

For a moment he looks too stunned to speak. Then the tiger comes roaring back. He stands, fists clenching at his sides, and I involuntarily lean away.

Abbie

"Do you have any *idea* how hard I've worked to make sure Jude has every little thing she could possibly want or need?" he says. "Do you know what it's like to be the sole provider for a family? The responsibility of it, the pressure of knowing it's all on your shoulders?

"For over a decade I've bankrolled my wife's—*ex-wife's*—theatrical dreams, supporting her financially and emotionally, making sure she could afford to turn down 'artistically unfulfilling' roles and still vacation in the Maldives with friends or jet off for a luxury yoga retreat whenever she felt the need for a 'spiritual refresh,' and all the while doing my best to juggle what was, in practice, *already* single parenthood with a very demanding and stressful career where I act as the spine of an entire international banking empire, not to mention a nightmare of a marriage which for the record was never even…that is…" he trails off, sinking back into his chair with a dazed look. I think both of us are in shock at his outburst.

He's breathing hard, and I realize he's just unloaded a lot of very personal, very raw feelings. Which I imagine he probably hasn't shared with anyone else. Ever.

"Everything I do is for Jude," he finishes, his voice quieter now.

"I'm sorry. I had no idea how difficult it's been," is all I can muster. I'm still floored he just let his walls down for five seconds, intentional or not. No wonder he's such a jackass all the time—he's been busting his ass for years to take care of everyone, but who takes care of him?

"I should get back to work," Graham murmurs.

"Okay. Sure," I say gently, backing toward the door. "I just thought it was important to tell you that your

Chapter 13

daughter needs you right now. And that I hope you can be there for her."

His head snaps up. "Are you sure you're talking about Jude? Or yourself?"

The question knocks me sideways. No amount of debate preparation in the world could have prepared me for this sudden personal jab. "Sorry, what?"

His stare feels heavy. "Clearly you're projecting your own daddy issues onto Jude. You can drop the façade of concern, Abbie."

"The—excuse me?"

"Don't play dumb, it insults you and me. We both know an Ivy League co-ed is smarter than that. But since you're here, we really should address this ridiculous crush you have on me."

Shit. So he *did* hear my phone conversation. And obviously—probably in an attempt to cover for his momentary display of vulnerability just now—the jack-assery is back in full effect.

"It's inappropriate," he goes on. "Unfounded. And it needs to stop."

Heart thudding in my throat, my mind turns in a hundred different directions, trying to unsink this sinking ship. Humiliated doesn't even begin to cover how I'm feeling, but I'm frustrated and angry, too. I know he's deflecting, trying to change the subject from his parenting skills and troubled marriage to something else entirely, I get that. *And yet.* I can't deny the clear truth beneath his accusation. Which is why I'm so goddamn flustered.

"That's not what I came here to talk about, Mr.

Abbie

Ratliff. At all." My voice sounds as uncomfortable as I feel. "I really do care about Jude."

"I'm done discussing my child." His voice is stern, his eyes flashing. "And honestly, I expected better from you. Your silly little attraction to me is becoming a distraction in the house. I'm not the only one who's noticed your fawning."

Oh, God. Everything is on the line now, not just poor Jude. "I'm sorry. I never intended to cross a line. I guess I misread the situation. I thought I noticed an attraction—"

"It's pathetic, really, how you mince about, trying to elicit compliments from me."

My jaw drops. "I don't—"

"You know you're an attractive woman," he continues, ignoring my denial. "Which is not up for discussion. But you've been acting like a silly schoolgirl. Frankly, I'm convinced you wouldn't be able to handle wherever my attraction might lead, though that's beside the point."

Everything stills. The anger, the indignation, the confusion. Where his attraction *might lead*? Meaning... he's into me, too? And he just admitted it?

Graham's deep blue eyes burn into mine. I can't breathe.

"As for dinner." He looks down and reopens his laptop. "I'm going out. With the woman I was forced to send home last night because of your irresponsible behavior."

Jealousy stabs me in the heart. My irresponsible behavior pushed him into the arms of another woman? He's the one who chased me down on my night off!

Chapter 13

"Mr. Ratliff," I say, trying to sound unperturbed. "If you would just—"

"Dinner *will* be for two, after all—Jude and you."

He returns to work and doesn't look at me again. I've obviously been dismissed.

Asshole.

Chapter Fourteen

Abbie

I DON'T THINK Graham came home last night.

Not that I waited up for him or woke up on the couch in the living room at an ungodly hour of the morning with a crick in my neck or anything. Not that I spent the entire evening compulsively scrolling on my phone, trying to distract myself from the fact that the man who owns my body in a very metaphorical way, who has been teasing and taunting me for what feels like an eternity, was out late with another woman. Allegedly.

I stumble upstairs to my room at six in the morning, desperate for a nap before the day begins, but knowing, with dread, that I need to get dressed. I have a job to do, even if I was up all night. Being an adult is horribly, terribly lame.

The only thing I'm grateful for is that Graham didn't catch me passed out on the couch. How embarrassing would it be if he knew I was up all night waiting for him? I need to gain control of this situation somehow, but he holds all the cards. I'm at a total loss.

Chapter 14

Upstairs, I freeze in my doorway. There's something laid out on my bed, waiting for me. As I get closer, I feel a flash of anger.

It's a classic schoolgirl uniform, with a pleated navy skirt, a white button-down shirt, thick knee-high socks, and a V-neck sweater. Did I mention it's summertime? Either this is Graham's kink, or this is his way of demanding that I change my clothes.

Based on literally every conversation we've had about clothing, and his attitude yesterday when I went to see him in his office, I know it's the latter.

Fuck him.

When did he even have time to drop this off? That narrow window between 4 and 6 a.m. when I finally drifted off? Graham needs to stop waltzing into my room on a whim. This may be his house, but this is *my* space. I'm entitled to privacy. That this man believes he has access to everything is maddening. And the worst part of all is that I'm disappointed to have missed him.

Everything about him is a duality of terrible and wonderful.

Okay, fine. He wants me to wear this garbage while I shuttle his daughter around from point A to point B and he pretends neither one of us exists? So be it. I'll wear the stupid outfit and I'll play the stupid game, but on my terms. I'm tired of being railroaded.

Once I'm dressed, I roll the waistband to make the skirt a few inches shorter and then tie the shirt hem into a knot, high enough so you can see my midriff. Graham can kiss my ass about the sweater and the socks. It's eighty degrees in the shade and Jude has half her lessons outside. No way am I going to parade around in that mess.

Should I wear pigtail braids with this Britney Spears ensemble? I give it a quick try, but it just screams *Fuck Me, Daddy*. And as much as I *want* to scream that, I don't think it would land well. I do still have an eight-year-old to keep an eye on. Not to mention, I really don't want Esmeralda to think I'm *that* kind of nanny. I really like her.

I put on three layers of lip gloss, way too much blush, and extra mascara. I look every part the saucy little tart. Perfect. Exactly what I was going for.

"Guess what I did today!" I announce, walking into the dining room. Only Jude waits for me. Graham is likely sleeping off whatever he did last night. I don't think I actually want to know, but not knowing is also killing me slowly.

"What?" Jude asks, lacking any sort of energy.

"I canceled all your lessons!" I clap my hands, trying to get some excitement rolling. "And I gave Cassie a call to set up another trail ride for us."

"Really?" her eyes nearly bug out of her head. She tries to settle back down, but the corners of her mouth keep shooting up into a little smile. "I don't have to do anything else?"

"Nothing else," I promise. "If horses make you feel better, then that's what you're going to get. A full day of horses."

Jude's excitement bubbles up into giggles. "I don't have to do any classes today? Not even Spanish?"

"Not. Even. Spanish."

Chapter 14

"Yes!" She pumps her little fists in the air. "Can we go now?"

"How about we eat first, so we don't starve out there on the trail?"

"Okay." She sounds disappointed, but only a little bit, and her smile is enough to warm my heart.

Jude eats her waffles and fruit at lightning speed, with me trying my best to catch up, and it's not even twenty minutes before we're trekking off to the stables. I casually scan the windows, hoping to see Graham's shadow, but see nothing. It's probably better this way. He'd probably lose his head if he found out I canceled all of his daughter's lessons for the day.

Tough shit. He hasn't been there for Jude, and he wouldn't hear me out when I tried to explain how badly his daughter needs him right now. I'm just doing what needs to be done to give her the break she needs. He's had every opportunity to do this himself, to be the hero who made the trail ride happen, but he didn't.

Now I get to be the hero.

Cassie meets us in the stables, dressed in the riding gear I would be wearing if I didn't have this ridiculous uniform on. She raises a brow as Jude goes running to her horse.

"Cute outfit..."

"Don't even get me started." I groan. "I know I should be in jodhpurs, but here we are. Thanks for doing this, by the way."

"Of course! Anything for my favorite munchkin. I'm not entirely sure how that outfit is going to work for you on the horse, but you seem like you can handle yourself."

Abbie

"That's exactly the kind of girl I am. Plus, I have my boots on, at least."

Cassie leans in conspiratorially. "So what happened the other night at the bar? Why'd Graham just show up like that? I've been meaning to ask you about it, but I figured we should talk in person."

I roll my eyes, more for show than anything else. "He's friends with my dad. I think he thinks that means I need more protection or something." It's the same explanation I've been giving myself. I conveniently leave out the part about me not being twenty-one.

"Ahhh." Cassie stretches the sound out. "I totally get it. Kind of a bummer, though."

"Yeah. I feel like I can't do anything fun now." I scrunch up my face in frustration. I want to be able to talk about this whole Graham mess with someone who actually knows him. Getting advice from Amanda only gets me so far when she doesn't truly understand who I'm dealing with. I'm tired of feeling so isolated in the house and in my mind.

"Man, but did you see the look on Graham's face after he pushed that boy? I thought there was going to be a fight," Cassie adds, her eyes lit up with excitement. "He looked *furious*."

"It was terrifying, honestly." I lean in and lower my voice. "I didn't even get that poor guy's number."

"Well." Cassie stands up straight and clears her throat a little. "He was just your warm-up, right?"

I stare at her for a moment. "Warm-up?"

She whispers, "You know. To get you ready for *Quinn?*"

Chapter 14

"Right!" How could I have already forgotten my lie to Cassie? "He absolutely was, but he was also really cute."

"Liquor makes everyone cute." Cassie winks at me. "But your boy is here now, and he seems to like the outfit."

Heart in my throat, I whip around to see Quinn on the opposite side of the stables, trying to look nonchalant while very obviously checking me out. *Right*, I remember as my heart rate returns to something normal, *Quinn*.

"Good job getting his attention," Cassie says with a laugh. "He looks like his eyes are going to bug out of his head."

"Victory is mine," I say halfheartedly. "So, are we ready to go?"

"Go? Are you kidding?" Cassie stares at me. "You better march your butt over there right now and flirt with the boy of your dreams. You didn't put all that work in for nothing."

"I don't know, Cass. I get so nervous when it's for real."

"Pretend we're back at The Flightless Pelican. Pretend I've just given you a shot of courage. You can do this."

The last thing I want to do is flirt with Quinn, but I can't exactly backpedal now. I need to at least put on a show if I'm going to save face.

I take a deep breath, nod at Cassie as she gives me an encouraging smile, and saunter across the hay-covered floor toward the boy with the big muscles and the even bigger grin.

Abbie

"Well howdy," Quinn offers cheerfully. "You look...different."

"Is that bad?" I ask, giving my hair a quick twirl. "Graham made me wear it."

"No, you look great. Did you say *Graham* made you wear that?"

"Well, I made a few adjustments." I laugh and touch his arm. His eyes light up. "But yes, he demanded I wear this hideous uniform. It even came with wool socks and a sweater." I'm really laying it on thick, but Quinn seems to like it.

"Damn. It's way too hot for a sweater right now."

"I *know*. But he's been on my ass about my wardrobe since I got here, and now I'm stuck wearing this thing." I pout my lips out just a little bit. Quinn licks his in response. "So I decided to rebel a little bit. Not sure it's up to code, though. You won't tell on me, will you?"

"I would never rat you out, Abbie." Quinn winks at me. "Besides, I like it."

"Thanks." I laugh a little and bat my eyes, hoping I look like a textbook flirt, when Quinn's eyes suddenly go wide.

I turn around and nearly fall over into a hay bale. Standing in the middle of the stables, surrounded by bales of hay and feed buckets and various tools, stands Graham Ratliff in a three-piece dark blue suit. God, he's hot. And fuming. He looks like the Devil himself.

My knees turn to pudding cups. He's immaculate in that suit. Dark, sexy, edgy. Delicious. It doesn't hurt that he's so mad he looks like he just might break something.

Chapter 14

His eyes are narrowed, his fists clenched, jaw set in a hard line that I want to run my fingers over.

My panties are so very damp, and I am also so very nervous.

"I need to see you in my study," Graham says. "Now."

Uh-oh.

Chapter Fifteen

Abbie

Graham stalks through his monstrous house without a single word to me or anyone else who mistakenly happens across his warpath. He fidgets with the cufflinks on his sleeves, never looking anywhere but directly in front of him.

I can practically feel him seething from behind.

I am, however, enjoying the view. Graham has a great ass, round and just a little bouncy as he walks. The angrier he gets, the more bounce he gets. I can tell he's ranting in his head, probably thinking about how he needs to punish me. Naughty visions appear before me, each promising something delicious. They startle me, but only a little.

How mad can he honestly be with me wearing the exact outfit he provided? He asked for this. This was his doing.

Esmeralda quickly steps out of the way as we round the corner and make our way toward his office. She goes a little wide-eyed when she sees the look on Graham's face.

Chapter 15

Then she flashes me a tiny, sympathetic smile and scurries away.

I thought men like him were supposed to have more composure than this. He must be really mad.

New realizations start to filter through my mind. When I planned this day and outfit, I was infuriated with Graham and his treatment of both me and Jude. I wanted to get back at him, frustrate him as much as he frustrates me, but I didn't think he'd lose his damn mind.

What if he sends me home?

Fear strikes me as I follow him into his study.

Graham slams the door, marches to the desk, turns around with a flourish, and sits down. He's angry, absolutely, but he looks much more calm than I imagined. His face is a placid lake of emptiness. His eyes are closed off to me, curtains drawn across the windows to the soul. Even his posture has relaxed now that we're back in his territory, his safe space.

"Sit." He points to a chair opposite the desk.

I oblige, swallowing hard, praying he's really not as upset as I thought.

Coffee steams on the desk. He picks it up, thinks better of it, and puts it back down. Then he clasps his hands together in front of him. When he finally speaks, his voice crashes over me like a wave of thunder, sending lightning to my core.

"What did you think you were doing today?"

So many things, Graham. I clear my throat and say, "You'll have to be more specific."

"I'll have to be more specific." He repeats it back to me, and huffs out a small, bitter laugh. "Yes, I suppose I have to clarify which transgression my atrocious nanny has most recently committed because there are so many to draw from, aren't there, Miss Montgomery?"

The way he says my name feels like a physical touch, with an extra squeeze around the throat. Not too hard, but enough to pose a threat. I shiver a little and force myself to pay attention to his words. I try to keep composure, the very real threat of being fired sinking into me.

"Are you saying you're dissatisfied with my care of Jude? Has she said something?"

"I don't look to my eight-year-old for advice on matters of any kind. She's a child." He cuts a look to me. "But no, your care of my daughter has been adequate."

Adequate? That actually hurts a little. I've worked so hard to get Jude to trust me, to boost her spirits, to help her realize she's important and special and *liked*, and he wants to call all my time with her "adequate"?

"So what is the problem, then?" I ask, trying to keep my voice level.

"The problem, Miss Montgomery, is that you canceled Jude's lessons without my permission."

I steel myself and lift my chin. "I did, yes."

"It was not your place to do so," he says, his voice like steel. "Jude is not your child. You do not pay for these lessons. You do not accommodate a small staff of instructors. She is not your responsibility beyond the rules I laid out upon your arrival." Graham seems to be reveling in his role as authoritarian, but his dictatorial attitude only serves to rile me up further. "Do you have a problem respecting my boundaries, Miss Montgomery?"

"She needed a day off," I shoot back.

Chapter 15

"You have *no idea* what she needs," Graham says sharply. I jump at his gruffness. "You will never again make any alterations to her schedule during the course of your employ, is that understood?"

None of this is about what's best for Jude, but instead about obeying Mr. Asshole here. God, how this man pushes all my buttons.

"She's overscheduled!" I explode. "She needs to have fun! And with parents who act like they don't give two shits about her, she needs something that makes her feel *loved*. The only place she's getting that right now is her horse. So yes, I absolutely canceled her lessons so she could go riding, because her mother abandoned her and her father can't even make time to join her for breakfast, and she's been a mess ever since she got home from her trip. Which I already tried to talk to you about, but it obviously didn't do any good because nothing changed!

"Look, I care about Jude, and I know you do, too. So I don't understand why you can't show up for her. Give her some time and attention. Show her you care." My voice cracks with emotion, and I have to clear my throat again. "You can't get these years back later. This is it."

I'm a little out of breath now, and honestly a little taken aback at myself for that outburst, but I'm proud that I stood up to him and defended Jude's honor. Said the things that I wish someone had said to my own father when I was young. Because Graham was right when he said I had daddy issues. I can admit that. But I'm not 'projecting' them onto Jude. I'm just recognizing what's in front of me. Calling it like I see it. Meddling, yes, but for good reason.

Abbie

I sit taller and watch Graham process what I just said. I start to think I may have actually gotten through to him, when—

"Be that as it may. You do not make these decisions without me. You do not make these decisions at all. You are here to ensure my daughter attends her lessons, eats her meals, and goes to bed after bathing. Otherwise, you are welcome to seek work elsewhere. In which case, don't dream of using me as a reference."

He leans forward, eyes blazing.

We stare each other down. He's said nothing about actually firing me over this, only giving me the option to quit if I can't obey his rules. Which is no option at all.

God, it's stupid how hot I find him when he's this angry. How can I be both so enraged and so turned on at the same time? This man is an enigma.

"I'd prefer to stay on," I say evenly. "For Jude."

"Very well."

"Is there anything else, Your Highness?" I ask, giving him a full mouth of sass.

"Yes, as a matter of fact. That is not how that skirt is supposed to be worn." The cold look on his face is replaced by something else, something intense, and my heart skips. "Nor is the shirt. You're obviously attempting to get me riled up."

Back to complaining about my clothes. Round and round we go.

"And obviously it's working," I snark.

"Going forward, you'll wear the uniform as it's meant to be worn," he says.

"I'm surprised you noticed my outfit at all, consid-

Chapter 15

ering the fact that your date went so well last night you didn't come home until dawn," I point out. "Was she not as distracting as you hoped? Or do you just have a wandering eye?"

Graham smirks. "If I didn't know any better, I might think you were actually jealous."

"Maybe I am. Want to spank me for it?" I ask. If he's going to treat me like a damn child, I might as well act like one.

Except he's not looking at me like I'm a child right now. Not at all.

His eyes lock on mine, and his voice drops to a low growl. "Don't offer it if you don't mean it."

Don't offer it if you... Oh.

My heart practically stops, because his words have shaken me to my core. My panties are damp in an instant. Still feeling defiant and brave, I decide to say something else I shouldn't.

"What if I do mean it?"

For a moment, Graham is silent. His eyes rake over my body. I try not to shiver.

"If my hands touch you," he says, measuring his words, "I'm not responsible for what happens after. Do you understand?"

Speechless, I nod.

He looks at me expectantly, and I realize he's waiting. Waiting for me to say more. Heat creeps along my chest, my pulse like a jackhammer.

I clear my throat. This is it. "What do you want me to do?"

A slow smile burns across his face. It almost looks

foreign on him, being so stern all the time. He pushes back from the desk and points to the space in front of him. "Come here."

Heart in my throat, I obey. I try to walk slow and sexy, like this isn't my first time doing something like this, like I know exactly what I'm doing. When I'm standing over him, I wait for my next instruction.

"Turn around," he commands.

Breathless, I obey again.

His voice is liquid silk. "Hands flat on the desk."

I lean over and lay my palms down, wiggling my ass a little as I adjust my stance for balance. Tingles explode through my body. I'm so aroused I can barely see straight.

After a few agonizing seconds, he says, "Now lift up your skirt."

Thank God the desk is here, because I'd fall right over if it wasn't. I'm nervous and excited all at once. Bracing myself on one hand, I reach behind me to pull my skirt up high, mentally applauding myself for wearing cute lacy panties today.

I hear the chair creak behind me, feel the heat radiating off his body as Graham gets closer. All of my senses are heightened, pulled taut as wire, and I start to shake a little. That's when I hear the crack of skin on skin as hot pain blooms sharp across one of my butt cheeks. A gasp escapes me, my breath catching in my throat.

He spanked me. He really spanked me. Like a child.

His strong, sure hand rubs my swollen cheek, soothing the sting away. "Did that hurt?"

"Yes," I whisper, closing my eyes, pushing my ass back into his palm.

Chapter 15

"Did you like it?"

I swallow hard, not trusting my voice. "Y-yes."

He spanks me again and I jolt, moaning a little this time.

"Thank you," I whisper.

"You're very naughty, Miss Montgomery," he chastises. "It seems you don't like to obey the rules."

"Mm-mm," I moan in agreement as he caresses my other cheek, the pain and pleasure mingling until I can't tell one from the other. I'm getting wetter by the second.

"You need to be punished." He spanks me lower this time, and more gently, his fingers grazing my center through the lace of my underwear. "Don't you?"

"Yes," I pant.

Graham doesn't move his hand away this time. Instead, his fingers find their way inside my panties. I hiss, pushing back against his fingers a little.

"You are very wet, Miss Montgomery." His voice is husky and rough as he traces his fingertips around my lips. "I think you like being punished."

My answer comes out as a moan. Him touching me is the most euphoric experience of my life. I can taste colors and see sound as his fingers slide up and find my swollen clit.

"What am I supposed to do with you?" he asks, almost quiet.

"Whatever you want," I manage.

Graham's fingers circle my clit and I nearly fall over. "I have very high demands."

"I'm a very capable woman."

He traces his finger back down to my center, barely

dipping inside my cunt with his fingertip, just enough to make me ache.

"Please," I beg.

"Please what?"

"I want more." God, I sound like Oliver Twist.

There's an edge of cruel humor in his voice as he says, "I'm not sure you can handle it."

"I can handle anything you give me, Mr. Ratliff."

"Hmm." He pauses, and I hold my breath. "I suppose there's only one way to find out."

His finger slides all the way into me then, so agonizingly slow that all I can do is pant my way through it. Once I'm full of him, he gives his finger a twist inside me, and I let out a yelp.

"Are you finding this to your liking, Miss Montgomery?"

I shiver a little. "Yes."

He slides his finger out and then plunges two back inside me, filling me tight.

"Ah," I cry out. It feels so good.

His fingers slide out again, then in again, spreading my wetness everywhere. I'm losing my fucking mind with every stroke. Again, he pumps into me. Faster. Harder. Pushing deeper each time.

The next thing I know I'm begging for more, spreading my legs wider, and he's giving it to me, letting me grind against his fingers as they pound into me, hard and deep and fast, just like I imagine his cock doing when I'm touching myself in bed at night. I grip the edge of the desk for dear life, eyes shut tight, floating on a wave of hot pleasure.

Chapter 15

"Yes," I whisper, over and over. I want to say his name more than anything, but I don't want to break whatever trance he's in or give him a chance to have second thoughts.

And then I realize I don't have any words anymore, only moans, because every nerve in my body is fully on fire and the only thing I can focus on is him finger fucking me to the brink of an orgasm as I'm bent over his desk.

He spanks me again with his free hand, fingers still pumping inside me, and that's all I need to come all over his hand. I cry out, climaxing so hard I collapse on the desk, panting and trembling as the shockwaves crash through me.

Graham pulls his hand back and a second later sets a handkerchief next to me on the desk. "Clean yourself up."

I obey.

Chapter Sixteen

Abbie

I WALK through the Ratliff mansion, flushed and confused, still catching my breath.

Objectively, I know and understand what just happened in Graham's office, but subjectively, I'm a mess. My fingers drag across the smooth walls, swerving around the framed art and tasteful family photos, like I'm unearthing the answers in the depths of the house. Divining rationale from the drywall. Why not? I haven't been able to understand anything happening in this house since I got here.

No one intercepts me on my walk of shame. I'm both grateful and disappointed; I kind of wanted Esmeralda to take one look at me, wrap her arm around my shoulder, and lead me to the kitchen for a mid-afternoon cup of tea. There, she'd pat my arm, telling me it wasn't my fault, that all men are pigs. They use us and cast us aside all the time. She seems like the understanding, matronly sort who would do it.

Instead, I'm greeted by an empty bedroom and an

Chapter 16

aching chasm in my center. Graham finally touched me, so why do I feel so hollow? The whole time, he acted so cold and removed. And then he sent me away. What the hell does that mean?

All of a sudden, a fit of giggles takes hold of me and I collapse slowly onto my bed, laughing like I've lost my damn mind.

That was, without a doubt, the single greatest orgasm I've ever had (not that I've had any experience besides with myself). Possible precedent set for the rest of my life. I was so turned on and it was so explosive, I don't know how to recover from it.

Maybe it doesn't have to make sense. Maybe it can just be exactly as it was and be okay.

My fingers stray under my skirt to the still-burning cheeks of my ass, tracing the hot skin where he spanked me. Sparks shoot through me at the faintest touch, and my pussy gives a little clench again. Everything surges up so strong in memory—his gruff verbal commands, the musk of his cologne, the skilled thrusting of his fingers. I can hardly believe that was me in there.

I climb off the bed and stare at myself in the mirror: cheeks pink, hair disheveled, clothes slightly askew, eyes gleaming. Who is this girl, and what does Graham Ratliff finally see in her?

His fingers were inside of me.

He made me come.

My knees go weak and I let myself fall back on the bed again. It wasn't a dream. It wasn't a fantasy. It really happened. And maybe it'll happen again.

There's a chirp from my phone as a text comes in,

Abbie

and I sit up suddenly, remembering the riding trails I was supposed to take Jude on with Cassie. Should I still go down there? Did Graham cancel the whole thing? I hope Cassie's the one texting me with an update.

And it is. She sends, *Graham called off the ride, but said Jude can have some extra lessons. I'll bring her up to the house when she's done. Are you okay? G looked pissed.*

I frown, unsure how to answer. On the one hand, I'm better than okay. On the other...

I'm fine—it was a verbal lashing, more or less—sorry if I got you in any trouble. ☹ I was just trying to help Jude, I text back, my hands shaking from the half-truths I'm telling. *Thanks for the check in.*

Anytime! Cassie replies quickly. *We were a little worried. Even Quinn.*

She ends the text with a series of winking emojis. Oh boy. Poor Quinn. He doesn't have a chance in hell, and I'm sure he thinks I'm into him after all my blatant fake flirting today. I know I got myself into this mess, but how do I get out of it? Should I give him the cold shoulder and hope he takes the hint? Tell Cassie I changed my mind? Let the flirtation play out (innocently) all summer, or will that just ruin any chance I might have with Graham? Ugh.

Desperate, I FaceTime my best friend.

"Help me understand men," I say when she picks up.

"Nice hair." Amanda laughs. I try to smooth it, but it doesn't really work. "I'm not good at men. I'm only good with frat boys who can drink more ounces of beer than they have IQ points. What happened?"

Chapter 16

I blush furiously, my mouth unable to get out the words. "Well..."

"Oh my God, did you sleep with him?"

"No!" The word comes out more forcefully than I expected. "No. But he...*we*...there was an incident."

Amanda leers at me through the camera. "Tell me everything."

So I do. I tell her about the uniform ("What a twat muffin. Who seriously gives someone that kind of uniform to wear while watching their kid?") and canceling Jude's plans. I tell her about Quinn's ogling in the barn ("Tell him you have a hot friend!!") and how Graham showed up, sexy and enraged. I tell her about how I stood up for Jude and for me, and how I sassed my boss back with all the sass I usually save for my dad, and what Graham did to me afterward.

"Oh. My. God." Amanda's eyes bug out on screen. "I'm so jealous. I need a hot, dominating man in my life." She sighs, then pauses, stares at me, and leans in. "Wait a minute."

My cheeks heat up again. "What?"

"You've had an orgasm before, right?"

"Oh my God, Amanda." Embarrassment eats through me. "Of course! Just...alone. You know?"

"This is incredible. He's your first, like, non-solo big O. This day needs to be commemorated! Should I send you a cake? We should celebrate this day every year!"

"Please, no." I groan. "I just need to figure out what to do next. I still can't figure him out, beyond that he seems to respond when I cop an attitude."

Amanda shrugs. "He's super rich, right? Maybe he's

tired of everything being handed to him. All the yes people. Maybe he likes the challenge."

"Maybe, but he definitely still likes being in control."

"Kinky." Amanda chortles with glee. "Does he have any hot friends who need nannies, too? I'm suddenly having a change of heart about my future."

"You're the worst." And then my stomach drops as I see another call coming in. "Ugh, I gotta go, my dad is calling."

"Your daddy or your dad?"

"Very funny." I roll my eyes at her. "Talk soon."

I hang up on my best friend and switch the call to my dad, voice only. Why is he calling now, out of the blue? It's almost as if he can sense that something happened. But after mostly ignoring his texts since I got here, I know I can't keep avoiding him.

"Hey, Dad."

"How's my baby girl doing in that big house?" His voice is familiar and comforting, soothing the homesickness that suddenly hits me. But I know what he really wants right now, and it isn't to comfort me.

"I'm fine. It's not so big once you get used to it."

"Don't get too used to it." He laughs. "So, what else? Any news to report?"

"Um. Not really." Not any that I'd like to share, thank you very much. "Just been pretty busy with Jude's schedule and everything."

"That's not the progress update I'm looking for and you know it, Abbie," he says, irritated. "You need to keep me in the loop. And if you aren't getting anywhere, it's

Chapter 16

time to quit that job and come back home. I'll find someone else."

NO. I can't go home. Not now. Not when things have finally turned a corner.

Not after Graham Ratliff has touched me in ways that no one else ever has.

"I *am* making progress," I insist. "I just need more time."

"We can't afford to have you dragging your heels," my dad goes on with his scolding.

"I'm not dragging my heels!" Frustrated, I fall backwards on my bed and massage the ache starting to pound in my temples. This is exactly why I've been avoiding his text messages.

"So what do you call the last several weeks?" he prods.

"Reconnaissance," I snap. "He's not an easy man to decipher, Dad. You told me that yourself."

He sort of snorts, but I can hear him relax. "Okay. Fair enough."

"Look, just...don't worry. He's interested in me. I'll have him hooked soon enough."

With that, I hang up.

Chapter Seventeen

Abbie

Graham isn't at dinner tonight, much to Jude's disappointment. And mine, I'll admit. Where the hell is he?

After everything that passed between us earlier, I guess I was hoping he'd actually make the effort to spend more time with Jude. And with me, if I'm totally honest. But no.

A mix of anger and dejection surges through my veins, so strong I can barely eat. Jude and I make quite the pair for Mary, who *tsk*'s us as our barely touched plates are eventually cleaned up from the table.

"You have to eat!" Mary waves the plate at Jude before she picks it up. "Is there something else I can bring you?"

"No, thank you. I'm not hungry." Jude is both miserable and polite, just like always.

Guess I need to have another talk with Graham. I'm not saying it will change anything—it hasn't so far,

Chapter 17

anyway—but God, Jude deserves better. Her happiness is something worth fighting for. And I don't care that it isn't my business. I *know* I'm crossing a line. But someone has to stand up for her, right? Maybe some naïve part of me thinks I can make up for my own messed up childhood by trying to fix Jude's. I don't know. Either way, I have to at least try.

Jude gets ready for bed and I read her a chapter from a book about mystery-solving orphans, but she's not asleep when I leave. She looks listlessly out the window, letting out a little sigh before saying good night. I wish I could make her feel better. It's all I can think about as I head down the hall.

The best thing about the guest room I'm staying in is its location. It sits on the back side of the house, with an amazing view of the stables, the tennis courts, the gardens, the pool, and the vast amount of property that comes with being filthy rich. It also happens to have a perfect view of the garage, which is packed full of expensive and foreign cars—or so I've been told. The only person who has access to it is Graham.

My room being positioned the way it is, however, also means there's no chance I'll miss Graham's return tonight. Those headlights are awfully bright if your blinds are open.

When Mr. Asshole finally decides to pull into the garage, it's well after midnight. His car swoops down the drive like a falcon and disappears into the garage. He spends a while in there, probably wiping the car down with a handkerchief or something equally ridiculous, before finally heading back into the house. He's alone, with no female to keep him company overnight. Though that's not to say he didn't already screw her.

Is he the kind of man who would do something like that? Give one woman an orgasm on top of his desk and give another woman an orgasm later? Bend her over a piece of furniture and punish her with his dick in the most delicious ways?

Desire curls through me. I should go to his room. I should knock on the door. I should tell him that he can't treat me this way, like a toy he can just take out whenever he feels like it and then put back on the shelf as soon as he gets tired of playing.

Except I'm honestly too chicken to ever do something like that. I roll over in bed, visions of him with that woman torturing me. Reliving how he looked at her when I caught them tangled up on the couch, how she splayed across his lap without any underwear on. It drives me crazy to think about him with someone else. Someone he sees as a "real" woman. I guess in Graham's eyes, I'm just a plaything. How the hell am I going to convince him to fall in love with me if he's fucking other women? It keeps me up half the night.

The next morning, Jude and I both look a little rough. I spend an extra five minutes on my makeup, attempting to conceal the heavy bags under my eyes, and give Jude an extra hug as she comes out of her room scrubbed and dressed and solemn. Seems like neither of us got much rest last night, and all because of the same man.

I hold her hand as we walk down to breakfast, and give it a squeeze as we enter the dining room.

Chapter 17

"Daddy?" Jude's voice cracks with wonder.

My head snaps up, and I'll be damned. Graham Ratliff is seated at the head of table, newspaper in hand. He hasn't eaten with us in over a week. What changed, all of a sudden?

"Good morning, princess." Graham offers the most genuine smile I've ever seen from him. He's wearing riding clothes today and looks like another human altogether without his bespoke suits and general air of distracted grumpiness.

"I'm not a princess," Jude tells him, rolling her eyes. "I'm a warrior."

"Well then, my little warrior, I have the perfect surprise for you today."

"A surprise? For me?" Jude nearly falls over herself in excitement, but I keep myself reserved. This is very atypical of him. I brace myself for bad news.

"I've canceled your day, Jude," he says, raising his cup of coffee. "We're going to go riding."

My jaw drops. "But you said—" I start.

"I realized we haven't spent nearly enough time together this summer," he tells Jude. "And I'm sorry for that. I want to show up for you. So...I took the day off, too. That's why I had to work so late last night at the office."

Is he serious? That's where he was last night?

"Yes!" Jude says, throwing her arms around his neck.

"You too, Abbie. We'll all go together." Graham looks over at me with an expression that is too complicated to decipher, but is full of command.

"Yes. Of course." I'm still dazed at all of this.

Abbie

"We're going riding! We're going riding!" Jude chants, jumping up and down now.

"We are. But only after you eat," he tells Jude, gently warning.

She plops into her chair and obediently digs into her scrambled eggs and toast, dancing a little in her seat. It makes me smile. Horses really do make this little girl's world go 'round. The rest of breakfast is much of the same, complete with a bizarrely cheery Graham. Undoubtedly, this is a side of him other people never get to see, and it's a shame. His broodiness exudes sex appeal, but there is something about the laugh lines around his eyes and the way he beams at his daughter as she asks a million questions about the ride that makes me want him all the more.

Your daddy or your dad? Amanda teased me yesterday. Heat travels through me.

After breakfast, Jude and I change into our riding gear and meet Cassie and Graham in the stables. They've already pulled four horses for us: Lucy, Desi, Donnie, and Daisy. Jude can't stop squealing as she runs to her horse.

"This is going to be the best day ever!" she cheers.

"Come on, slowpoke!" Graham says. "We've got a full day ahead of us!"

Who is this man, and did he seriously just say "slowpoke"?

We set out across the property, Cassie leading us on some easy trails. She works smoothly at keeping the conversation going, all the while periodically casting me concerned glances as we go. I give her a reassuring smile

Chapter 17

of gratitude. She must have thought this whole thing was so bizarre after Graham shut it down yesterday. Then again, she's been here a long time. Maybe she's used to his changing moods.

"Come this way, Jude." Graham pulls ahead of the pack. "I have a surprise for you."

"I love surprises!"

"I know you do, buttercup. That's why I have an extra special one." Graham actually sounds fatherly and tender. He helps guide Jude's horse down an adjacent path, offering her guidance the entire time. I can't help staring after them, still floored by the change in Graham.

"How are you holding up?" Cassie asks in a low voice after she maneuvers her horse to ride alongside mine. "I see you're in proper riding gear today."

"I'm fine." I give her a smile. "It's just strange seeing him play dad like this today, especially after the way he acted yesterday. I really did think he might fire me."

"He must have given it some thought. Realized how important it was to Jude," Cassie offers. "He's a very loving father. You just sometimes have to work around the gruff."

"If you say so." I frown and duck under a tree branch as we ride. "I mean, I do remember him and my dad laughing a lot. And Graham being more...laid-back, I guess. But now? He's like an entirely different person from my memories."

"I think he changed a lot after the divorce."

"That's what I've heard. I get the impression the change has not been...received well."

"He's a good man," Cassie says kindly. "He loves

Abbie

Jude. More than anything. You just have to be around enough to see it. Because yeah, he's definitely a textbook workaholic. But I think it's his way of hiding from the mess Mrs. Ratliff left behind."

Fair point, but that doesn't make up for how miserable and neglected Jude is. I keep this thought to myself, though. Up ahead, Graham stops his horse near a river, gesturing for us to do the same. Cassie hops down and unloads a picnic basket from the back of her horse. Jude squeals again in delight, and dismounts quickly to tackle her dad with a hug. He helps her tether Desi to a tree, all the while smiling and speaking softly to her.

"I used to come here when I was a child." Graham gestures around him. "I loved it here. My favorite spot on the property."

"But I thought you grew up in London," Jude says, spinning around in a circle, checking everything out.

"Little smarty." His grin is wide and I want him to turn it toward me more than I've wanted anything in my entire life. For him to show me that kindness, that joy. "I did, but my godfather used to bring me here in the summers. Belonged to some uni friend of his. It was like my own Wonderland. That's why I bought it."

"Whoa."

"And this tree here?" Graham moves past Cassie and me, still tying up our own horses, and pats a sizable tree trunk. "I used to climb this. I felt like Sir Lancelot up there."

"I want to be Sir Lancelot!" Jude eagerly follows him over. "Can you help me?"

Chapter 17

"Up you go." Graham kneels and gives her a boost up into the low-hanging branches of the tree.

Watching him play daddy really is a remarkable aphrodisiac—trying not to drool over it is a struggle. I help Cassie set up the picnic, which consists of crackers, cheese, fruit, and bottled lemonades from Mary. We fan out the blanket near the riverbank and set out the platters of food while Graham and his daughter play around the tree.

A little scream cuts through the trees as Jude tumbles from a low branch, landing on the ground below. Graham rushes to her side before we can get there. Her riding pants are torn and dirty and her knee is scraped and bleeding, but Jude cries like she lost a whole limb. She sobs and hiccups and panics as Graham goes to take a look at it.

"Don't touch it!"

"I just need to look, sweetheart," Graham says soothingly. The tone of his voice cuts straight to my core, instantly triggering memories of him playing nurse for me when I cut my finger and had to go to the ER all those summers ago. "Can I see?"

Jude nods, her lower lip trembling. I'm sure she's legitimately freaked out about her fall, but the girl is milking this for all it's worth. And honestly, I don't blame her. She's finally getting the attention from her dad that she deserves—I'd probably do the same.

Cassie and I try not to hover as Graham coddles his panicked (but minimally injured) daughter. He rolls up her pant leg, taking care not to brush her knee, and gently presses around it.

Abbie

"Does this hurt?"

Jude shrugs, her lower lip quivering.

"It doesn't look so bad," I say, squatting down next to Graham. Her knee is still bleeding, but the wound isn't deep. "I think you've just scraped it up a bit."

"I-I n-need a Band-Aid," Jude hiccups through her tears. "It h-hurts. And my pants r-ripped."

"I'll bring you back to the house, then," Graham says.

"Actually, why don't I just ride you over to the stables?" Cassie says to Jude. "It's a lot closer and I have a first aid kit in there—plus there's ice cream in the break room fridge."

"Ice cream?" Jude says, glancing at her dad. "Can I go with Cassie?"

"Of course. And you can have as much ice cream as you like," Graham agrees.

Cassie holds out her hand and Jude takes it, letting Cassie pull her to her feet.

"Come on, Judey. Let's go doctor up that knee. We'll give it a good clean and a bandage and you'll be good to go." Cassie mounts up and pats the saddle in front of her.

"Plus ice cream," Jude reminds her.

"Wait—should I go, too?" I ask as Graham lifts Jude up onto the saddle in front of Cassie, giving Jude's knee a tender kiss. "It's my job. I can help."

"Nah. I think I can manage it," Cassie says with a wink.

"Thank you, Cassie," Graham says. "That's very kind of you."

Jude sniffs out some goodbyes and then Cassie's horse heads out of the clearing.

Chapter 17

"I'll hang back and clean up the food here, if you want to follow them," I say, going for the picnic blanket. "It shouldn't take long."

"Nonsense," Graham says, towering over me. "I'll help you."

Chapter Eighteen

Graham

Cassie rides off with my daughter, trotting carefully through the trees. She's been a good and loyal member of my staff for a few years now, and no one else can really compare. Other than Esmeralda, of course. Cassie is good with Jude, excellent with the horses, and understands when her presence is no longer necessary. All qualities I value greatly. Particularly this afternoon.

I've been waiting to get Abbie alone again, ever since my disastrous attempt at a date failed so miserably to distract me from her, though I didn't think it would be so soon after our encounter in my office. She's irresistible in her riding gear, a refined woman who is capable of strenuous things. I like my women strong, fierce, and mouthy.

My ex-wife was all of those things. She was a pillar of steadfast stubbornness that made her likewise irresistible. But Natasha was also unfaithful, which entirely negated all of her merits in the end. Infidelity is one transgression I won't stand for.

Abbie, on the other hand, is fresh and innocent. She's

Chapter 18

not yet aware that her beauty can be used as a weapon, harnessed into something awful and terrible. She's stunning. Ripe. Yet sometimes that innocence bleeds into a childishness that I cannot stomach. That attitude, that youth, that naivete. Typical for a nineteen-year-old, I suppose, but certainly not what I need.

What I need is a woman.

"Thank you for doing this for Jude today," she says, kneeling down to wrap up the food on the picnic blanket. "I know we got into it yesterday, but I do know that you care a lot about her. And she really needed this break."

She snaps the lid on a container and opens her mouth to continue, but I cut her off.

"I don't want to talk about my daughter."

"Okay."

She sits up, blonde hair cascading down her shoulders. I want to wrap my fists in it, force her onto her knees. Rip those tight pants off her and feel that hot wetness waiting for me once again. Just thinking about my fingers in her cunt sends a jolt to my dick. Subconsciously, I smell my fingers as though the sweet scent of her musk still lingers.

I jacked off to that scent. It was magnificent.

Her eyes meet mine, and she freezes. My interest unsettles her a little, I can tell, and she tries to distract herself with the picnic. I crouch so we're eye level and hand her a container of strawberries. When she looks up, our hands brush and she looks at me expectantly.

"So then...what *do* you want to talk about?" Abbie asks. She starts twirling her hair, batting her lashes like she learned how to flirt by watching Britney Spears videos.

I don't bother answering, instead helping her pack up the picnic Mary sent with us.

Meanwhile, I grapple with urges, battling my lust. I remind myself that Abbie is so obvious in her attractions that it takes all the appeal out of it. She gasps and giggles and sighs. It's pathetic, really. I prefer her mouthy, not girlish. Defiant, not compliant. I want fire in her veins and poison on her tongue.

My eyes tear across her body again, lingering over the way her breeches skim her ass, the way her riding jacket hugs her curves. She is as exquisite as a rose. She keeps stealing glimpses at me, and each time she sees my face, she blushes.

She thinks this is a game she wants to play. She does not understand the power I wield, both in the office and in the bedroom. She has no way of comprehending what I would require of her. In some ways, that makes her attraction to me even more forbidden, in turn more sensual. If I grabbed her by the throat, fear would tickle her eyes before the pleasure came. In that moment, that power? Delicious.

After being quiet for a while, Abbie starts up again. "You're a really good rider." Oh God, mindless flattery. Another of her embarrassingly transparent flirting tactics. "But you have really good horses. Which is great, because this is such a great estate to go riding—"

"Stop," I command. Her mouth closes. "I'm so bored with people kissing my ass."

Chapter 18

Her eyes spark and I very nearly smile when she stands up, clearly pissed off.

"I'm not trying to kiss your ass."

"Aren't you, though?" I ask, adding a layer of disdain to my voice.

She scoffs indignantly. "You're an asshole, you know that?"

"No. Tell me about it."

Tell off your boss, little girl. This is a dangerous game you're playing.

"Tell you about it? You want a list?"

"Why not?"

Abbie swears. "You're impossible. You're arrogant and an asshole and impossible."

"Is that all?"

She narrows her eyes, and I feel my cock stir. "You really want to do this? Okay. You're a distant father who gives no fucks about the emotional needs of his daughter, not to mention his staff, or anything else going on in his house. You think the whole world should tiptoe around you because you're wealthy. You act like the king of your estate instead of the man paying the freaking mortgage. You're cruel and rude, and, yes, arrogant and impossible."

I can't help the grin on my face now. "Big words for a little girl."

"I'm not a little girl. I may not be the oldest adult in this house, but I am still an adult. One who cares for your child on a daily basis, unlike you, and I should be respected for it."

"Respect is earned."

"If you didn't respect me, why did you hire me to take

care of Jude? Who you claim to care so much about? This isn't about respect. You just like to lord your power over people."

I nod, as if I'm considering her outburst. "This *is* less boring, I'll admit."

"For fuck's sake! Sorry I'm not as fascinating as one of your socialite friends who doesn't wear panties."

"There's that jealousy again. It isn't a cute look on you," I fire back.

She slaps me. It barely registers, but I grab her hand and push her up against a tree. I press my nose to her ear. "Oh, little girl, is that how you want to play? You like it mean?"

Abbie shivers, but there's no more childish gasping. "Let me go."

"You do like it a little mean." I unpin her hand and place mine against her throat instead. Not enough to hurt, just enough to let her know I'm there. Dominant. In charge. Her body tenses and she breathes heavier, her breasts rising and falling against me. "You like it a little dirty."

Her gaze flicks to the side, but I've already caught the look in her eyes. They're large and blue and hungry. "You don't know what I like."

"Do you?" I ask. For once, it's a genuine question.

"Yes," she says, with a fire in her voice that grabs hold of my cock and hangs tight.

I don't have a condom, so I can't properly fuck her the way I want, but I am going to have this woman and I am going to have her now.

Chapter 18

"Then show me." I drop my hand and take a step back, calling her bluff.

She takes a deep breath, and there is such desire etched into every line and crease of her face and eyes that it takes all my willpower not to start calling out orders.

Turning around, she grabs the tree trunk for support and pushes her ass out toward me, arching her back. "Spank me," she says. Her voice quivers, but it's strong. Just the way I like it.

I walk over and oblige, meting out the punishment she's asked for, reveling in the way her whole body tightens up and then sags with relief after every strike, her soft moans getting deeper and longer with each slap of her ass. Before long, I can't take it anymore. It's time to see if she is capable of playing games with the adults.

"Enough," I say. "Don't move. My turn."

Abbie freezes where she is. I drag my hand slowly down the back of her riding jacket, over the curve of her ass, and then I reach up and pull her tight breeches down to her knees in one smooth motion. I can see the red marks on her derriere, perfectly round, perfectly fuckable.

I spread her ass with both hands until that pert little hole is revealed. I have a hunger to dive into it, but now is not the time or place. Still, I press into her slightly with my thumb, just enough to tease her.

"*Oh,*" Abbie moans. She likes it. How maddening.

I cannot wait until the day that little mouth is around my cock.

For now, I settle for fingering her pussy, finding her all but dripping with the wetness I had suspected was waiting for me. I knew she was turned on, but this is still like discovering the last jammy donut. It's a delicious treat.

A soft groan inadvertently escapes me, and I use my free hand to unbuckle my own pants. My cock springs forth, hard and ready, and I use it to trace a line from her pink lower lips up the crack of her ass, slicking both of us up with her juices. She's soaked, and now so am I.

Pushing her ass cheeks together with my hands, I create a sweet, tight channel to thrust into. Each stroke of my dick back and forth between her firm, flawless ass cheeks sends electricity through my body. It's not the same as being inside of her, no, but it gets the job done. Wet, hot, tight. Delicious friction.

As I fuck her cheeks, she makes sounds like a little mouse, squeaks and high-pitched moans, too caught up in what I'm doing to her to form coherent sentences. I think about reaching around to tease her nub, but the feel of her forbidden flesh against my cock overwhelms me.

I move faster, and the harder I thrust, the louder and more turned on Abbie gets. She begins pushing back against me, matching the rhythm of my strokes, lifting her ass and tilting her pussy to beg for penetration. I don't give it to her, but the pressure in my balls builds into something bigger than myself. I follow the rabbit down the hole, groaning louder than I have in my life as I fuck her ass cheeks until I finally feel myself slipping over the edge. When I come it's like an avalanche, and I spurt across her lower back, grunting through each hot wave until there is nothing left but a shell where my body was.

Grabbing the picnic blanket on the ground, I use it to

Chapter 18

clean myself and then zip my pants back up. Abbie is still arching her back, waiting expectantly. She thinks I will reciprocate, and give her another orgasm. *This was the reciprocation, sweet Abbie.* I made you cream all over my hands, and now I creamed all over your ass. This is how things work.

Though I do like her hunger, her passion, her desire. It feels good to be wanted so carnally by someone so feisty.

Instead of going to her waiting body, I climb up on my horse and throw a handkerchief from my pocket at her. She must know where she stands in my house.

"Clean up," I tell her and turn my horse to trot back to the house.

Chapter Nineteen

Abbie

I can't believe he just walked out on me, *again*!

And without even getting me off!

I have never been that intimate with anyone in my entire life. I never let anyone get that close to me; not any of the boys from college, not any boys from camp or high school, not ever. They've tried and I've sent them all running. But with Graham I served my body up to him on a silver platter, and he left me once he got what he wanted. That's never happened to me before.

I'm furious and confused in equal measure as I slam the remains of the picnic supplies into the basket.

Graham Ratliff is the devil. That's the only way to explain this. He's the devil in human form, hell-bent on destroying me. The way he stared at me when we were alone in the woods was unreal. So cocky. So hungry. So alpha. And so damn sexy that I let him do whatever he wanted to me. Expose me, use me, leave me.

I didn't hate what happened—I hate how it ended.

There are so many new things I just learned about

Chapter 19

myself. I like being pinned against trees. I like when he grabs me by the throat. I liked that a *lot*. Everywhere he touched me set off fireworks behind my eyelids. He was so forward, so forceful, so demanding. And I *loved* it.

Briefly, I consider pleasuring myself to take the edge off. Get what I need so I can do something more than stew over this whole stupid situation. I could, too. I could stretch out on this picnic blanket, covered in the juices he shot all over me, and finish the job. The thrill of doing it in the woods, exposed, where anyone could see? Doing something forbidden and naughty, pleasuring myself at the memory of Graham's hands emblazoned on my body? I almost come just thinking about it.

I want to be fucked in the woods, my moans echoing all around me. Maybe with someone else watching when they shouldn't. I guess that makes me some kind of exhibitionist.

This I've also learned about myself.

And then I remember how he left me. How my whole body felt like it was pulled taut as a wire, fireworks thrumming through me, and how it was all taken away. In an instant. And he was so cruel about it, throwing a handkerchief at me, just like last time.

Who actually carries those stupid things around anyway? And why the hell does he treat me like this? Why does he insist on being so cruel when it's clear that he wants me, too? Is this how it's always going to be? Getting him in bite-sized pieces, mere crumbs, instead of the full dessert I crave? Angry thoughts swirl in my mind as I ride back to the stables.

When I came here, I didn't think my crush on him

Abbie

would be an issue. It was years ago, I've blossomed since then and met plenty of cute boys my own age, and time heals all wounds. But I cannot get my mind off him. I cannot purge Graham from my brain. Every glance, I've logged and scrutinized. Every touch I've received, I've begged for more like a starved puppy.

In the wake of the cold left by his most recent desertion, I worry that I can't do my job.

Maybe it's simply time to give up. Because what kind of man does this to someone? What kind of man leads me on like this, touches me like this, and then leaves me half naked in the freaking forest? Not a man worth my attention. That's what Amanda would tell me. And yet.

By the time I get back to the stables, I've settled on murder as the solution. Murder sounds nice. Graham deserves it.

Daisy takes me straight to her stall, three down from Donnie. Graham is in there, brushing his horse and speaking softly to him, feeding him shiny red apples from a nearby bowl. He's so gentle, a far cry from how he handled me, and he's caring for the horse himself instead of leaving the chore to one of his staff members. That surprises me. A lot.

"Men are trash, Daisy." I lead my horse into her stall and give her an apple. "Absolute garbage."

Just because he's doing something decent, it doesn't make him a decent person, I remind myself. A decent person wouldn't have left me in the woods. A decent person would have reciprocated the act. Graham Ratliff is indecent, even if his horse doesn't hate him. Clearly, Donnie is only so happy because he's being fed apples.

Chapter 19

His real care comes from Cassie and Quinn, not Graham.

"Trash," I reiterate to my horse. She nickers softly, which I take as an agreement. "Exactly."

"Who's trash?" a voice asks behind me. "Got a healthy pack of raccoons somewhere?"

"What?" I turn with an eyebrow raised, and find a beaming Quinn. I shake my head in confusion. "Raccoons?"

"They love trash." Quinn flashes a bright smile at me. "I figured you were talking about them."

"Oh, no." I flush a little and shrug, hoping to look innocent. "I meant men. In general."

Quinn claps his hands over his heart and staggers around the stall. "Ouch. That hurts."

"There might still be time to change my mind," I say with a laugh.

In some ways, it's almost too bad about Quinn. He's genuinely attractive in a wholesome, all-American boy kind of way, which isn't exactly exciting, but it's not terrible either. He's sweet and good-natured, and fun to flirt with. Plus, he's always nice to me. If I didn't have my eyes set on darker, broodier prizes, he would be the perfect summer fling.

I can already picture it: nighttime skinny-dipping in the river, making out in the hay bales in the afternoon, swapping jokes over s'mores. Talking to Quinn feels like going to summer camp: hot, fun, and over quick enough to not become tedious. But he seems so into me, and that's also a nice perk.

You have a job to do, I remind myself.

Abbie

"How was the ride?" Quinn asks, fully righted now instead of hunched over like I impaled him with my opinions. "See anything cool?"

I bite my tongue as memories of our ride zip through me. I definitely saw a few cool things, learned a lot more interesting things, and now have settled on murdering my boss. *Can't forget about the murder*.

I mean, not actual murder, but slapping him again would feel so gratifying right now.

"We went to the river that cuts through the property. It was really pretty." Was it? I don't even remember what the river looks like. I know there were trees, and water, and probably a few bushes, but past that, I can't recall where I literally just was. All I remember is the small purple violets I stared at as Graham pushed me up against that tree and ripped my pants down...

I shiver.

"You okay?" Quinn asks, a smile quirked up on half his face. "You spaced out there for a minute."

"Yeah. Just thinking about how nice the river was."

Is that a snicker I hear, from a few stalls down? Is Graham eavesdropping on my conversation? Anger floods through me again. This man is going to be the death of me and my frayed emotions. He wants to leave me alone after he comes on my ass? Fine.

Two can play this game.

"You know, I *really* would have liked to be able to stay out there longer...but Jude scraped her knee pretty bad, so we had to pack up and head back early," I tell Quinn innocently.

He takes the bait, changing his entire body language

Chapter 19

from friendly to flirty. "I've been down there with the horses a few times, actually. There's a lot of really beautiful spots on the property, especially if you know where to look."

"I'd love to see them all." I lay my hand on Quinn's arm, and then quickly pull back and look away, as if I'm shy about touching him.

"Maybe I can take you sometime."

Jackpot.

I let out a bubbly little laugh. "You know," I say, leaning closer, "I never noticed how green your eyes are. They remind me of the pines out by the river."

Quinn grins wide, and he actually gets more interesting as he does. He has a crooked grin and two teeth just out of alignment on the bottom, an enticing "imperfection" not often seen in my circles after decades of braces. Yes, I could definitely like Quinn.

"And yours are really blue." Quinn nods. "They remind me of the sky. In midsummer."

"Really? What's different about the sky in midsummer?" I twirl the tips of my hair, just a little. Quinn moves in closer; this is something he definitely likes.

He gently takes the brush from me and begins brushing down Daisy in short strokes, right by my shoulder, closing the gap between us. Moving in closer, with just a hint of subtlety, he explains, "It's the most beautiful sky of the year. Never seen anything a deeper blue than that. Blue, with a hint of purple. It's stunning."

"Wow. You don't sound like any stable hand I've ever met."

"Well, I'll let you in on a little secret." Quinn gets

Abbie

conspiratorial, leaning closer, so we're barely a breath apart. "I'm an art major."

"An art major who works in a fancy man's stables?"

"Guilty as charged."

Laughing, I walk out to get another apple for Daisy, and spy Graham finishing up with Donnie. He doesn't look at me or make any sort of movement to show he's been listening.

"You're so funny, Quinn." I play it up, raising my voice a little. "The funniest guy here on the estate."

"Well, thank you kindly, ma'am," he says, affecting a cowboy accent and flashing another bright smile at me. "I don't mean to be forward, but can I take you out on a date?"

My heart races, just enough to be noticed. The thrill of being asked out still hasn't died. I cast another glance at Graham, who continues putting up his brushes and tools without a single care in the world. No sign at all that he just came all over me in the middle of the woods after I all but begged him to spank me up against a tree.

Fine, then. Game on.

Turning back to Quinn, I say, "I'm off tomorrow."

I hear footsteps behind me, and when I look over my shoulder I see Graham gliding away so imperiously, I can't even be sure he's been paying attention to me and Quinn at all.

Chapter Twenty

Abbie

I'm on a date in the middle of the stables, with an extremely good-looking boy who I don't actually want to be on a date with. Will wonders never cease?

"You look beautiful." Quinn hands me a single long-stemmed rose. Red, of course.

I blush a little and swat at his arm. "It's just my riding clothes. But you're sweet to say so." I admit, I did go kind of heavy on the Teenage Fantasy.

"I hope you aren't opposed to riding horses for our date?" He gestures to the two dapple grays waiting for us in the corral. "You seemed so disappointed that your trail ride got cut short, I figured I should take you out again and show you my favorite spot. I got us some dinner, too."

"Aww. That's perfect!"

Amanda told me to enjoy myself tonight, because if Graham gets to have two ladies, I get to have two gentlemen. I reminded her Graham is the devil, not a gentleman, and she told me to shut up and just *enjoy myself already*. And she's right. I'm here for a job, but that

Abbie

doesn't mean I can't enjoy myself along the way. Besides, Quinn is fun to flirt with. It's nice to have something go easy for me just once in this big, stupid house.

We saddle up and Quinn leads us down a familiar route, but then cuts sharply north.

"I know you saw the river," Quinn shouts over at me, casting me a shy smile, "so I'm taking you up to the highest point on the property. You can see the whole estate from there."

By the time we get up in the hills, we're exhilarated and a bit out of breath.

We tie up our horses and find a nice grassy area where we can sit while we eat. Quinn tells me the gyros, mixed olives, and lemon potatoes are from a local spot in town, and I let out a little groan as I bite into my food.

"I can't believe how good this is," I say after I wash my first bite down with cherry Coke. "Not to mention this view. Incredible."

"Can't go wrong with the Adirondacks in the summer." He beams.

"Beautiful." I mean it.

For a while, we sit in companionable semi-silence, eating and occasionally asking each other about school and extracurriculars or what there is to do in town (not much, according to Quinn), or on the Ratliff property (also not much, according to me, but that's only because I rarely have time to swim). It's a much nicer date than I anticipated, really low key—until we're done with our food and Quinn suddenly leans close, like he wants to kiss me.

And I think about it. I really do. I haven't been kissed

Chapter 20

in what feels like forever at this point, and having a make-out session surrounded by trees and mountains and the rushing of the nearby river sounds incredibly romantic. But the problem is, it's Quinn.

"Look. I have to be honest," I say, gently resting my hand on his chest to keep him from moving any closer.

As I try to find the right words, Quinn blinks those big eyes at me and I feel terrible.

"I really like you, Quinn. You're sweet and extremely attractive and fun to be around. It's just...there's someone else."

Realization dawns on his face. His lips quirk up and he nods, leaning back. "It's okay, you don't have to explain."

"It's not like that," I rush to say, even though I'm not sure what "that" is exactly. "We're not technically official or anything, but—"

"I kinda guessed you weren't really interested." Quinn shrugs, which causes a weird feeling in my chest. I almost wish he was more upset. "Based on how many times you glanced over at Mr. Ratliff when he was in the stables. It seemed obvious you still have a crush on him. I remember you from three years ago, you know."

My cheeks run hot, and then my mouth starts running and I can't stop it. "It's not a crush. It's just...a secret. A huge secret."

Quinn nods and reclines back on his palms, looking like he's ready to listen. I know I'm playing with fire by telling him any of this, but it feels so good to say the words out loud to someone besides Amanda. Someone who knows Graham, knows how intimidating and untouchable he can be, and therefore understands how monumentally huge this whole thing is.

"The thing is, Graham doesn't want anyone to know about me and him," I blurt.

His eyes widen a little, but he quickly recovers. "Ohhh. I get it. I can totally understand that whole forbidden attraction thing."

"Really?"

"Really," he says. "Makes perfect sense. You're talking to someone who was in love with a married woman for years before realizing it was never gonna happen."

"Ouch," I say, and he nods.

"It worked out for the best," he reasons. "I've been playing the field ever since."

"So that's why you're such a ladies' man," I tease. "It all makes sense now."

God, it's nice to finally have someone treat this like it's legit, not just some silly little imaginary relationship I made up in my head. Even Amanda acts like it's a game half the time. I feel myself warming to the subject, hungry for the chance to talk about my dalliance with Graham as if it's more than just a summer fling that the two of us are pretending isn't happening.

"So I'm just a pawn, huh?" Quinn laughs, but it sounds a little forced. "Though I guess I should be flattered you've been flirting with me, even if it was only to make him jealous."

"No, don't say that! I like flirting with you, and I do like you—honestly," I insist. "But yeah, I feel like a total jerk now. It wasn't fair to get you involved in our...lover's

Chapter 20

quarrel. Still, I'm glad we got to come on this ride and hang out. It's nice to have someone I can talk to."

"Has it been going on this whole time?" Quinn asks.

I chew on my lip. Pretending life is going exactly as I want it, instead of rapidly spiraling out of control, is one thing. Outright lying is something entirely different.

"A lady never kisses and tells." I twirl my hair at Quinn, hoping it's enough of a deflection to wind down the conversation.

He laughs and holds up his hands. "Fair enough. No hard feelings, either. I probably would have done the same thing."

"Really? Mr. Art Major would stoop so low as to make his lover jealous?"

"If I thought it would work? Yeah." He grins his crooked grin again, and for just a minute, I wish things were different. I wish this was summer camp, and Quinn was a hot counselor, and we could sneak into the mess hall and kiss in the humid night air.

But that isn't real life.

"You're really nice, you know that?" I say. "You deserve a really nice girl."

He shrugs. "So do you, Abbie."

"What, deserve a nice girl?" I tease.

His face goes delightfully crooked. "Well, sure, if you like. But I meant you deserve someone nice, too. Someone who's going to treat you well."

Quinn looks at me very seriously, and I know he's talking about Graham. He's right, too. I deserve a lot better and I deserve a lot more. But I'm going to keep chasing what I want—because I'm stubborn as hell when

Abbie

I know what I want. And because it's also part of my job.

It's really too bad about Quinn, though. He'd be such a perfect summer fling. But he doesn't seem like the type to pin me to a tree by my throat. He would never pull my pants down in the middle of his private forest and spank me.

These are apparently now dealbreakers for me.

We spend the rest of the date talking about our dreams after college and our hopes for the future. It's almost like a real date, but without the pressures of what comes next, and it's nice. Quinn only has good things to say about his friends and family, and he has big dreams to move to L.A. to be an animator. He makes me laugh and reminds me that men aren't all awful.

It's over too soon. I clean up while he readies our horses, and we trade jokes on the way back to the house. Even when we put up the horses, we're laughing. He tells great stories about his siblings and the hijinks they got into as kids. He also offers to walk me to the house, like a proper date would.

"I'm so sorry," I say again as we walk up the drive. "It was cruel of me to do that to you."

"I appreciate the apology." He nudges me with his shoulder. "But I'm glad to have made a new friend."

"Absolutely." I grin big at him and hold out my hand. "To friends?"

The massive front door swings open, causing us both to jump.

In the doorway, Graham stares us both down. Anger

Chapter 20

sits around his eyes and I suddenly don't know what to do with my hands.

"You." He points to me. "In." Then he looks over at Quinn. "You. If you want to wake up with a job tomorrow, I suggest you go."

"Yes, sir." Quinn pales a little and nods his head. He casts a regretful glance my way as he turns abruptly to leave.

Graham shoots me a withering look and then thunders down the hallway just as he did a few days ago, furious with me then, and furious with me now. I remember what happened the last time I enraged him. My ass remembers what happened, too. And my pussy remembers both his ire and his demanding penance.

As I follow him in, I have to repress the smile from blooming across my face.

Chapter Twenty-One

Abbie

Graham stops at the bottom of the stairs, and memories of the night he cornered me down here fill my brain until it's all I can think about.

I remember the way he pinned me to the wall, the way he ran his nose across my skin, the way I almost lost myself to his touch when he didn't even come close to an erogenous zone. The way he spanked me across his desk, drawing an orgasm out of me with his bare hands. The way he took his pleasure from me out in the woods, like an animal, primal and brutish, riding off into the sunset afterward.

I've never let anyone else touch me the way Graham has. I've spent the last three years saving myself for him.

Waiting is agony.

He turns around and stares at me for a long moment. It's like a million conversations happen between us without a word ever being said. Our eyes meet, the air thick with tension.

He's nothing like Quinn.

Chapter 21

And everything, everything I want.

I put my hand on my hip and give him a little sass. "You interrupted my date. Again."

"Is that what that was? A date?"

"You mean a social outing where a cute boy takes me out, treats me nice, speaks to me like I'm a human being instead of a piece of furniture? Yeah, I'd call that a date." I twirl the tips of my hair around a finger and cock my head at him. "Would you like some tips on how it works? I'd be happy to share some advice."

He sucks in a deep breath and mutters something I can't quite make out.

I take a step toward him, emboldened by the fact that I'm getting to him, that he can't contain his fury. "What was that?"

"I said I'm going to make myself a drink." His voice is tightly controlled and even, but I can see the muscle flexing in his jaw, the amount of effort that's clearly being expended so he can continue to appear to be in charge.

"Okay..." I'm still not sure exactly where this is going.

"*You* are going to feel a little disappointed I ended your date for you." He adjusts his cuffs and straightens his shirt, then looks at me again with that searing gaze. "So while I pour the scotch, you can decide if you're going up to your room to get yourself off thinking about that little boy—or if you're going to be naked for me in my bed, ready to see what a real man is like."

The air is stolen from my lungs, hearing him talk so explicitly to me. Where did this come from? What changed his mind? Why now? My brain short-circuits, my knees weakening as I process the filthy words that just came out of his mouth. The implicit offer he's made.

It's no choice at all.

I can't even manage a response as he stares at me with a look so feral, so possessive, I almost come on the spot.

My God, it worked.

It really, truly, *fucking finally* worked.

"You have ten minutes." Graham heads down the hall toward his study, leaving me to stand there alone, still in shock.

As soon as he's gone, I race upstairs to my room to take the world's fastest shower, piling my hair into a bun on top of my head and then quickly soaping up and rinsing off the smell of horse and grass and sweat. The whole time, my hands shake with excitement and fear.

I've never done this before, but I remember how *ready* I felt with Graham when we were in the woods. He could have taken me then. I *wanted* him to. But he didn't make his move. Yet.

Should I tell him he's going to be my first?

No. I won't tell him. I want the full experience. I want a real man. I want to know what it's like to really *be* with him, without him treating me differently because I'm a virgin.

A quick look at my phone tells me I only have two more minutes to get to his room, so I throw on a strappy little sleep chemise, let my hair down so it falls in soft waves to my shoulders, and then run all the way there on silent feet.

Cautiously, I crack open his door and find the room decadent, immaculate, and empty. The carpets are plush,

Chapter 21

the walls lined with monochromatic art, and the bed is massive and imposing, all dark wood and starched white linens. A true bachelor pad for someone who can afford an interior designer to toss in some masculine-looking industrial lamps.

My heart beats double time as I approach the bed. This is really going to happen.

As soon as I slip off my chemise, leaving it in a silky puddle on the floor, the nerves stop and pure excitement hums through me. This is what I've wanted so badly. The mere idea of finally having it makes me dizzy. I take a deep breath. He's going to be here in seconds.

Climbing onto his mountain of a bed, I find the mattress softer than expected. I sit in the middle on my knees, with my legs spread, and push my chest forward so my breasts are the right amount of perky. I may have practiced this pose in the mirror several times.

The door clicks open and Graham walks in, carrying a whiskey tumbler. As his eyes rake over my exposed body, my pulse pounds in my ears. He says nothing, only surveys me as he sips his drink. Our eyes lock and I feel like I'm scorching in the sun.

"I see you've made your choice," he says, the barest of smirks crooking up one corner of his mouth.

"What fun is getting myself off if someone else can do it for me?" I try to sound experienced and confident, smoldering at him as best I can, afraid to move from my spot, afraid of breaking the spell.

Graham walks over to the bedside table and sets his glass down, removing his cufflinks one at a time. "This is your final chance to leave my room untouched."

Abbie

I turn to face him and take a deep breath to steady myself. "I know what I'm asking for."

"Do you?" Next are the buttons on his crisp white shirt. One by one, they come undone. My mouth is watering. "Have you ever been with a man like me?"

A flash of guilt sparks at keeping the fact of my virginity from him, but I resolved not to tell and I stand by that now. I don't want him to be gentle; I want him to ravish me. I want him to take all that fiery passion he seems to have for work and pour it into me with his dick.

As he drapes his shirt over a chair, leaving him in his undershirt, I subconsciously lick my lips. I'm ready.

"Have you ever been with a woman like me?" I reply, throwing his words back at him.

He grins, an honest-to-goodness real grin, but it's tinged with danger and heat. "I've been with a lot of women."

"But none of them like me."

"No. None of them like you."

It's probably the first honest thing he's said to me since I arrived.

Graham tugs his undershirt over his head, exposing a broad expanse of chest, sculpted shoulders, and two columns of abs that would make every boy on the swim team jealous.

Anticipation comes in the form of goosebumps all over my body. I run my hands through my hair and cock my head to the side, pouting just a little, pushing my small but shapely breasts forward more. I have no idea what comes next, but I can't wait to find out.

Finally, Graham unhooks his belt and drops his slacks

Chapter 21

to the floor, revealing a pair of tight, dark boxer briefs. He hooks his thumbs in the band and slides them down slowly until his engorged cock springs to life before me. It literally steals my breath. Thick and long, perfectly proportioned, rock hard and ready.

It's the first penis I've ever seen with the lights on and just thinking about it sliding into me gets my juices rolling and my heart pounding even faster. Every nerve ending is wrapped around an explosive, ready for a light.

Completely naked now, he stares at me like a lion before a gazelle. I want him so bad, just sitting here is killing me. I go to move, but he stills me with a flick of his hand.

"Stay."

If I wasn't oozing before, I am now. *Tell me what to do, Daddy*, I want to purr at him. Instead, I run my hand down my chest, between my breasts, holding his gaze taut.

"Come." He points to the space on the bed before him.

So I crawl over there, pushing my ass high in the air. His cock is so close I could open and suck him right into the back of my throat, stroke his girth with the wet walls of my mouth. So help me, if I don't come this time, I'm going to kill him.

With a wry grin, he pushes my shoulders, gentle enough not to bruise, firm enough to dictate his desires to have me on my back without a word. I spread my legs wide, imagining myself a gift ready for him to open. His fingers trail up my stomach, through the valley between my breasts, and across my throat.

Abbie

As I struggle to breathe evenly, Graham explores my body with his hands. Slowly, thoroughly, leaving nothing unchecked. His touch is rough and hungry. He squeezes and caresses, pinches my nipples and cups the swells of my breasts. But he never touches the part of me begging for him the most. He skirts around my swollen nub like a thief in the night, stealing only the occasional stroke across the outside of my innermost lips before dashing away again.

By the time he's done with his exploration, I'm knotted up inside, panting for him, as desperate and hungry as the look on his face. I didn't know it was possible to feel this way, to be so tightly strung and so gratified all at the same time.

"Please." The word drops from my lips before I can stop it, along with a throaty moan. I try to thrust into his hands, but he pulls away again. "Please, Graham."

The look on his face is positively diabolical. "You've been very naughty. Playing games you don't know how to play."

"Teach me," I moan.

"Toying with the emotions of a puerile young staff member in an effort to get into my bed." He tsks at me as his hands move lower, slower, gliding along my inner thighs in such a way that I'm ready to climb the walls.

"Yet here I am," I point out.

"Here you are." With that, his fingers dip into my innermost center and then slide up to give a long, slow, wet stroke around my clit. Tears spring to my eyes and my breath freezes in my lungs. "Are you hungry, naughty little girl?"

Chapter 21

"For you," I whisper.

He could be the devil himself and I would bow naked to him every day. He takes his cock in one hand and toys with it near my opening, circling my slick little mouth, the pleasure causing his eyes to close for just a moment.

"Divine," he whispers. "You're soaking. Are you a horny, naughty girl?"

I thrust my hips against his length and let myself moan as loud as I am frantic.

"Tell me," he commands.

"Yes," I murmur.

"Yes what?"

So help me God, I will tell him whatever he wants as long as he stops teasing me.

"I am a horny, hungry, naughty girl," I say, drawing the words out breathlessly, my eyes burning into his. "And I need you to fuck me right now."

His smile both terrifies and emboldens me. "That is exactly what I wanted to hear."

Chapter Twenty-Two

Graham

Her pussy tastes like candy. Not literally, not an unnatural sweetness that lends itself to lollies and chocolates, but rather an inherent sweetness. The kind that leads to addiction.

I'm not a sentimental man, but it's taking me back in the best way.

I feel ten years younger, fifteen years younger, using her as a time machine to transport me out of the cycle of bullshit I've been living in. Sex has always had the capacity to be completely impersonal to me, just another activity that doesn't require a relationship to be enjoyed. But this has a flavor to it that I rather like.

I run my tongue down the length of her sweet cunt and she quakes under me again. Every lick brings more shivers, her body cracking open under my attention. Abbie is so sensitive, so young, that every motion is like a new exploration. She hasn't had the time to learn how to become jaded and impersonal with sex like I have. She

Chapter 22

still moans and groans like a kitten having its belly rubbed for the first time. It's exquisite.

I wrap my mouth around her clit and suck, slipping a finger inside her, pulsing gently as I suck, and the sounds she emits...they do things to me.

God, I could drown in her youth. I could get lost in her body. For once, I am Graham Ratliff again and not the suit and tie that I have to keep up. I can be rough, rugged, and youthful myself. Forget everything weighing on me, making demands of me—everything except her.

I pull hard on the nub of her clit and she bucks against me. She's so responsive it makes my cock leap against the edge of the bed. I want to feel her heat wrap around my shaft, but she's got to be properly primed. Not that it's ever been an issue with her. This feisty little thing has been throwing herself at my feet since the minute she first stepped foot on my property. I was able to fuck her ass cheeks in broad daylight without a care in the world. I bet I could have opened her tight hole that afternoon and left us both more than satisfied.

Abbie is hungry for me, and I her. In my own ways. She's got the cheek and feistiness I enjoy, when she isn't turning herself inside out to appease me. Seeing her with that stable boy nearly drove my blood to boiling. I've never thought myself a jealous man, but it pulled something out of me today. I didn't wake planning to cross the line again so soon, but the tension has been building between our interactions. I almost wish we were in the stables, where that boy could find us, so he would know: Abbie is mine and mine only.

Standing, I slap her pussy cruelly with my cock and

survey the map of her body before me. It's exquisite. Soft mountains, tight valleys, everything pert and perky and sweet. She reminds me of a nymph, a classic Greek goddess with flushed pink cheeks and creamy skin. She reminds me of freedom, of fast boats and faster cars, of laying in the middle of a field in the middle of summer, lazily watching the clouds roll by. I've never fucked someone this much younger than me, but it's delicious.

"Turn over," I command. "Get on all fours. I need to find a condom."

Obediently, like a hungry little puppy, she flips over and pushes her perfect nineteen-year-old ass in the air. I palm it, relishing in the firmness under my hand, and give her a good smack. Abbie moans and backs her ass toward me.

I was wrong; she's not like a hungry puppy. She is still very much like a desperate kitten. Every touch sends her into a frenzy, begging for more.

I pull open the bedside table drawer and rifle around until I find what I'm looking for. As soon as I have the condom on, I line my cock up against her wetness and press against her, just enough to split her lips open, just enough to tease. She's panting before I'm even inside.

"Please," she begs again. It's her favorite word right now, the only one she seems to know.

As much as this Abbie gives me a thrill, I miss her sass. She always starts so fire-filled and then disintegrates into something so childish. I don't want childish, not like this. I want the sassy woman who talks back, the one who I know can handle the kind of sex I like.

So I smack her ass again and push harder into her to

Chapter 22

silence her pleading. The second my cock begins to stretch her, she stops begging and gasps a little, moaning softly, music to my ears.

"You've never had anyone as big as me, have you?" I ask, not unkindly. It's not arrogance or ego on my part, just the fact her body has gone so still all of a sudden, as if she's not sure how to take it all in.

"No," she admits.

"Try to relax," I say as I ease deeper into her, steady and sure, taking my sweet time until I'm fully sheathed. I feel her cunt clenching tight around me and can't help letting out a low groan, my eyes closing. Her warmth saturates me, promises this is exactly what I want, even when she resumes her pleading.

"Mmm, fuck me," she whispers, her voice throaty with lust, tilting her hips just enough to drive me mad. "Please, Graham. Fuck me and don't stop."

Her wish is my command.

My motions start slow, so that both of us have a chance to savor every inch of pleasure, the sweet progression of friction, but I can't hold back for long. Soon, I'm thrusting my cock faster and harder, building intensity. With each thrust, she melts against me until we're nothing but a rhythm of bodies slapping against one another. I grip her firm ass, holding tight as she grinds back against me, letting loose sharp cries of passion with every pump of my cock.

"Oh my God," she whimpers, over and over again. I think I can hear tears in her voice.

This is the kind of sex I like. Little talking, lots of thrusting. Too many women want to talk, but I'd rather just fuck. At one point, Abbie looks back at me with big doe eyes laced with passion, and it reinvigorates me. I put a hand on her shoulder and push her from her hands down to her elbows, forcing her hips to tilt farther, allowing an even better angle for penetration. Then I pick up where I left off, drilling into her deeper and deeper.

"There is no one else," I hiss aggressively, remembering the look on her face when the stupid stable boy was walking her up the drive. How she looked so... pleased. So content.

That boy had her smiling in ways I've never seen, as though he had the secret combination to the lock within her. He took her to a place I've never gone, this girl who wanted nothing more than to be around me when she was a mere teenager. The power of my attraction wasn't enough to stave her away from someone else, a mere schoolboy from the stables.

I slap her ass again, wiping away the memory. "Say it. You do not flirt with anyone else."

"No," she moans. "Y-you can't make me."

Still thrusting, I smack her ass again. Harder.

"I can and I will. If you want this cock again, Abbie, there will be no one else." Just to prove my point, I pull back, leaving only half of my length inside of her—as if it's that easy for me to stop. Which it isn't—but she doesn't need to know that. God, but she's hot and wet, wrapping thick fingers of pleasure around my shaft. A shudder rolls through me. "*Say it.*"

"I can talk to whoever I want," Abbie says, copping

Chapter 22

that familiar attitude. She looks back at me again with those big, sultry eyes. "You aren't the boss of me."

The urge to come washes over me as her mouthiness prolongs the pause in our fucking.

"I am exactly your boss." I pull all the way out and then slam back into her, sending electricity through my entire body.

She arches her back and pants as we continue to take our pleasure from one another.

"You will talk to no other little boys," I tell her, slipping a hand between her thighs to rub her clit as I thrust. "Not at a bar. Not in my home."

"You're greedy," she accuses between sharp breaths. "You just want me all to yourself."

I lean forward to whisper in her ear, still stroking her nub. "That's what *you* want, isn't it?" I let myself go, jackhammering into her even faster. "Well, I am greedy. I will have you. All to myself. Whenever I want."

She moans happily in response, meeting every thrust.

"Yes, yes, yes," she chants like a mantra. "*Graham.*"

"Mine, mine, mine," I chant back.

I close my eyes and curse under my breath, focusing on nothing but fucking her hot little hole as hard as I can until I'm barely keeping myself together. I start to slow down, attempting to ease the pace and prolong the pleasure, but it's already too late. This feels too good.

I'm about to pull out when suddenly I feel her walls constrict around me, and then she starts bleating the helpless, high-pitched cries of an orgasm. I circle her clit faster and fuck her even harder, relishing her tightness, until I can no longer fight the urge to come.

Graham

I slide out of her, start to peel off the condom, ready to spurt hot cream all over her ass, when I see red streaks on the latex. Abbie collapses on the mattress, facedown, still moaning.

Wait. Fuck. Was she—

It's too late now, there's no stopping what's started, so I drop the condom and come all over her lower back, groaning as I do. The orgasm is like dust in my mouth, there but unpleasant, which frustrates me. There wasn't enough blood to say she was on her monthly, just enough to confidently say it was the first time she's been touched like this. Anger rises in me as realizations color the evening's activities in a different light. No longer do I feel like I was rolling through the hills of my youth.

"Were you a *virgin?*" I demand, grabbing my undershirt from the floor to clean up.

She says nothing as I swipe the mess I made off her skin.

"Answer me," I bark, seeing the smudges of red on her creamy thighs as she rolls over. The answer is clear as day. Meanwhile she looks like a child rebuked, which only upsets me further. "What the hell were you thinking?"

Abbie sits up, eyes wide. "I didn't think...I mean, why does it—virginity is just a social construct anyway, it's entrenched in the patriarchy," she babbles desperately, somehow managing to be both brilliant and completely naïve in this moment. "Please, Graham. I—"

"Get out," I command. "Out. Now."

She hurries off the bed and slips back into her night-

Chapter 22

dress. Then she casts one more look at me before running out of the room, the door slamming behind her.

"Fuck!" I throw my shirt across the room and grab my scotch.

That's why she was so sensitive to every flick of my tongue against her clit. That's why she was so tight and so wet. Hell, that's why she was so fucking desperate in her pursuit of me. The damn girl had no clue what the fuck she was doing.

"I'm a goddamn idiot," I mutter, sinking onto the bed to take a deep swig of my drink.

Time to have a good think about my foolish choices. This is going to get so messy.

Fuck.

Based on her behavior and her bold pursuit of me, I was sure Abbie had screwed plenty of boys from her university, if not during her high school years. I thought her heightened response to me was simply due to the fact she'd never been with an experienced man before, not that she'd never been with *anyone* before.

And now? She's going to be insufferable after this. She's going to be hanging off my every word, more so than before, because despite her big talk about social constructs, I've just taken something precious from her.

I don't want attachment. I had attachment in the form of Natasha, and it was arguably the worst experience of my life. The divorce threatened to kill me. This was supposed to be fun, a means to an end, a dip into the dessert tray. A fantasy fuck. That was all it was supposed to be.

I'm thirty-five goddamn years old. I have a child,

several mortgages, an ex-wife. I'm sixteen years her senior, old enough to be her dad. Hell, I crossed several lines just touching her because of my relationship with her father. He and I have been friends for years and I let my cock do the talking. Because Abbie was so sassy, so irresistible. Other women I've been with, plenty of them have been desperate too, but they lacked her youthful optimism and glow. They lacked her sweetness.

And so, like the fucking sod I am, I let lust and desire make my choices for me.

I know I have to let her go. I won't keep fucking a virginal teenager, no matter how sweet her pussy, how tight her ass, how irresistible her moans. This ends now.

I get dressed and storm back downstairs to my office, ready to work my way through the night just to avoid the darkness and fury of my own thoughts.

I can't believe I just fucked my best friend's virgin daughter.

And that I'm already hard thinking about when I can do it again.

Chapter Twenty-Three

Abbie

I'm in the ornate living room, flipping through *Architectural Digest*, with an eye on the door. I need to talk to Graham, but I haven't seen him anywhere in the house since he kicked me out of his room last night.

He's not in any of the common areas or his office or the study, meaning that he's either sequestered in his bedroom in a space I cannot currently infiltrate, or that he's left the estate. Probably the latter. Although the house is the size of a shopping mall, so it's hard to say exactly. All I know for certain is that I can't find him, thus I can't even attempt to apologize or have an adult discussion about what transpired between us.

Which feels fucking awful.

Especially considering that—after all my epic initial failures—I'd finally gotten exactly what I wanted. Graham and I had sex, *good sex*, and even if it hurt a little it was still incredible to be with him like that, to feel him inside me. To come with him. It was like every fantasy I'd ever had about him brought to life.

Abbie

But it all fell to pieces the minute he finished, just because he realized I was a virgin.

So here I am, sitting on this sofa in a bathing suit and cover-up dress, flipping through pages of gorgeously decorated homes of other celebrities, bouncing one leg on top of the other in anxious agony. Hoping against hope he'll waltz through the door before Cassie picks me up.

Beach day with me and Jude? Cassie's text had said this morning. I'd said yes immediately. I desperately need to be distracted, to get my mind off of what happened.

I'd texted with Amanda last night, too worried about being overheard to do a voice call, and immediately she'd responded with, *Did you like it? Did it hurt? Did you come? Tell me ALL THE THINGS.*

But I was so overwhelmed by the whole thing that I wasn't in the mood to give her the full rundown, so I'd sent a short reply (*Yes, yes, and hell yes*) and then told her I was falling asleep and promised to spill all the details soon, when I could get some privacy.

In reality, I'd been up half the night staring up at the ceiling, replaying the whole sex scene in my head on repeat and imagining how it would have gone if I'd told Graham I was a virgin beforehand. Answer: it wouldn't have happened at all. I'm sure of it. So I guess, in a way, I don't regret keeping my secret from him. But on the other hand, I realize that it might (probably?) mean he never touches me again. Fuck.

There's something else bothering me, too—Graham and I still haven't actually kissed. I've imagined it so many times in my head over the years, I keep almost forgetting that it hasn't really happened yet. But honestly,

Chapter 23

something about it makes me feel a little used, like we weren't fully intimate when we had sex. And I feel like I haven't gotten the full Graham Ratliff Experience. I mean, Google says it's normal not to kiss during intercourse, but...I don't know. I can't help wishing I could do it all over again with his mouth on mine.

Cassie's going to be here any minute. Deciding I need to exhaust every avenue of inquiry so I don't regret my cowardice later, I drop the magazine and go upstairs to Graham's bedroom. I hesitate outside his door and then steel myself and give a loud knock. My heart pounds as I wait, slowly counting to ten. Nothing. I knock again.

I feel like a stalker, but I hate that he's avoiding me. I didn't mean to trick him. That wasn't my intention at all. I just didn't want him to hold back or think less of me. Never in my life would I have thought this is what the result would be.

I'm debating whether to knock again or just give up when I hear footsteps at the other end of the hall.

"Abbie?" It's Esmeralda.

"Oh, hi! I was just, um, looking for Graham?" I babble, trying to look casual. "I haven't seen him all day and Cassie invited me to the beach with her and Jude so I figured I'd, you know, let him know."

"It's Saturday—you don't need his permission to have fun on your day off," Esmeralda says kindly. "Besides, he's on his way out. I believe he's packing up the car now."

Shit. "Okay, great. Thanks, Esmeralda!"

I take off at a full run, hoping to catch him before he pulls out of the garage. When I get there, he's just ducking into the driver's seat of his gleaming black BMW.

"Graham!" I can't help the desperation in my voice.

His door slams, and my heart freezes in my chest—but then his window slides down and he leans his head out. He isn't frowning, but he's stony, statuesque, an impenetrable ivory tower.

"I'm going out of town." His tone is clipped and curt. "Today notwithstanding, obviously, I expect you to fulfill your duties as nanny while I'm gone. That is all."

"Please, can we just talk for a second? Just a quick second? It's important—"

"For God's sake, come off it!" he snaps. "This is pathetic, self-indulgent behavior. You're my employee. Act like it."

"But I—"

"*Enough*, Abbie." He doesn't yell, but he may as well have. "I'll be home in a few days. I need to clear my head. In the meantime, I strongly suggest you pull yourself together."

I'm too stung to respond. All I can do is force myself to nod as the car window slides back up and Graham guns the engine, roaring out of the garage without another word.

I think I see Esmeralda out of the corner of my eye, watching, but when I turn to look, the doorway is empty. I hope she didn't overhear any of that.

Blinking back tears, I march back to the house, trying to forget what just happened. By the time I reach the entry stairs, Cassie is already waiting there with Jude, both of them chattering excitedly.

Chapter 23

"Abbie!" Jude exclaims happily, the scent of sunscreen wafting off her heavily. "I was afraid you weren't gonna go anymore. Mary packed us a cooler!"

"Don't you worry about a thing," I tell her, flashing an apologetic smile at Cassie. "I'm ready to rock. Just need to grab my bag from the living room, okay?"

Seconds later, we all troop out to Cassie's Jeep together, laughing and smiling in the summer sun, and all the while I try to pretend I wasn't just shunned by the man I've been pining over for years, the man I've had late-night dreams about since I was sixteen years old. I try to ignore the fact that I just got everything I ever wanted, only to have it ripped away from me.

The beach is only a twenty-minute drive from the house, but once Jude realizes that Cassie and I are both wearing bikinis, she gets this sad look on her face about the stodgy black one-piece that she has on. Her father picked it out, I'm certain. Who else would dress their eight-year-old daughter in something so dour?

"You know what, Jude? I have an idea," I say, turning toward the back seat to face her. "Why don't we stop at one of the cute little shops by the beach so we can get you a new suit?"

Her eyes widen. "Really?"

"Yup. You can pick out whatever you like. My treat. If Cassie doesn't mind stopping."

"Sure thing," Cassie says, beaming.

Jude squeals with glee and thanks us both, and once we get to the tourist shop, she takes off toward the kids' suits and goes absolutely nuts, running her hands along

Abbie

every single brightly colored row of little girl bikinis, eyeing them all like she's a kid in a candy store.

"Oh my gosh!" I hear her exclaim. She comes running over to me clutching an adorable tie-dye tankini covered in rainbows and unicorns. "This one. This one, please, Abbie?"

"It's perfect!" And it is. This girl is so into horses—with or without horns—it hurts.

Cassie gives the suit two thumbs up, and after I pay for it, the staff remove the tags and let Jude change in the dressing room.

While she's changing, Cassie nudges me. "You okay? You seem a little...off. I thought you'd be bouncing all over the place after your date with Quinn."

My stomach feels funny at the question and I suddenly wish I was anywhere but here. Still, Cassie is a friend, and she's been nothing but kind and compassionate, and I just want to talk to someone.

"It's a long story."

"I've got nothing but time." She winks.

"Are you sure this is okay?" Jude peeks her head out of the changing room curtains tentatively. "I'm worried my dad won't like it."

"Silly girl, your dad isn't here!" I swallow down my feelings and summon a bright smile. "Plus it's a girls' day, which means you can wear whatever you want. Let's see!"

"I bet you look amazing," Cassie encourages.

Jude steps out, cheeks pink, her hands in nervous fists at her sides. She looks adorable. The suit is perfectly innocent enough, with brief-style bottoms and a spaghetti

Chapter 23

strap tank on top, which leaves just the barest hint of her belly exposed. Graham would probably shit himself, but I think she looks perfect and I tell her so.

"You think so?" She can't hold back a smile.

"Do a twirl!" Cassie claps.

Jude does a timid twirl, and the ladies behind the registers clap for her, too. The more we clap, the more confident she gets, until she's curtseying in the middle of the store and laughing. We pile back into the Jeep, after thanking the staff profusely, and head to the beach parking lot.

While Cassie and I set up the umbrella, the beach blanket, the small cooler Mary filled with juice boxes and water and snacks, and the lightweight folding chairs, Jude settles herself a little ways from us and starts building a sandcastle. Cassie gives me a knowing look, like she wants all the dirt ASAP, and I'm not sure what to do. I know I should keep the whole sordid affair to myself, but I'm dying to talk about it.

"So? Tell me about the date!" Cassie pokes at me as we slather ourselves in sunscreen.

"Quinn's great," I tell her. "He took me out on a ride and we had a picnic and talked, and he's...really, really nice."

"But...?"

I sigh. "I don't know."

She tilts her head at me. "I think I know what's going on here." There's another knowing look from her, but she seems a little hesitant. "Can I take a guess?"

"Go for it." There's no way she'll actually guess what's going on.

Abbie

"You said you were into Quinn, but when we all went riding together the other day, I sort of got the impression that you and Graham have some...tension?"

I go very, very still.

"Don't get me wrong here, but I think he's into you." She takes a long pause. "And I think...maybe you're into him, too."

I look away, watching Jude fill up her bucket with seawater and then pour it into the moat around the mounds of sand that I can already tell are going to shape up into horse stables.

"Am I wrong?" Cassie prods gently. "Did I offend you?"

All the complicated feelings in my chest war with each other, weighing me down like boulders. I'm so tired of pretending. So I hold out my pinkie finger and wiggle it at Cassie. She laughs and hooks her pinkie finger around mine.

"I can keep a promise," she says sincerely.

"Look, Cassie, I don't even know what's going on." I sigh and recline in my chair, closing my eyes. "I really want him to be into me. I'm really into him. I have been for years. But everything I've tried, all the flirting, all the skimpy clothes, even trying to make him jealous with Quinn...he's impervious. Nothing works."

I can't tell her the full truth. That making him jealous with Quinn *did* work, or at least it seemed like it did last night, until he realized I was a virgin and kicked me out afterward. I just can't divulge those kinds of secrets to other people who work for him—only Amanda is safe. Plus, I don't know what Cassie would think of me if I told

Chapter 23

her everything. But it's relieving to unload what I can. Even sharing this much feels so much more freeing than holding it all in.

"I think I gave you the wrong advice." Cassie digs around in the cooler for a bottle of water, then cracks it open and takes a long swig before turning to me again. "You know, when you asked me a few weeks ago. About Quinn."

"How so?"

"Well, I thought you were into Quinn, so I gave you advice for Quinn. But he's nothing like Graham Ratliff."

"Tell me about it."

Cassie smiles. "I think you just need to be yourself, Abbie. Be you, and you should be able to land him."

"Even though I'm sarcastic and mouthy?"

That has her laughing. "Especially that. Graham doesn't like people kissing his ass. Besides, have you *met* Natasha Ratliff? That woman is mouthy as hell and they only split up because she got caught cheating and then walked out."

I mull it over. He *does* seem to respond to my mouthiness. Even last night, it seemed to work him up even more when we were...in the middle of things.

Well, okay then. O-fucking-kay.

I've got a new plan.

Chapter Twenty-Four

Abbie

Jude cannonballs into the pool in her new unicorn tankini, splashing water everywhere and spattering me with droplets. I let out a squeal and try to protect my hair, fully knowing it's fruitless, that my outstretched palms will do absolutely nothing, yet still I try.

She surfaces like a baby seal, grinning from ear to ear, hair plastered to the side of her face.

"An eight!" I tell her. "The judges deducted points for getting wet."

"It's a pool!" Jude gently splashes at me. "You're supposed to get wet!"

I splash her back, only with more water. She squeals and ducks too late, getting drenched. "I'm only in here because you are and that's what responsible adults do," I point out.

"Being a responsible adult sounds boring. Be a kid instead. It's way more fun."

I chew on this, because my eight-year-old bestie often drops some adorable truth bombs. She scurries up the

Chapter 24

pool ladder and gives herself a running start before hurtling into the water again, her arms wrapped tightly around her legs. This time, she manages an even more epic splash that gets water all over the deck and almost capsizes my donut float.

Jude pops up from the water like an eager puppy. "What do the judges say *now*?"

"Perfect ten." I clap around the sweating tumbler of blueberry lemonade in my hand. Mary makes a mean blueberry lemonade. "Excellent form."

"Yes!" She pumps her fist in the air in victory. And then her eyes grow wide as she spots something over my shoulder, and the biggest toothy grin splits her face. "Daddy!"

I whip around so fast I nearly slip off my float. Graham Ratliff, freshly home from his trip out of town, stands by the back door in a linen suit, surveying us behind dark-tinted sunglasses. His blazer hangs over his forearm, expensive leather carry-on bag at his side, a wayward lock of dark hair falling over one eye. He looks just casual and disheveled enough for me to forget he's a billionaire asshole instead of an Italian runway model.

My heart is in my throat as I eat him up with a hungry gaze, even as shame and anger knot in my belly over the way he fled the estate after taking my virginity. He's just so stupidly, terribly, oh-my-God beautiful. It's honestly hard to even keep my thoughts straight when he looks like that. But no matter: I have a new plan.

Just like Cassie said, I need to be my mouthy, sassy self with this man. That's how to get him. Plus, I've got youth and infatuation on my side. He obviously wants me

Abbie

to some degree—we've had three trysts over the last several weeks, which has to mean something. So Graham can try to deny it all he wants, he can run away trying to "clear his head" and forget about me, but it's obvious that the attraction is mutual. At least some of the time, when he lets his guard down.

I just have to figure out how to harness my power and get him to keep his guard down *all* the time.

Jude has already squirmed her way out of the pool and raced to her father, dripping chlorinated water all over his expensive shoes and suit. To his credit, he doesn't push her away, but wraps her in a towel and lifts her in his arms in a big hug. She giggles and coos while he does, happier than I've seen her in the last several days.

"Come swim with us!" Jude begs. "It'll be so much fun!"

"No thank you." Graham sets her down and slings his leather bag over his shoulder. "I just got home. I have unpacking to do. Is that a new bathing suit?"

Crap.

"Abbie got it for me. You like it?" Jude asks, doing a little twirl. "See the unicorns?"

I hold my breath.

"Hmm. I'd say it definitely...suits you," Graham says, cracking one of the worst dad jokes of all time. "It's perfect."

Jude laughs.

"Come in the pool, just for a few minutes. Pretty please, Daddy!" she insists.

"Yeah, Daddy. It'll be fun." I splash at him with my

Chapter 24

sassiest smile, even though I might well be ruining his nice suit. I can't do this halfway.

As a few drops of water splash Graham and Jude, she shrieks in delight. Graham looks less amused. Oh well. It's time to be myself: mouthy and irreverent, skimpy bikini and all. I arch my back on my float a little, pushing my girls to the forefront to take full advantage of my string bikini. Then I give Graham a little wave.

Jude doesn't notice, still wrapped around him. "Come *on*, Daddy. I missed you so much and you don't ever play with me and I just want you to come swimming with us! We can have races and competitions and you can show me how to do a cannonball—"

"You don't need any help there!" I call out, pulling down my own dark shades so she can see me wink. "Jude is a champion cannonballer. I don't think you can take her."

Graham shifts his bag strap on his shoulder, glancing between me and Jude. She continues gazing up at him with that pleading look in her eyes, outlining every last game and race we could have if he stays. Finally, he shakes his head good-naturedly and gently peels Jude off him.

"I'll see you in a few," he tells her, then turns around and heads into the house.

My heart sinks. What does that mean? Is he actually coming back? Or did he mean he'd see us later, like at dinner? God, this man is about as easy to read as a brick wall, all his motives hidden behind that stony expression.

I settle back onto my float and let out a sigh. But when I see how deflated Jude looks, I switch back into high-energy mode and get her back in the pool for some more cannonballs.

"You think he's really going to swim with us?" Jude asks breathlessly when she surfaces.

"Maybe," I say.

She paddles over to my float and pushes the wet hair out of her face. "I hope so. Daddy never plays anymore."

I give her a gentle smile. "I'm sure he wants to, it's just...he seems like a really busy guy, huh? The kind who hardly ever takes any time off."

Jude shrugs. "He used to play, though. Before Mommy left." Her mouth droops, but she shakes her head, as if physically pushing away the sadness. My heart hurts for her a little. "But now he's working in his office all the freaking time. Or at meetings. Or gone."

"Sounds like you miss him a lot," I say.

"I—Daddy!" Jude squeals, her voice hitting an agonizing pitch.

I slide my sunglasses up on top of my head and look over my shoulder. Graham has shed his suit and joined us in a pair of dark orange swim trunks. The sun illuminates his abs, accentuating each defined ridge as he walks. He looks perfectly tanned, which is actually pretty impressive for someone who lives in suits all the time. He even walks like a runway model, sauntering over to the pool and casually tossing an extra towel onto one of the loungers.

"Am I too late for the cannonball competition?" he asks, a grin on his face.

Wow. It's a bit of a shock to see him looking so genuinely happy to be here with us. When he sped off in

Chapter 24

his sportscar a few days ago, it seemed like a dark cloud was hovering over his head. One that wasn't going away any time soon. Now? He's acting like a completely different person.

What exactly happened while he was away?

Then again, does it matter? This version of Graham is definitely preferable to the old one. And there's something about him showing up for Jude that always makes me melt.

"Jump with me!" Jude is already back out of the pool, standing by the rock waterfall. She walks out to the end of the diving board and puts her hands on her hips. "Abbie can judge us!"

"Maybe I should be the judge." Graham dives smoothly into the deep end, barely leaving a splash in his wake.

He'd make a terrible cannonballer—Jude could definitely kick his ass. He surfaces near my float and stretches his arms out behind him on the deck. "Abbie can cannonball with you."

"Yeah, Abbie! Come cannonball with me! Daddy can judge us now!"

"Go on, Abbie." Graham splashes at me. "Show me what you've got."

Ooh. The edge in his voice does delicious things to me, and another sip of blueberry lemonade helps this moment feel like the perfect lazy summer evening. The warmth of the waning sun, the water, the lemonade, Graham back home and in a good mood. I debate begging off, but then remember every movie where some sexy actress climbs out of the water, hair slicked back, water dripping down her curves, and suddenly I want to have that exact same experience with Graham.

"You should know, I'm a champion cannonballer." I set down my lemonade at the edge of the pool and slip out of my float. "Best of the best. Fair warning."

"Until you met me!" Jude challenges. "Bring it on!"

Graham laughs. "Looks like there's going to be some stiff competition."

"How can I trust you to be an impartial judge?" I toss back at him, leaning into the banter. "You seem like the kind of guy who plays favorites."

"Playing favorites in a cannonballing competition?" Graham scoffs. "Where do you think we live? Russia?"

"You never know. Comrade." I climb the steps out of the pool and then join Jude near the diving board. "How do we do this, Jude? Who goes first?"

"You!" she says, a little devilish grin reaching up to her eyes. She reminds me so much of her dad. "On three, ready?"

"Oh, I was born ready."

Jude counts me down, and on three I take a running leap into the pool, water exploding everywhere when I hit the surface. All I can hope is that I soaked Mr. Italian Runway Model over there. I swim back to my donut, taking long strokes to show off my skills, and slide back on my float, maximizing my time sliding out of the water. In my head, it's sexy as hell.

"What say the judges?" I ask.

"Hmm. A solid five," Graham says, not looking at me. "What?!"

Chapter 24

He shrugs and offers an almost-secret smile to Jude. "The form was iffy."

I fold my arms and lean back a little on my float. "Iffy! Clearly you must be joking, sir."

"All right, Jude!" he calls, flashing me a wink. "Let's see what you've got!"

Sweet lord. I could take this version of Graham every damn day. He's sexy, he's charming as all get out, and he's so good with his daughter it makes me swoon.

Jude bends down deep and jettisons off the diving board, falling in near-perfect form, little waves erupting all around her. We both clap and she does an eager lap around the pool, like she's waving to her fans.

"Perfect ten!" Graham calls.

"Yes!" Jude jumps up and down in the water.

"Favoritism!" I laugh. "Blatant favoritism!"

"What's that?" Jude asks. "It means I'm your favorite?"

"You're definitely my favorite," Graham says, giving her a quick dunk. Jude pops back up and hoists herself out of the water to continue the cycle of cannonballs.

I gently kick off the side of the pool so my float bumps into Graham. "Whoopsie."

"Whoopsie? Are you ninety?"

"Only one of us here is old enough to be a grandpa," I tell him. "And it's certainly not me."

"Nice suit, by the way." Graham changes the subject without looking at me. His tone clearly implies sarcasm, but I just smile.

"Why, thank you," I say sweetly, needlessly adjusting

Abbie

the positioning of the triangle cups on top just so I can tease him with the sight of my cleavage.

"Setting an excellent example, I see," he adds, his eyes now glued to my chest.

"Can I get one like Abbie's?" Jude asks, surfacing near us out of nowhere.

Graham laughs. "I'll have to think about it."

"Yes!" Jude smiles and splashes away, going under to chase after the diving toys that Graham threw out for her.

Graham gives me a look. "See? Kids are always watching."

"If that's the case, I might not be the only one who should be worried."

"Are you suggesting we're both bad role models?" His little smirk makes it look like he might actually enjoy that idea.

Hot damn, Cassie was right after all. He does like me saucy. And I like sparring with him, too. It's fun. Seeing him *like this* is fun. Having him be so domineering in the bedroom was hot, but this feels more my speed, trading jokes and teasing each other a little. I don't want this afternoon to end.

"What a picture-perfect family moment," a snide female voice interrupts.

Graham and I both look behind us at the same time.

It's Natasha Ratliff.

Chapter Twenty-Five

Graham

I HADN'T MEANT to lose track of time in the pool. I thought I could do a quick dip, appease Jude, maybe get a sense of Abbie's mood toward me while I was at it, and then hurry back out for my meeting with Natasha. I didn't expect to actually enjoy myself, nor have such a good time with Abbie, who seems to be back to her usual, irreverent, irresistible self. But I did.

And then Black Death in Stilettos walked into my house like she owns the place and ruined everything.

"Mommy!" Jude yells from the pool.

"I'll be ready shortly," I tell Natasha coldly, all my good feelings immediately draining away. "You can wait inside." I get out, grab my towel, and give my ex-wife a hard stare.

She merely returns it, refusing to be cowed. "I'd prefer to wait here with my daughter."

"This is my house," I point out.

"This is my kid," she shoots back.

"Only when it's convenient for you."

Natasha grins with her shark teeth. "I'm not the one who instructed me to wait inside, away from her."

Inside, I seethe. Outside, I remain still and nonplussed. "Wait where you wish, then."

"I believe I'll do just that."

Instead of returning her barbs with more of my own, I grit my teeth and towel off as I head for the door. I'm in no hurry. Jude is no doubt excited to see her mother, but that witch walked straight through my house without an invitation, which means she can wait for me as long as necessary.

If I wanted to make things easier for Natasha, I would have met her down in Manhattan at some point over the last few days when I was at my apartment in Central Park West trying—and ultimately failing—to eradicate my raging lust for Abbie. But I didn't care to meet Natasha then and I certainly don't care to meet her now. Unfortunately, I must.

I change into a dry pair of shorts and a T-shirt, making sure I don't put much effort into what I look like. Natasha doesn't get that from me anymore. Besides, we're only going to a café.

Back outside, she's watching Jude show off in the pool while Abbie looks visibly distressed by her presence. Natasha always had that impact on our staff. They were all terrified of her and her moods. Still, Abbie needs to be able to hold her own—because of the joint custody situation with Jude, Natasha's occasional presence is a given for any nanny. Call it a test of sorts.

Chapter 25

"All ready now?" Natasha asks, cutting a glance my way.

"As I'll ever be," I respond dryly.

"Can you stay for a little bit after you get back, Mommy?" Jude pleads, hanging off the edge of the pool. She pouts her bottom lip, something that always melted me from the time she was a small toddler who learned how to work her father's poor heartstrings.

"I don't see why not." Natasha bends down to kiss her on top of the head and avoid my gaze. "If that's what you'd like."

Abbie's lips press into a hard line, but she stays silent. I simply hold up my keys and jingle them at Natasha. "We can discuss it over dinner."

"I'll be back." Natasha gives Jude a little wave as she follows me out.

Why can't she be a more attentive mother? She didn't just walk out on me—that I could handle. We're both adults and these things happen. But she walked out on our daughter, too, and that is something I cannot forgive. I work long hours and still make time for my child as best I can, but Natasha can barely be bothered to make a phone call once a week.

Not to mention that when the mood strikes her, she'll walk right into my house like she still owns the place, like she never left. As though her absence hasn't been noted by anyone. As though Jude doesn't still cry herself to sleep some nights over her missing mother.

Graham

"The City is just magical. So many more choices for food," Natasha muses, poring over her menu at the casual beachfront place I've chosen to host Satan herself at. "I don't know why you insist on staying up here when you could be staying in Manhattan."

"We like the quiet."

She smiles that winning smile that no longer works on me. "California is beautiful, too. And quiet."

"Los Angeles is hardly quiet," I respond.

"It's a whole different animal than Manhattan. The vibe is much more relaxed. It's green everywhere. And the people are so—"

"Am I missing something?" I interrupt. "Are you saying you want to move to L.A.?"

Natasha huffs. "I'm just being conversational, Graham. Relax."

I don't want to be conversational. I only arranged this meeting so I could update her on Jude, and discuss whether she'd like to have more weekend visits with our daughter.

Unfortunately, friendship between us is completely off the table. We can hardly speak to one another without bickering, much less maintain a halfway decent relationship.

"My new show opens next week. I'd like to bring Jude to the dress rehearsal to meet everyone." Natasha flags down our waiter. "God, the staff here is so slow."

"It's a beach town." I cock an eyebrow at her.

"So is L.A."

The waiter appears at our table with sunburnt cheeks and a cheery demeanor. Natasha orders shrimp cocktail,

Chapter 25

two summer salads, and a bottle of champagne. She used to do this often, ordering for the pair of us without consulting me, but I let it slide. If letting her order means she'll be more affable, then so be it.

I don't like the fighting. I don't like that we do it in front of Jude. I don't like that we can't have a single conversation without it erupting into an argument. I don't like how dirty she plays. I'd rather she just see her daughter on a regular schedule and leave me out of it.

Now she's drinking champagne, which means things can take a turn for the worse if we aren't careful. Or she could get a light buzz going and be as pleasant as Abbie. It's impossible to predict with Natasha.

"So. The reason I reached out is that I wanted to talk to you about Jude," I tell her, ignoring the champagne in my glass. I see nothing worth celebrating in this moment.

"We can talk about Jude when we aren't in public." Natasha arches a heavily made-up brow at me and, without breaking eye contact, drains her entire glass. Then she trades her empty glass with my full one. "You should know better. Paps are everywhere, darling."

"Looking to add Public Intoxication to your rap sheet?"

"Touché," she says, dropping a wink and sipping from my champagne glass anyway.

I found it incredibly charming once, her casual disregard for rules and social mores, but now I'm only frustrated by her carefree attitude—it's just one more example of the way she casts me and my concerns aside. I didn't lie when I told Abbie I was tired of people kissing my ass, but I also don't appreciate the blatant disrespect Natasha offers up at every opportunity.

She does nothing but natter on about her career and the lives of people I don't care about as our food comes and goes, and more glasses of champagne meet their end on her side of the table. I stay sober and take it all in stride. Perhaps the conversation is best had at home, anyway. I'll be more comfortable on my own turf.

Her spirits are upbeat as I drive us back to the estate and park in front of the house. But as soon as we enter the living room, the entire outing turns sideways.

"I'm so glad you finally asked me out," she coos. "It's time to put all this silliness to bed."

I raise a brow. "Haven't you been to bed with enough men, Natasha?"

"Oh, stop it. Neither of us are angels. We can be adults about it."

She checks her lipstick and snaps her compact shut. I know her well enough to realize it's a warning, so I go to the liquor cabinet and pour out two scotches, trying to ignore the twitch between my shoulder blades. Silently, I remind myself I can handle her.

When I turn around, Natasha is smoldering at me, tossing her hair over her shoulder. Things she used to do that drove me wild. "We belong together, Graham. Tell me we don't."

Ah. Apparently, my ex-wife assumed I had very different motives for inviting her out to dinner this evening. Bollocks.

"We don't," I say flatly. "We really don't."

I hold out the glass of scotch, and she wraps both

Chapter 25

hands around it, one eyebrow cocked, before spinning back around and sauntering to the chaise longue. She steps out of her heels and drapes herself across the furniture dramatically. Everything about her has always been dramatic.

"That's a lie and you know it." She takes a healthy swallow of scotch. "I've missed you."

I don't move because I'm not sure what I want to do about this. "I find that very hard to believe."

She sets the scotch on a side table and then sashays over to me, gazing up into my eyes. "You don't believe that I've missed you?"

It's a credit to her acting ability that I actually have to make myself think about it.

"No."

"Oh, Graham." She drapes one arm after the other over my shoulders, pressing into me.

"What are you doing?" I ask quietly.

"What I should have done six months ago," she whispers.

When Natasha kisses me, I let her. Some part of me needs to know if I still feel anything for her. But I don't feel that tug of excitement and arousal, or the muscle memory of emotional warmth. When she kisses me, all I taste is champagne and regret, the lingering bitterness of her betrayal. And if I'm honest with myself, it's Abbie who flashes through my mind. Not my ex.

Taking her by the shoulders, I gently push her away. "You have the wrong idea. I didn't call you here to discuss us. I called you here to discuss your parenting skills."

"My parenting skills?" Natasha's eyes flash and she

rears back. "I'm gone *one year* and all of a sudden you're all high and mighty about parenting? Last time I checked, you were busy flirting with the teenager you're paying to raise *my* daughter. In fact, where is my Judey?" Natasha pushes past me and storms toward the hallway. "I want to see her."

"It's past her bedtime," I say, pointedly checking my watch. "She's asleep."

"I want to see her."

"Another time."

"You can't keep her from me, Graham." She crosses her arms, glaring at me, her lipstick smeared from our kiss. In this moment, I almost feel sorry for her. "She's just as much my daughter as she is yours. You can't hoard her."

"*Hoard* her? Are you joking?" I can't keep the outrage from voice. Her venom won't curse me, not here. "You barely even see her, and it breaks her heart! You don't call, you can't be bothered to text her back, and you don't come around unless you're looking to stir the pot."

"I don't stir pots."

"I beg to differ."

"I'm a very busy woman." Natasha leans over and grabs her shoes unsteadily. I reach to steady her, but she jerks away. "Don't touch me. I'm not going to stay here and take this."

"No, because you're going to walk out, just like you always do."

"That's not fair."

"It's the truth."

"Fuck you." Natasha struggles to get the strap of her

Chapter 25

purse over her head, infuriated and still tipsy. "Fuck you and your superiority complex, Graham. You spent our entire marriage acting like you were better than me because you came from money, but you're just an entitled little shit who built his empire with his daddy's money. Must be so hard, having everything handed to you in life. I guess that's why you don't know how to share."

Rage coils in my gut and I have to be careful to swallow it down. In the old days, this is when the fights would just start to get good. On the precipice of her hurling priceless heirlooms across rooms and me dodging irreplaceable art pieces as they soared past my head. I would yell loud enough to wake Jude in the opposite wing, yell until Natasha was trembling. But I am not that man anymore and I no longer have to endure her abuse.

"You will not verbally assault me in my own house," I tell her. "And seeing as you're under the influence, I'll have Ronaldo take you home now."

Natasha glowers. "You don't know what you just threw away."

Ignoring her, I pull out my phone and dial my driver's number. When he picks up, I turn my back on my ex-wife. "So sorry to bother you this late, but can you please bring the car around front? My ex-wife will be needing a ride back to Manhattan tonight. Yes. Wonderful."

"You're unbelievable," she mutters as I hang up.

I grab her firmly by the elbow and escort her to the door. When I open it, Ronaldo is already waiting with the car. He nods his head in respect and opens the back door, extending an arm toward Natasha. Instead of taking it, she just glowers at me.

"This isn't over," she hisses, storming to the car, sliding into the back seat, and slamming the door shut.

Ronaldo casts an apologetic glance my way. I wave him off and go back inside, head pounding, eager to finish off those abandoned scotches.

Chapter Twenty-Six

Abbie

Cassie is really friggin funny. We've been texting all night, which has done wonders to keep my mind off the fact that Graham took Natasha out to dinner, and the fact that I still have no idea where we stand after his little impromptu trip out of town.

Watching him leave with his ex-wife left a heavy rock in the pit of my stomach. So, after Jude and I had our own little pizza party in the den while watching Disney Plus, I put her to bed and then curled up in my room with my laptop to catch up on the latest episodes of my favorite guilty pleasure—this ridiculous teen vampire TV show. Hey, it can't always be *The West Wing* or *Veep* or *Scandal*. Sometimes you just want to turn your brain off.

But halfway through my episode, Cassie texted. It turns out she also loves the show, so we've spent the last hour discussing how absurd the plot is this season. My favorite characters torpedoed their relationship, the best friends got turned into vampires, and there's this new subplot where one of the side characters being kissed by their enemy is the only way to break a curse. In all actuality, I kinda love it. Enemies to lovers is my jam. Cassie feels the opposite.

What a cliché! Not to mention, totally unrealistic. Enemies never become lovers IRL. In fact, that's a harmful trope, she types. *BESIDES all that, kissing away a curse is so fairy tale.*

Because vampires are soo non-fictional? I text back with the thinking emoji.

I mean no, but...vampires are so much more than "once upon a time," don't you think?

Laughing to myself, I tell her I'm going to get back to my episode but that I'll let her know how I like it. She's all caught up on the series already.

Gerald is the absolute worst, I can't help typing to her just minutes later. *I can't wait 'til he's properly beheaded.*

Cassie immediately shoots back, *I love a girl who can get behind a solid beheading.*

We're soulmates, I text, feeling a pang of guilt over the fact that I've been avoiding Amanda lately.

The thing about Cassie is, she's right here in the eye of the storm. She sees everything, she knows everything that's been going on with me and Graham—at least, she knows as much as I've been able to tell her—and I trust her to keep my secrets. It's not that I won't spill it all to Amanda eventually, but...right now, I'm grateful to have Cassie as a friend and ally.

On the screen, Gerald is hunting my favorite character, Mika, on a dark city street. I pull the blanket up to my nose. I like the show, a lot, but the dark scenes always creep me out. There's something a little too real about

Chapter 26

young women being stalked by predators, even though I know I'm just watching actors on a soundstage, and I end up spending the next day or so running from light switch to light switch to keep the lights on in dark hallways.

Gerald sneaks up on Mika, eyes glinting, ready to pounce, when a loud knock on my door makes me shriek and jump.

"Abbie?" Graham's voice pushes through the door, full of concern.

I burst out laughing, embarrassed, and hit pause, Gerald's pearly fangs out on the screen. Then I close the laptop so Graham won't see it when he comes in here to... scold me? Was my volume turned up too high? I have no idea why he's outside my door this late at night.

Jude is already in bed, and despite our cordial interaction in the pool this afternoon, Graham has still barely spoken to me since discovering the whole virgin thing. I want him to be here to talk to me, to apologize for being so terrible after our first time together, but I know better; he's not the kind of man to do that.

The robe hanging on the back of my door catches my eye, and I look down at the camisole and short-shorts pajama set I'm wearing, and then think, *fuck it*. I happen to wear skimpy pajamas because I'm more comfortable that way, and I'm not going to cover up just to make a better impression on my boss. It's too late for that anyway. So I open the door, sans robe, preparing to stand my ground and keep my chin up no matter what this little visit is all about.

"Sorry, you scared me," I say. "I was watching—"

The rest of my words die on my tongue. Graham

stands there in casual shorts and a T-shirt, slightly disheveled, a wild look in his eyes. I want nothing more than to grab him by the collar and drag him into my room, push him onto the bed, and climb on top.

"What frightened you?" he asks, glancing over my shoulder into the room, oblivious to the dirty thoughts running through my head.

"Nothing. I, umm. I was watching a scary TV show. This vampire thing..." His mouth twitches just enough to let me know he's holding back a smirk, and I'm left feeling a little silly for divulging my favorite show. I try to shrug it off, folding my arms. "So. Can I help you with something?"

His hot gaze rakes over me and the vibe in the hall shifts into something...potent. Primal energy radiates off his skin. It's suddenly very obvious he's not here to talk about Jude.

"What's the name of that lipstick you like so much?" he asks, his voice low.

I don't know what I was expecting him to say, but this wasn't it. "Teenage...Fantasy?"

"That's the one." His eyes sear into mine. "Put it on. Now."

"Why should I?" I shoot back, all my anxiety and frustration boiling to the surface even though I love taking orders from this man. "You can't just...fuck me, and then run away to New York and act like you want nothing to do with me, and then decide to turn around and come back here acting like nothing's changed and expect me to just...just do whatever you say at the drop of a hat—"

Chapter 26

"I want you," he says, cutting me off. "I'm not going to fight it. That's what I decided. You know what I did while I was away? I spent days pacing my flat all alone, not getting any work done, ripping my hair out in frustration, trying to convince myself to let it all go, to just fire you and content myself with somebody else, but...in the end I couldn't do it. I want *you*. There it is."

His eyes burn into mine, and I see the slightest flash of vulnerability hiding behind his steely gaze. And something else. Sincerity. He means what he just said, every word of it.

Immediately I feel my heart drop into my stomach as my center turns warm. I didn't expect this. He wants me. He wants *me*.

He spent days in Manhattan with just about any woman he could want a mere phone call away, spent a night out with his flawless, famous ex-wife, and in the end he still came home to *me*.

Victory. This is what victory tastes like.

"I want you, too," I whisper, even though I'm sure he already knows it.

I take two steps backward into the room, leaving the door half open for him. Graham steps inside, closing the door and turning the lock. We stand toe-to-toe, my breath catching in my throat, and then I glance over at the lipstick sitting on the vanity. His eyes follow my gaze.

Then he walks over, picks up the tube, and brings it back to me.

"Put it on," he repeats, pressing the lipstick into my hand.

Using muscle memory, I apply a few liberal swipes to

my lips, cap it, and set the tube on the dresser without ever breaking eye contact. We're breathing in tandem, rough and deep.

"Now get on your knees." His voice is so deep it reverberates in my chest.

I have no choice but to obey. There is nothing else my body will do, or wants to do, then whatever commands come out of his pouty-lipped, accented mouth. Fact: everything sounds better in a British accent.

Graham unzips his shorts and pulls out his massive cock, already stiff and ready for me. I wasn't wrong about its size and shape last time—it's fucking perfect. My mouth begins to water.

"So you hadn't had sex before." He gives himself a long, hard stroke and it makes me weak, watching him expertly touch himself. "Have you ever given a blow job?"

His coarse language makes me even hotter, my knees going weak against the soft carpet.

I shake my head no. "Not yet."

"It's time you learn, then. Open your mouth." His grin isn't kind. It's hungry.

My heart pounds as I open up, trying to keep my jaw relaxed, thinking I know exactly what to expect. But nothing prepares me for how full my mouth suddenly is, the way his cock hits the back of my throat, triggering my gag reflex. He chuckles to himself as I choke, pulling out so I can cough and catch my breath. My eyes are watering, but I'm determined to try again.

"You really are a virgin." The way he says it makes it sound so dirty. "We'll go slow."

Chapter 26

This time, his head stays in the front of my mouth. I feel like Magellan, exploring this smooth, slick, pulsing thing in my mouth. Every lap and flick of my tongue sends him groaning. He grabs the sides of my head, gentle enough not to hurt but firm enough to keep me still, and slowly thrusts himself against my tongue.

I follow his lead for the first few minutes, learning the pace he likes. Then I start swallowing against him, focusing on keeping my throat as relaxed as possible, and he mutters an, "Oh *fuck*" for the first time.

Yes. I feel like I could fly. Like I could come on the spot just listening to him moan like that, moan because of what I'm doing to him. My chest goes warm.

I'm getting more confident by the second. I can make this man feel good. I can make this man feel *really* good. So I get *really* into it. I smear lipstick all over his cock, bobbing and twisting my head. Alternating between hard suction and soft licks, putting to good use the, ah, education I've received on the internet over the last few years of self-discovery.

Graham likes it when I suck hard, and he *really* likes it when I brush my thumb over and around his balls. His knees buckle a little, brushing against the silk of my pajamas. I follow the contour of his balls back into a secret little spot Amanda once told me about. She called it the magic button, said every boy would be on his knees with it.

Making Graham feel good brings me a surge of power and control that I've never felt before. Nothing can fuck with me, nothing can make me feel better than this. This is my purpose: bringing powerful men to their knees. So I take him deeper in my mouth and give that little button a press, starting gentle and extending it into something more firm as his groans grow.

"Don't stop," he moans. "Harder."

I obey.

His thrusts get deeper, faster, more erratic, until he's almost choking me again. I can tell by his breathing that he's almost there, right on the edge, about to lose control. So I start moaning against him, as if I'm about to climax myself, and that really does the trick. He's fucking my mouth now, really going at it hard, gasping and jerking and then—

Graham's orgasm is glorious. He fills my mouth with his hot cum in powerful bursts, grunting as he does, and I'm surprised to find that I can swallow it all down easily. I drag my mouth over him slowly after each thrust and his groans get so deep, so sensuous, that my fingers find my center nub and begin to rub furiously over the fabric of my shorts. I moan against him some more, fingers of pleasure already tugging at me.

This must be what he felt like the first time he gave me an orgasm across his desk.

I want to feel this way every day.

"Naughty girl. You shouldn't know such tricks yet." Graham pulls out of my mouth and steps out of his shorts, away from me. His breath hitches a little as he watches me sit there on the floor, my back against the foot of the bed, pleasuring myself. "You naughty minx."

"I think you like me naughty." My voice is husky, my body already electrified.

Chapter 26

"Get on the bed," he commands. "I want to see you get yourself off."

I do as he asks, but when I start to slide my shorts off, he stops me.

"Pajamas stay on." His voice is rough. He spins the vanity chair around and takes a seat. "Your nipples are immaculate beneath the silk."

"My nipples are always immaculate. Sure you don't want to come help?"

"I want to watch," is all he says.

I lie back against the pillows and let my hands roam slowly over my body, pulling the silk of my pajamas tight over my aching nipples and across my swelling pussy. I play it up a little, arching my back, turning myself on with my own moans, letting one camisole strap slip down over my shoulder. Every nerve is on fire as I engage in this intimate dance, this private thing I've never done in front of anyone before. Maybe this should be more difficult, more awkward, but this is Graham. I've dreamed about doing this kind of thing with him a thousand times. It feels...right.

And I'm still drunk on the power of bringing this powerful man to his knees.

Feeling emboldened, I meet his gaze, a little shy at first, with a burning in my heart. I see want etched across every inch of his face. I could recognize that look, that desire, anywhere. He's taken off his shirt and sits there naked in my vanity chair like a king.

"Faster," he orders from his perch.

"I like it slower," I sass, but rub myself with extra vigor anyway.

Abbie

"You like to argue with me." It's a statement, fact, nothing left to question.

"You like it when I argue with you." Speaking gets difficult as the intensity ramps up, hot little pulses I can feel shooting from my clit to my toes.

I close my eyes and lean my head back, letting my mouth fall open, lost in the sensations.

"You haven't the faintest idea what I like," he growls.

"It's okay to admit you like me," I tease, breathy. I'm soaking wet now, my juices seeping through the fabric. I slide my hand down the front of my shorts, my fingers gliding easily around my slick lips, dipping inside me, then back up to swirl around my clit.

"We're adults, Abbie. We don't have to like each other."

Graham's voice is tight. One peeked-open eye shows me he's pleasuring himself again while watching me, jerking off as he sits in the chair.

I feel oh-my-fuck amazing as I continue my circuit of pleasure. Sitting up to adjust my position, I stare him straight in the eyes and suck hard on my first two fingers. Then I reach down and shove them as far inside me as I can again, moaning softly. "I like you, too, Graham. Mmm."

He grunts, frustrated or aroused, maybe both, and gets up to walk over to me, his big hands pumping his cock with each step. Streaks of Teenage Fantasy stain his hands. We abandon all words and simply stroke ourselves with desperate, barely restrained moans, gazes locked, until I have to shut my eyes, losing myself completely in the rhythm of my motions.

Chapter 26

I'm riding my fingers, two, three of them, the fingers of my other hand rolling my nipple, my hips rising and falling faster and faster as I imagine it's Graham spearing into me.

"*Graham*," I moan. "Yes."

The orgasm is sudden and bright and almost dizzying, making me feel like I'm flying over the estate. Quickly, Graham's own moans deepen and join mine and I feel squirts of warmth hitting my pajama top. I open my eyes to watch him, licking my lip as he squeezes the last drops of his seed onto my chest. When he's finished, he sits on the bed and reclines back, panting.

"I didn't think guys could do that twice in a row," I blurt before I can stop myself.

He cracks a grin, an honest-to-God grin. "You are so very inexperienced."

"Doesn't seem like you mind."

He turns his head to look at me. "I'm sorry about the...unfortunate state of your pajamas."

"I'm not," I sass, getting up to go shower, shutting the bathroom door behind me and not looking back.

It isn't because I don't want to stay in bed with him after what we just did—it's because I do. More than anything.

And I'm smart enough to know how foolish that is.

Chapter Twenty-Seven

Abbie

"Gooood morning!" Jude bops into the dining room for breakfast, already dressed, with a massive smile on her face.

"Excited?" Graham cracks a smile almost as large as hers, and I'm pleased to see he doesn't have a newspaper to hide himself behind. "It's hard to tell."

"Ha ha, Daddy," Jude says drolly, but then perks right back up. "Exhibition days are the best days ever! I finally get to show everyone what me and Desi can do."

"What Desi *and I* can do," he corrects.

"That's what I said," Jude sasses.

"I can't wait." I offer a small toast with my orange juice, still feeling the glow of what I did with Graham last night rushing through me. "I know you and Cassie have been working really, really hard."

"My little equestrian." Graham smiles again, and I'm afraid to look at him, but it's hard not to. He's just...in such a good mood. It's contagious. And sweet.

"Cassie says I should be a shoo-in for at least two

Chapter 27

ribbons," Jude mumbles around a bite of sausage. "I think I can get three."

"You're a Ratliff," Graham says, gesturing at her with his fork. "You can do anything you put your mind to."

"My mind says I'm going to get three ribbons today." Jude flashes three fingers at me.

"It's been so long since I've been to an exhibition," I say. "I'm excited, too."

"Me, too. So hurry up!" Jude commands, shoving half a pancake in her mouth.

"Slow down!" I reach for her, mildly horrified I'll actually have to put my Heimlich Maneuver training to use. "We have plenty of time. I don't want you choking."

"I'm fine," she insists around the massive blob of food in her mouth.

"Now Jude," Graham warns. "You won't be able to compete if you've choked to death on a pancake first."

She rolls her eyes, swallows hard, and cuts a slightly smaller piece. Then she daintily pushes it into her mouth and chews robotically while holding her dad's gaze with a very "Are you happy now?" look on her face. I kind of love her. A lot. Best tiny BFF I could have asked for.

Graham shoots me a look of parental exasperation, but he says nothing and finishes his coffee. Meanwhile Jude talks a mile a minute between bites, going over all the training she and Cassie have been doing. I finish my food as quickly as I can, while Graham picks idly at his croissant—miraculously managing to get nary a flake of pastry on his shirt, might I add.

"Nerves?" I tease him.

"Something like that."

Abbie

"Daddy takes my riding very seriously." Jude licks syrup off her finger and hops out of her chair. "Let's go, let's go, let's go!"

"We are going to be so unfashionably early," Graham says, but he stands anyway and follows after Jude, who all but runs out of the room. "Careful that you don't get cramps, Jude. That was quite a lot of food all at once."

"Gotta carb up before the competition!" Jude throws over her shoulder.

Graham and I share another look, him shaking his head. I laugh. There's a kind of warm buzz between us now, one I'm afraid I'll jinx simply by acknowledging it in my head—so I'm trying not to dwell on it too much. On the other hand, maybe I'm just imagining it. Wishful thinking, me hoping that he's being honest with me, that he doesn't want anyone else, that he's not just using me as a rebound or something.

The thing is...it doesn't feel that way. It really doesn't.

But what if I'm wrong?

"Can we put on my mix in the car?" Jude asks as she puts on her shoes and Graham gathers up her bags. "I need to get hyped!"

Graham looks perplexed and I have to laugh again. "I made her a playlist of fun songs to get her pumped up for the competition."

"Should I be worried about what's on it?" he asks dryly.

"Of course not, Daddy," Jude says, rolling her eyes at him. "It's just music."

Once we're all buckled in and heading down the driveway, I pull up the playlist on my phone and plug it

Chapter 27

into the car, filling our ears with lots of girl power jams. Jude sings at the top of her lungs to Fifth Harmony, which sets Graham a little on edge, but watching her bust it out fills me with joy.

When we get to the equestrian facility—a forty-acre horse park with sprawling, impeccably manicured grounds, competition and show arenas, a covered equidome, riding trails, and a main building with restrooms and refreshment vendors—the chaos has already begun. Seeing all the kids strutting around in their freshly pressed jodhpurs and natty black jackets and riding helmets, I can't help but miss my riding days. Getting my hair specially braided by my mom the morning of, the thrill of chasing ribbons, maybe flirting with cute boys in their riding gear. Sigh.

Jude grabs Graham's hand and leads him through the crowd toward the stables, waving to a few girls she knows and all but skipping as she moves along. I follow behind them, just soaking up as much as I can.

My parents withdrew me from my lessons when I was in tenth grade, saying I wouldn't be able to balance lessons and my course load at school, but I knew better. I heard the conversations about money through the walls when they thought I was asleep. Saw the unopened bills piling up, noticed the calls my parents suddenly dodged. It was subtle, but I got it.

Watching Jude get to live out my childhood dreams is a little bittersweet, but it's also going to be thrilling to watch. Cassie collects Jude at the entry to the stables and shoos me and Graham away before escorting Jude further inside, tossing me a friendly wink over her shoulder as they go. Behind her, I catch a glimpse of Quinn oiling up some equipment. He must feel my eyes, because he looks up and sees me, offering a head nod in hello.

Then he side-eyes me and Graham a few times while he chats with Jude and Cassie, but I try to ignore it. Graham is here for Jude, and so am I. No reason for anyone to look twice.

"I've heard the lemonade is good here. Care for a glass?" Graham turns to me, business in the stables finished. "We could take it to our seats."

"I would, but I think I ate too fast," I beg off. "There's no more room at the inn."

He laughs and puts a hand on my lower back, ever so lightly, to escort me to the bleachers. For just a moment, I let myself imagine this is my real life: Graham Ratliff escorting me places, the two of us laughing over fancy lemonades, cheering on Jude and her horse as they perform for everyone. Maybe ice cream for all of us afterward. A girl can dream, right?

We take our seats as the first batch of riders take their place in the ring. It isn't Jude's group yet, so Graham spends the next several minutes talking horses with me, pointing out the different breeds and how much they typically go for at auction. I don't bother telling him I already know these things because he seems so focused and involved. I just...want to enjoy him, enjoy the way he seems so fully at ease with me, so fully in the moment.

Until someone near us murmurs, "Look! It's Natasha Ratliff!"

My head whips up on its own, and sure enough, there is Jude's mother, picking her way through the crowd with

Chapter 27

a bright smile and a slight wave, her gigantic sunglasses screaming "Look at me, I'm a celebrity!" if nothing else about her is.

Graham tenses next to me, just enough for me to notice his body going taut, but his face never changes. He's like a statue: beautiful and stoic and unchanged.

"Mind if I sit?" Natasha asks, taking the seat next to him and blasting us with that dazzling smile.

"What are you doing here?" he asks, keeping his voice low. "You never come to these."

"Shh." She waves him off, pointedly scanning the arena. "My daughter is riding."

"She's not even out yet." Graham's lips form a tight line.

"They all look the same from here." Natasha frowns, and then perks right back up, waving to a tiny body on a horse being led out to the corral. "Look. She's right there, Graham."

Graham's jaw tightens for a moment, but he says nothing. I press my thigh slightly against his, hoping it telegraphs a bit of reassurance, but otherwise keep my eyes forward, afraid to find myself yet again at the receiving end of Natasha's judgment and insults.

Luckily, she decides to ignore us and pulls out her phone to record Jude's performance.

Soon enough, I forget Natasha is even there. Jude plays her part marvelously. Every move is performed with the air of a trained professional, confident and smooth and expert. She and Desi maneuver around the arena like they're doing ballet, like they're part of the same body. They exhibit the kind of bonded, synergetic

Abbie

relationship every rider yearns for. That she's achieved this level of skill so young is a testament to both her dedication and Cassie's careful, guiding hand. I make a mental note to commend Cassie later.

Graham looks on, incredibly proud, fully engaged in watching his daughter compete. He and Natasha make small talk about Jude's performance, and he seems to really enjoy it. I love seeing this version of him. The version of him I wish Jude could see more often, too.

In the end, Jude gets all three ribbons she was aiming for, looking especially pleased with herself after the final ribbon is awarded. She hugs Desi around the neck and graciously accepts a colorful bouquet from Cassie afterward, even though I can tell from here that she's itching to pump her fists and celebrate with a big whoop.

Celebrating is for later, though. Now is for poise, class, self-possession. That's what we're all taught, and Jude plays the role brilliantly.

"I need to talk to Cassie about making arrangements to see Lucy this week," Natasha announces, rising from the stands after the award ceremony has finished. "Do you mind?"

"Not at all," Graham says. "She's your horse."

"I miss that little devil," Natasha says with a smile. "Lots of little devils I miss."

She looks at Graham when she says it, but he's too busy replying to an email on his phone to even notice her attempt at flirting. She scowls at me, just for good measure I suppose, and then folds herself into the departing crowd.

Chapter 27

"Shall we?" Graham pockets his phone, stands, and extends his arm for me to go ahead of him.

By the time we get to the stables, I assume Natasha has already talked to Cassie, but the former Mrs. Ratliff is nowhere to be found.

"Haven't seen her," Cassie tells Graham with a shrug. "Jude just ran to the restroom; she'll be right out."

"She was amazing," I gush. "*You* were amazing."

Cassie waves me off. "Jude is an excellent student and an excellent rider. Her passion for horses is where it needs to be for someone of her caliber. You've got a good one, Mr. Ratliff."

"She is remarkable," he agrees good-naturedly.

I suddenly hear an ear-splitting giggle and look over to see Natasha with her arm wrapped around Jude's shoulder, holding her daughter captive while she chats animatedly with a group of people who appear to be fans of hers. Jude's smile looks a little stiff, but Natasha doesn't seem to notice as she tosses her hair and laughs again loudly, sprinkling fake smiles around like glitter.

As Graham stands beside me, watching the shenanigans unfold, I wait for him to march over there and say something incendiary. He doesn't like waiting around, doesn't like waiting on anyone. Especially not Natasha. But instead of trying to tear her away from her fans or drag Jude away or start a fight, he just leans back to rest his elbows on an empty stable door, watching her ham it up with a mild look on his face. When he catches me looking at him, he gives me a little shrug, then pulls out his phone.

Abbie

He looks downright relaxed. I don't think I've ever seen him this mellow, this laid-back.

Is it possible that it has something to do with me? That maybe…I'm good for him?

God, what if it's true? Maybe Graham Ratliff gets something real out of what we have. Something he didn't even know he was missing. Maybe…hell, maybe he needs me a little.

Maybe I should…be more than myself. Be honest. Tell him the truth. All of it.

But if I do that, who knows what would happen? I can't predict how he'd react. Especially after seeing how he responded to the revelatory bombshell that was the fact of my virginity.

So then…maybe not.

Maybe the truth just isn't in the cards for us.

Not if it means I might lose him again.

Chapter Twenty-Eight

Abbie

AFTER WE GET BACK to the house, Jude runs upstairs to her room for a shower and some well-earned screen time. She clutches her ribbons to her chest as she goes, beaming like the proudest little bear cub I've ever seen. It's hard not to get emotional myself, watching her work so damn hard these past few weeks and now seeing it all pay off.

Graham smiles after her retreating form and then walks down the hall, toward the study. For a moment, I consider going up to my room too. It's been a long day, and a hot shower really does sound good. But then Graham pauses mid-stride and looks over his shoulder.

"Care to join me in the study?"

I don't think I can keep the shock off my face as I try to process his oh-so-casual invite. What does it mean? Is this an invitation to actually talk, or just to fuck? Or both? Or to...hang out? And then I realize the obvious: I don't care. Whatever it is he's offering me, I'm in.

"Sure," I say, trying to echo his air of nonchalance.

My pulse starts kicking as soon as I move toward him,

standing there in the doorway waiting for me with a look of amusement on his face.

Doesn't he realize that the reason I'm so keyed up is because every interlude we've had, every private moment, has been fraught with unbalanced power dynamics? Graham, the boss. Me, the employee. Graham, the teacher. Me, the student. Graham, dominant. Me, submissive (if not a bit mouthy). Everything that's happened between us has been delicious, but we haven't been on equal ground. Not at all. He's always seen me as young, naïve, inexperienced.

Which, fair.

But now he's holding out an olive branch, an invitation to join him in his private chambers—instead of issuing a command. It's an *offer*. He's never offered before. This could mean something big, some seismic shift between us, or it could mean absolutely nothing at all. I just have to see how it all plays out.

From the corner of my eye, I spy Esmeralda dusting a statue down at the other end of the hall. When she catches my gaze, she immediately turns away and hurries off. For some reason, her reaction weighs heavy on my shoulders. Does she know there's something going on with me and Graham? Is she casting judgment? I used to think we were friends, but everything feels a little cool between us lately. Or maybe I'm just being paranoid.

I make myself shrug it off and follow Graham into the study. He closes the door behind us and makes his way to a leather wingback chair, gesturing for me to take the chair across from him. I do, but all I can think about is the fact that we're alone in here. Instantly, memories of what

Chapter 28

we did in my bedroom flood through me, and I can feel my cheeks go hot as I remember the intense power I felt with his cock in my mouth.

It didn't feel like he held the power, like I imagined it would. I always assumed it was a power play for men, a way to assert dominance, sticking their dick in someone's mouth and demanding to be sucked. But it wasn't like that at all with Graham. I felt like I was the one in control. It was an intense high, bringing a man like him to weakness, making him come for me.

Is he treating me differently now because I was eager to learn, eager to obey, eager to play his game? Did that somehow earn me points in his mind, or respect?

I break out of my reverie long enough to realize he still has that amused look on his face. Almost as if he can tell what I'm thinking.

Thank God he can't.

"Can I make you a drink?" I ask, suddenly unsure what to do with my hands or body, temptation raging through me. Keeping myself occupied feels safe, at least for now.

"Scotch, neat."

I get up and head over to the liquor cabinet, wondering if he's watching me.

My fingertips dance across the cut-crystal decanters until they settle on the one I've seen Graham drink from the most. I think about holding it up to ask, but decide against it. He likes confident women. I could bring him the wrong drink entirely, but if I did it with enough confidence, I bet he'd drink it anyway. I pour two tumblers of

Abbie

the stuff and walk them over to the chairs, oozing as much self-confidence as I can.

I want him to feel the same way about me as I do him. I crave it more than anything else, except maybe the touch of his lips to mine. Maybe I crave them equally.

Sinking back into my chair, I raise my glass. "To Jude."

Graham raises his. "To my checking account."

I go to take a sip, mimicking the motions I've seen him do since I've never drunk straight whiskey before. But the second the alcohol touches my lip, I freeze, nose scrunching up. It burns, and it smells absolutely awful. Like smoke and burnt rubber and cough medicine.

Lowering my glass, I see Graham smirking at the face I'm making.

"See, this is why I've never offered you any," he quips.

"If I had wanted some, I wouldn't have waited for an offer."

He full-on grins. "You do tend to take what you want."

We settle into mostly comfortable silence as he sips his drink. I hold my breath and take the tiniest sip. My eyes start to water as it burns my throat, causing Graham to laugh out loud.

"How can you drink this?" I sputter.

"I've had a lot of practice. And really, it's an acquired taste."

"So I have to learn how to drink scotch to like drinking scotch?"

He nods. "Indeed."

Chapter 28

"What more do I need to know, besides open mouth, insert liquid, and swallow?" I bat my eyelashes at him innocently, then try another tiny sip. I manage to swallow it down without shuddering. It's a small victory, but mine all the same.

"Better?" he asks.

"A little." I clear my throat and let a few quiet moments pass before I blurt out what I've been thinking all afternoon. "I thought you handled Natasha very well today."

He raises a brow.

"I'm not kissing your ass," I add. "I've just seen quite a bit of parental discord as of late, and you were...very good."

Graham laughs. "Thank you. I'll take it."

I pause and then plow onward. "Especially considering your last few interactions with her. I know I should stay in my lane and all, I just...I wanted to say, it's good for Jude to see. It's really hard when you're her age and your parents are always fighting."

"Your parents fight a lot, then." It's a statement, not a question.

"Well, my dad makes the money and my mom spends it all, so..." I try a larger sip of scotch this time and immediately regret it. "I'd say 'fighting' is sort of a generous term."

"Marriage isn't easy." He takes another deep drink and swirls the glass around, eyes transfixed on the moving liquid. "Finding someone to spend the rest of your life with is a daunting task, no matter what the wedding industry wants you to think."

Abbie

"Almost everyone I know has divorced parents," I offer with a shrug. "I'm just sort of waiting for it to happen with mine. Maybe they'll be happier once they're apart."

He nods, looking like he's mulling over my words.

"I don't like fighting with Natasha," Graham says suddenly. "I know it wears on Jude."

"So why do you, then?"

He frowns a little, but he doesn't look angry at me for asking, but rather angry at himself for the answer. "If I'm very honest, I'm still angry at her for leaving. I don't mind that she left me, I mind that she left Jude. You've seen what it does to her, having her mother appear and disappear whenever she likes." He shakes his head. "And Natasha...she uses Jude for show. She likes to take her to dress rehearsals and interviews and show her off at exhibitions, but she doesn't want to do the hard work, be a real parent. Natasha didn't want a child, she wanted honors."

I can't help myself. "Poor Jude."

"Indeed. Natasha took an entire *year* away, like a teenager larking about on a gap year. And now she's back she expects us to do everything she asks at the drop of a hat, and all on her terms."

"And you don't want to play by her rules."

"Not anymore." His voice is a little bitter, a little sad, and a little stony. "That's done."

After draining his scotch, he refills his glass and then tells me more about his side of the divorce. I don't know how to respond to most of what he's saying, so I don't.

Chapter 28

He's never opened up to me like this before and I'm not about to risk chasing him off with the wrong words.

Finally, his story trails off and his eyes find mine. "I shouldn't be telling you all this."

"It's fine. Really." I give him a tiny smile, trying to break the heavy mood with a little teasing. "Besides, now I know why you're afraid of intimacy."

I'm joking, but I mean it.

"Just because you've *been* intimate with me doesn't mean you know me intimately," Graham points out.

"Oh, I think I know some things." I raise a brow, as if I'm teasing him, but inside, I'm not laughing at all. Because the truth is, I *do* know some things about Graham by now. Things that have given me a whole new perspective on him.

Based on what he's told me, I've come to realize how used he felt by Natasha during their marriage. It's obvious she took advantage of him and the financial security that his wealth offered her, and it also seems like she was more interested in the access he could grant her to the power players in the entertainment world—in New York and London and Hollywood—than in Graham himself. I can't help wondering if getting pregnant with Jude was a calculated move on her part as well, but that's only speculation. I certainly hope that's not the case.

Regardless, I don't want to be another lying woman in his life. I won't be.

I need to confess.

So I close my eyes, swallow a large mouthful of drink, and take a deep breath. I don't have to tell him every-

Abbie

thing. Just my part of it. He'll understand. He'll respect me for coming clean.

I'm just about to open my mouth when—

"Daddy?" Jude's head pops through the door. "It's my bedtime. Abbie, can you tuck me in?"

Before I can say anything, Graham offers, "I'll do it."

Then he sets his drink down without looking back at me and follows her out of the room, leaving me alone with my cursed thoughts.

Chapter Twenty-Nine

Graham

Jude tucks her favorite stuffed horse under her arm, her new dressage ribbons tacked up on the wall beside the others. She said good night to the ribbons before settling into bed in a way that brought a smile to my face. She's got a pure, beautiful heart, something my ex-wife knows nothing about.

Maybe it's for the best Natasha isn't around often. I can protect Jude's innocence and compassion all the better.

"I love you, Daddy," Jude murmurs sleepily.

I bend down to kiss her gently on her forehead, smoothing the hair away from her face and tucking it behind her ear. "I love you too, my little warrior queen."

"I'm glad you got to see me and Desi win today." She's already drifting off, her breathing starting to level off. "I wanted you to be proud."

Her words dig into the soft space beneath my heart. "Oh, Jude. I'm always proud of you. You don't need any ribbons for that."

But the words, truthful as they are, only serve to remind me how infrequently I say them. Self-reproach washes over me. I need to do this more often. Tuck her in, take her out, make the time for her. But I work so much, have so many meetings, so many fucking work trips, that the bulk of her care necessarily rests on her nannies. Am I as guilty of ignoring my daughter as Natasha is? Am I around as often as I need to be?

Abbie certainly doesn't think so. She's said as much more than once.

As I turn out the light and gently close the door—open just a crack, the way Jude likes it—I admit to myself that my daughter deserves so much more than I give her.

I prefer not to examine the maelstrom of emotions starting to emerge, so I push them away and let my feet take me down the hall of their own accord as I stew. I had wanted to talk to Natasha about her parenting skills, but I need to sit down with myself about mine.

I grew up not thinking my father loved me. I cannot—will not—do the same to Jude.

My steps have taken me directly in front of a closed door that isn't mine. This is Abbie's room.

Before I can think about it enough to change my mind, I rap softly on the door.

A second later it opens; the sight of her momentarily takes my breath away. Hair in loose curls, her lips parted, body wrapped once again in a silk pajama set. Abbie looks miraculous in silk.

"Hi." She smiles and it's beautiful.

I'm struck with the sudden urge to kiss her. I haven't yet because I didn't want silly ideas to bloom in her head

Chapter 29

about us, didn't want her to think this could be anything besides casual. But now, it's all I can see or think about. Her perfect mouth, those soft pink lips, that clever tongue.

I step into her room, pushing her backward as I go, gently cupping her cheek. As my intent becomes clear to her, I see her eyes widen. Slowly, carefully, I lower my head and brush her lips with mine. She gasps a little, a trace of scotch still on her breath, and I hold her steady and kiss her again. As our open mouths meet, a foreign sensation builds in the pit of my stomach, something I haven't felt in a long time. A kind of magnetic pull. A yearning.

My hands drop to her ass, pulling her into me, and my next kiss is harder, prodding her to open wider with my tongue, and she groans softly as she accepts me. She tastes sweet, like a ripe strawberry, the tang of youth and beauty mixed with a fierceness that I cannot get enough of, no matter how many times I tell myself it's in bad form.

I want this woman. I've made it absolutely clear. And tonight, I will have her.

I break away from her just long enough to kick the door shut with my foot. "Abbie, I want to take you to bed again. But I won't take anything that you don't want to give."

She lets out a half gasp, half laugh, as if what I've said is somehow incredible to her. "I want you too, Graham. I already told you that."

This time she comes to me. Our lips mash, tongues tangling, adrenaline kicking hard. She takes my hands and drags them down her chest to rest on her perky breasts, her nipples already hard and waiting. I lift her up and let her wrap her legs around my waist, walking straight to her bed, relishing the taste of her mouth and the responsive strokes of her eager tongue on mine.

When my knees hit the footboard, I push her off me and onto the bed, crawling after her.

"Sit up," I tell her, and when she does I slide the straps of her silk tank off her shoulders, running my hands down her arms to slide her top down completely.

Leaning back, I take her in, try to imprint this view of her in my memory. Pupils dilated, lips wet and swollen from kisses, chest heaving with her quickened breaths and those small breasts naked and bared to me. They are perfect in all the ways I like: perky but petite, elegant even, with a gentle curve beneath and pert, deep pink nipples crowning them in the center. I dip my head to give each one a soft, sucking kiss and she moans.

"You are perfect," I murmur against her nipple. I suck on it again, softly, enjoying the way she arches her back. "And so responsive. It doesn't take much to get you moaning."

"Maybe you just know exactly how to touch me." Her voice is a low purr, laced with desire.

"Don't you know how to touch yourself?" I tease.

"Of course I do. You watched me, remember?" She sighs a little as I suck on her other nipple, her nails digging deliciously into my scalp.

"I remember. In fact, it's all I can think about." My voice is husky as the truth comes spilling out. "I wanted to be the one to make your body move like that."

Chapter 29

A little laugh interrupts her heavy breathing. "Lucky for you, I've got all night."

I let out a groan, abandoning her breasts so I can pull her silk shorts down her soft ass and run my hands back up her body, caressing her smooth calves and taut thighs.

"Naughty girl, going commando," I tsk, stroking her wet center with one finger.

"Mmm. I never wear underwear to bed."

"As well you shouldn't," I say, taking my finger back and giving it a lick. "Lie down."

Abbie obeys, as always, and spreads her legs wide, her knees up. She's immaculate, laying nude in the dim light of her room. I can never let myself fall for her, because it's child's play to do so, but I can give myself this. I can make love to her, at least this once.

Her scent is intoxicating, subtly sweet, and I realize her pussy is something I could eat forever. Each lick and suck and nibble only reaffirms that this is what I truly want. I can fall into her and forget everything else, all the bad, all the guilt, and for one night feel completely at ease again. This is what she can give me. This is her power.

I lap in upward strokes right between her lips, keeping the drag of my tongue slow and steady against her, two fingers pumping her hole gently as I work her with my mouth. She is so incredibly wet, her fingers in my hair, her hips moving in time with my finger thrusts.

"I'm going to come if you don't stop," she pants. "*Graham.*"

Instead of stopping, I increase my pace. Shorter, harder licks. Faster fingering. When she starts moaning, I moan along with her, letting her pull my hair as she rides my mouth. She climaxes quickly, shivering. Her orgasm tastes so good, her sharp little moans so hot and desperate, I know I'll be jerking off to this memory for ages to come.

"Graham," she whimpers, over and over.

I feel like a king.

Once she's ridden out the shockwaves, I pull away and trail kisses over her hips, up her belly, across her rib cage until I reach her breasts once again, enjoying the feel of her getting helplessly turned on all over again under the direction of my tongue. I pull a condom from the nightstand drawer and rip open the package.

Again our mouths find each other, and the heavens open as her sweetness pours into me. Her fingers tug insistently at the buttons on my shirt, and I lean on one arm to allow her the access she craves. Her touch is soft but frantic as she moves down to my pants. I barely have time to get the condom on before she grabs my cock and pulls me inside her, hot and wet and perfect. God, she fits me like a glove. I don't usually go for missionary, but this feels…fucking exquisite.

Abbie looks up into my eyes and wraps her legs around me, thrusting against my length as I start to spear into her.

"I need you," she whispers. "All of you. *More.*"

It doesn't sound childish. It doesn't sound juvenile. It is the voice of a woman with needs that only I can meet. So I oblige.

Our bodies commune and the world goes silent, save for the breathy gasps from her sweet mouth as I gently push in and out of her warmth, our slow rhythm punctu-

Chapter 29

ated by hot kisses. She's insatiable, Abbie, now that our lips have touched. And admittedly, so am I.

Everything else melts away. It is only us, rocking together endlessly in a tender motion, the pleasure building and building, impossibly higher and higher. I don't feel less for fucking her in this manner; it's the opposite. I feel more powerful than ever, watching her face twist in pleasure with each thrust. Her mouth makes the perfect O shape as I begin to thrust harder, letting myself get lost in the sensations.

"That's it. Don't stop," she pleads, breathy and frantic. "Oh, God, Graham. Don't stop. Don't fucking stop."

Hearing my name on her lips is my undoing. I want to hear it a thousand times.

"Say my name again," I whisper in her ear.

"Graham," she purrs, her nails digging into my back. "*Oh*, Graham. *Graham, Graham, Graham.*"

As my name drops from her lips, I feel an orgasm swelling inside me. I chase it, desperate, relentless, fucking her until I'm out of breath and we're both panting hard, gasping for air. Her hands move to the back of my neck and pull me down for another kiss, deep and wet, perfectly in time with our thrusts. All it takes is that final connection, and we both come crashing to a climax together. Skin slapping, breath heaving, moaning into each other's mouths until we've ridden out the last shuddering wave.

I collapse beside her, still catching my breath, still tasting her pussy on my tongue, watching the smile bloom on her face.

Graham

"God. You're...amazing." She turns her head toward mine so we're facing each other.

"You're not so bad yourself," I joke. I take her hand and stroke the soft skin of her palm, her fingers, stopping when I see the small raised, crescent-shaped scar on the side of her pointer finger. "Is this from that summer you were here? The knife accident?"

"Yeah," she says, looking away as if embarrassed.

I still remember that day. How she'd passed out right in front of me, how my adrenaline had raced as I carried her to my car, how terrified she'd been in the hospital. Turned out she'd never broken a bone, never had surgery, never had stitches before. She was in a panic. I hadn't left her side.

Lifting her finger to my mouth, I kiss the scar gently, then think better of it and give her entire fingertip a gentle suck that has her moaning softly. I cover her moans with my mouth and we kiss for a while. It's more relaxed this time, more exploration and less tongue fucking, though I'm already getting hard again.

"Can I tell you something?" she asks, pulling away for air, then dropping her head onto my chest. My fingers make lazy circles over her hip, up her side, down her arm.

"Don't tell me you love me," I warn.

"Ha, no." Her voice brushes me off, but she's tensed up against me. I tilt her chin with my finger to get a better look at her, and find she looks terrified. "I just wanted to be honest with you after everything you said about Natasha. I want you to trust me."

"Okay," I say carefully, unable to fathom anything that would cause her so much distress.

Chapter 29

"So, I..." She pauses and swallows hard. "I have to admit, I came here with an agenda. I came here specifically in hopes of seducing you."

God, she's kind of hilarious. Did she really think I couldn't tell from the get-go, from the moment she walked into my house, that she was trying—albeit somewhat poorly—to seduce me?

"And you did a good job." I keep my voice light.

But she doesn't look relieved. If anything, she looks even more panicked. "The thing is, my dad—"

"I don't want to talk about your dad right now." I kiss her forehead and pull her on top of me, wrapping my arms around her, my erection settling between her warm thighs.

"I just need you to understand something," she pleads.

"I understand plenty." I place a kiss on the side of her neck. One in the middle of her throat. One on her lower lip. Her body relaxes as she melts against me. "But if you really need to open your mouth, I think I have something you can put in it."

She laughs. "You're ridiculous."

"That doesn't sound like a no."

A grin quirks her lips. "That's because it isn't."

"Come here, you naughty girl."

Chapter Thirty

Abbie

IT'S A BEAUTIFUL DAY OUTSIDE. Puffy clouds dot the sky, sunbeams spill over the world, and the weather is that perfect level of summer warmth and gentle breeze that keeps us from needing to hide out inside to escape the usual humidity. Birds call out lazily as Jude and I eat our afternoon snack under an umbrella by the pool, creating a symphony that serves as our soundtrack.

Jude gulps her blueberry lemonade and picks at a charcuterie plate of fruits, cheeses, and sweets. She wears her two-piece unicorn bathing suit and a pair of sunglasses. Our hair is in matching French braids, and I even gave her a quick swipe of mascara and cherry Chapstick when she begged, under a solemn vow that she never tell her dad.

Jude had a half day today, so all her lessons were finished already...and I figured what Graham doesn't know won't hurt him. At least, that's what I told Jude when we linked pinkies to swear it was our secret.

"How do I look?" Jude had asked, draping a blanket

Chapter 30

over her shoulders and doing a catwalk walk around her room like a supermodel at Fashion Week.

"Like perfection," I had told her, giving her a big hug. "Absolute perfection."

"Can you do my hair like yours too?" she'd begged.

"Um, of course!"

As soon as I was done, my tiny bestie and I headed out to the pool to enjoy the remainder of the day.

So far, today has been perfect. Everything has been perfect since last night.

Because being with Graham now—and knowing that he wants me, that he isn't going to fight it anymore—is so much better than I could have imagined. It's better than the first time he touched me in his office. Better than when he put his hands around my throat against a tree, surrounded by trees and birdsong. Better, even, than the power I found when I took his cock in my mouth. I know I'm playing with fire, and I have no idea how this thing between me and Graham will end up when summer's over, but I'm ready to find out—even if it breaks my heart. I'm just going to enjoy the time that I have with him, and try to live in the moment as best I can. No regrets. Because this thing blossoming between us is…well. It's incredible. And even if what we have is temporary, it's worth fighting for.

Last night was more beautiful than this gorgeous summer day. My lips still tingle at the memory of his kiss and my center contracts every time I remember the feel of his hands against my bare skin. My pussy still feels like a bruise inside, just a little, and every time I feel that deep ache again it instantly transports me back to the moment we came at almost exactly the same time. We didn't just have sex, we made love, and it was perfect. That it was my second time ever is inconsequential. Graham *changed* last night.

He used to simply demand things from me. Order me around. He always kept things cold and distant, and I always went along with it because I was desperate for his attention. But last night, the choice was all mine. He lowered some of his walls, and he was actually *present* with me. I'm hungry for more, and soon. He's all I can think about.

"...so then I told Sara that she can't talk to Megan that way, no matter where she rides, because Megan is my friend and you don't talk to my friends that way." Jude interrupts my thoughts with the story she's been on for a while. I want to pay attention, because eight-year-old drama is a delight on a whole other level, but my thoughts keep spiraling back to her dad.

"So what did she say?" I ask, dropping my sunglasses to look at her, let her see I'm invested in the story.

Jude grins triumphantly. "Nothing. She left the stables and didn't bother us for the rest of the exhibition." She pops a grape in her mouth and looks like an adorably cheeky little chipmunk. "Megan is the one who got second place."

"Because you got first."

Jude's grin widens and she does a wiggle dance on her lounger. I pretend I don't notice, letting her have her moment to celebrate. Just then, my phone vibrates against my leg. DAD, the screen flashes. Again.

Chapter 30

I want to take the thing and hurl it straight into the pool.

"Shouldn't you answer that?" Jude's brows draw together behind her sunglasses. "What if it's my dad with an emergency?"

If it was Graham, I'd answer it in a heartbeat, but it's not Graham.

"It's my dad," I tell her. "I'll call him back later." Which is a lie.

I don't *want* to talk to him. In fact, I haven't returned his calls in weeks.

Yes, things are going exactly how they were supposed to, which he'd probably be thrilled about...except there's just one itty bitty problem: I wasn't supposed to fall for Graham. I wasn't supposed to develop real feelings for him. I told my dad, back at the beginning of the summer, that it wouldn't be an issue. That I could handle the job.

Seduce the billionaire.

Get photos of the billionaire being inappropriate with his nanny.

Blackmail the billionaire.

Easy peasy.

But the second I set foot in Graham's office, I should have known this was not going to go as planned. I didn't have a choice, though, did I? I'm trapped in this just as much as Graham is now, only he has no idea what's going on. I *tried* to tell him. I really did. I don't want to lie to him anymore; I just want to *be* with him. But that wasn't the plan. It was never the plan.

I failed, and I failed big time.

There's no keeping this from my dad, either.

Abbie

Avoiding him is probably just making things worse, telling him everything he needs to know about how not-successfully the plan is going. Hell, last time we talked he was ready to pull the plug on the entire thing and have me go home. But I can't. I can't leave Graham. I can't leave Jude. I can't leave this beautiful house. My home is nothing short of a nightmare, and going back to it simply isn't an option right now.

"Wanna know something? Your dad has a special ringtone on my phone," I tell Jude.

She turns her head toward me. "Really? What is it?"

"Wanna hear it?" I ask conspiratorially.

Jude bounces up in her seat. "Yes!"

I grab my phone, ignoring the dozen alerts for text messages from Dad, and scroll through my contacts app. One push of a button later, and an ominous song plays from my phone.

Jude looks confused for a minute, but then a smile spreads across her face and she starts cracking up. "Darth Vader's theme song? Because he's your evil boss?"

"Exactly." I wink at her over my glasses. "You're such a little smarty."

"Is he a bad boss?" she asks, suddenly serious. "Is he mean? Are you scared of him?"

"Oh, honey." My heart hurts a bit at the question. "He can be pretty intimidating sometimes, you know that. And yeah, I used to be a little scared. But not anymore. He's just got a lot on his plate. And he works really hard to make sure you're well taken care of."

"Yeah. He's not around a lot." She's stopped eating

Chapter 30

now, and starts scratching her ankle, not looking at me. "Sometimes I think it's because he doesn't like me."

A knife to the heart, that's what this is. Her fears are all too familiar to me. "Jude, sweet pea, it is not because he doesn't like you. Not at all. He loves you more than anything. That's why he's always working—so he can make sure you have everything you need. He told me that, even. And you know what? He's strict with me, too, because he wants to make sure that you're getting the best care. How you're treated is the most important thing in the world to him."

"Really?" She casts a furtive glance my way. "You think so?"

"I know so. Believe me, I know it can be really hard when your parents are always busy or they get in fights when they're together. I know exactly what that's like. But they still love us more than we can understand."

"How do you know?"

"Because I talk to your dad." I reach over to give her knee a squeeze. "There isn't anything else in this world as important to you as him. How did you feel when he put you to bed last night?"

Jude's face squinches up as she thinks for a minute. Finally, she settles on, "Loved."

"See?" I give her a bright smile.

My phone vibrates again, another message from my dad that I can't avoid this time because my phone is open. I quickly swipe it away in case Jude sees it, just like I did.

If you won't come home, I'll come get you myself.

NO. This is where I belong right now. This is my home. This is everything I've ever wanted. Leaving is not

Abbie

an option. My dad's probably bluffing anyway—he would never risk coming here himself; he couldn't even drive me up from Connecticut because he was too anxious to set foot near the man he claimed to be his closest friend for years.

My time here has only confirmed what I've been trying to deny to myself for years: that my dad is a piece of garbage. So then what does that make me, the girl who agreed to go along with his shitty plan? What does that make me, for actually going through with it? What does that make me, for living this lie?

I have to tell Graham, soon. I have to tell him the whole truth. He needs to know what my dad is planning. Graham is a smart man, surely we can come up with some kind of a plan. Together.

Guilt clogs my throat and I have to swallow it down with a large swig of lemonade.

"I'm jumping in!" Jude announces, taking off her sunglasses and heading for the diving board.

"Don't splash the food! Nobody likes soggy crackers!" I tease, shoving everything else out of my mind.

As Jude takes her first cannonball into the water, I start to delete the texts from my dad, trying not to read any of them. Then I stop. Should I show these to Graham? What if he doesn't believe that my dad, his longtime friend, is trying to fuck him over? What if I need proof?

I scroll through the lengthy text chain, adrenaline rushing through me, still making sure to check on Jude every few seconds even though I know she's an expert swimmer. Footsteps sound behind me suddenly and I

Chapter 30

jump, my heartbeat racing in my ears. I lock my screen and try to nonchalantly hide my phone, every bit the innocent sunbather.

"I didn't expect to see you again so soo—"

The words die in my throat. It's not Graham. It's Esmeralda.

"Oh, hi." I smile brightly, guilt still tugging at my gut. "We never see you out here!"

"You never see me anywhere." Gone is the friendliness from Esmeralda's voice. Icy disdain replaces it. "But I see you."

The smile starts to slide off my face. "Is there something I can help you with?"

"I'm not the one who's going to need help."

It's only now that I realize she's holding a pile of magazines in her hand. She throws them down on the table in front of me, then steps back and watches me with her arms crossed.

I slide my sunglasses on top of my head and lean over. It takes a minute for me to understand what I'm looking at, and why Esmeralda is looking at me the way she is.

As I start flipping through the covers of each trashy tabloid, I realize they're each screaming the same headlines in huge block letters.

BILLIONAIRE BANKER SEDUCES TEENAGE NANNY—THE SCANDAL EXPLODES!

GRAHAM RATLIFF FINDING RELIEF IN THE HELP?

NANNYGATE

RATLIFF AFFAIR WITH BARELY LEGAL NANNY.

Abbie

My stomach drops, my mouth runs cotton-dry, and I suddenly can't breathe. Every single one of these magazines is covering the story.

"Good luck," Esmeralda bites, turning on her heel and storming away.

I can only sit here and stare at the grainy, blown-up photos of me and Graham on cover after cover, unable to stop myself until I've looked at every single one in the stack.

And the headline on top?

NANNY CONFESSES ALL.

Graham and Abbie's story continues in The Billionaire and His Scandal...

When Abbie Montgomery arrived, I knew she would destroy me.

My best friend's daughter, virginal and still harboring her childhood crush on me, was completely off-limits.

Of course, forbidden desires are always the sweetest. Watching her bond with my daughter during the day, giving into sweet, soft temptation at night... I always knew it couldn't last. I always knew it would end badly. But I never expected the spark between us could explode my entire life.

Find out what happens in The Billionaire and His Scandal.

Paige Press

Paige Press isn't just Laurelin Paige anymore...

Laurelin Paige has expanded her publishing company to bring readers even more hot romances.

Sign up for our newsletter to get the latest news about our releases and receive a free book from one of our amazing authors:

Laurelin Paige
Stella Gray
CD Reiss
Jenna Scott
Raven Jayne
JD Hawkins
Poppy Dunne
Lia Hunt
Sadie Black

Also by Sadie Black

HIS NANNY TRILOGY

The Billionaire and His Nanny

The Billionaire and His Scandal

The Billionaire and His Forever

About the Author

Sadie Black lives in her head as an ex-member of the British royal family, a current fashion icon, and couldn't be more annoyed that she has to pay taxes on a job called "governess."

Made in the USA
Middletown, DE
30 August 2024